Intelligent Designing for Amateurs

T0096985

Intelligent Designing for Amateurs

Nimue Brown

TOP HAT
BOOKS

Winchester, UK
Washington, USA

First published by Top Hat Books, 2013
Top Hat Books is an imprint of John Hunt Publishing Ltd., Laurel House, Station Approach,
Alresford, Hants, SO24 9JH, UK
office1@jhpbooks.net
www.johnhuntpublishing.com
www.tophat-books.com

For distributor details and how to order please visit the 'Ordering' section on our website.

Text copyright: Nimue Brown 2012

ISBN: 978 1 78099 952 4

A CIP catalogue record for this book is available from the British Library.

Design: Stuart Davies

Printed in the USA by Edwards Brothers Malloy

We operate a distinctive and ethical publishing philosophy in all
areas of our business, from our global network of authors to
production and worldwide distribution.

No actual history was harmed in the making of this novel. Dedicated with much thanks to the lovely people who have inspired me, or contributed in technical ways to making it possible... in no particular order... Autumn Barlow, Sarah Gothard, Paul Alborough, Lee Ann Farruga, Edrie Edrie, and Tom Brown. For the purposes of not being sued, I'd like to thank the good people who inspired the penance biscuits by very carefully not mentioning who they were!

Chapter One

Anthropological observations of the curious habits of personages native to Barker Street

Hopefully there would be dead people next door. That would liven things up tremendously. Ever since the new tenant was first mentioned, Temperance had been trying to imagine what an archaeologist would look like, and had become stuck somewhere between the beard and the muddy boots. Granny said an archaeologist dug things up, which had formed most of her impression. Temperance had never encountered an actual archaeologist before, and until recently, hadn't even met the word in person. It was one of those large, pleasing, hard to spell words that she liked to roll around in her mouth. There were others. Obsequious. Crepuscular. Epigrammatic. Meanings did not always excite her young mind, but a word that came with a person had more appeal. Granny told her something about digging up iniquities, or possibly aunties. Antimacassars? Digging up definitely suggested mud, and led Temperance to think from there about the likelihood of dead people. Dead people went into the ground, so it stood to reason they could come out of it again. What else was there to unearth aside from coal and ore?

"Nothing at all like a body snatcher," Granny had insisted, when the subject came up at breakfast, but Temperance wasn't sure. What else would anyone want to dig up, really? Treasure might be nice, she supposed, but that seemed more like pirate business.

Still, having a new neighbor would cheer the whole street up. The bigger, separate house next to their little terrace had been empty all winter. Seeing the dark windows at night always inclined her to feel sad.

"How's that sweeping going, then?" Granny demanded from inside the house.

The sweeping had not, in fact, started, the girl having entirely forgotten about the broom in her hand. Pushing curls of escaping brown hair out of her face, Temperance surveyed the twig strewn path to her grandmother's door. Sweeping seemed so pointless. The wind would bring it all right back in no time. She sighed heavily, feeling very sorry for herself.

Before she could start on the job, the sound of hooves and wheels drew her attention to the street again. All of the delivery people had already done their rounds for the day. Horse-drawn vehicles were otherwise unusual here. The inhabitants of Barker Street were all very decent people, but not equal to carriages, excepting for weddings and funerals. Temperance loved funerals, but the approaching wagon lacked the plumes and splendid display of misery. Instead she saw a neat little trap, followed by a heavily loaded cart where a great many things were piled up behind the driver and passengers.

With a little squeak, she dropped the broom and ran to the garden gate. Then, because she did not want the archaeologist to think her childish, she slowed down. Walking in what she hoped was a dignified way, she soon reached the next property just as the tired horse came to a halt.

The person inside the trap was carefully helped down, and then approached the front door. There was no beard whatsoever, and no obvious signs of mud. Perhaps there had been a mistake? The trap itself took off at a jaunty speed. Temperance wondered if this was the archaeologist's wife, come on ahead to make their new home nice. The man himself would probably be in a hole full of bones at this very moment, Temperance reasoned.

One of the men got off the cart. He had wild hair and a big coat. On the whole he seemed a better candidate for the adventurous life, and Temperance watched him expectantly.

"All to be unloaded here?" he asked the woman.

"If you please." She nodded to the girl who was sitting on the cart. "I assume you can find the kitchen, Mary?"

The girl nodded and hurried inside. The two men set about unloading items of furniture from the cart and taking them into the house. Temperance felt rather puzzled by all of this. There weren't any bones being unloaded just usual, household things. Unless the bones were in one of the tea chests. She supposed that would make sense, even if it was a disappointment.

"Hello girl," said the tall woman, with an accent that clearly came from another place.

Temperance had spent hours planning how to make her introductions to the new neighbor. She had already established herself as being absolutely essential to Charlie Rowcroft, Barker Street's resident inventor. Now, she meant to impress the archaeologist, or for that matter his wife, with her clever, useful nature. Thus, she would gain free access to their home as well. Staring up at the new arrival's face, she couldn't remember any of the planned speech and found herself instead saying, "Have you got any dead people?"

The woman smiled. "Not on me, no. Why, are you in need of one for some reason?"

As a short-term measure, the best answer she could think of was to run back and tell Granny all about it.

Granny Alice swept in, a rounded but immaculate form in an old dress and ruthlessly polished boots. She liked to make an impression, her tightly bunned hair and stern expression deliberately misleading. Depositing a large laundry basket on the kitchen table, she was relieved to find some free space for a change. The owner of both wash load and table, Charlie Rowcroft, did not take much interest in tidiness. It held true for her disheveled appearance, as well as the chaotic state of the house.

"Seen much of our new neighbor?" Alice asked, wondering

what the eccentric pair would make of each other.

Charlie looked up mournfully and shook her head. "I've not been out at all this week. I didn't even realize anyone had taken number seven."

"No wonder you look so pale and pasty. Some fresh air and a good meal wouldn't go amiss." Granny reinforced the observation with a few tuttting noises.

"It's no good, I've got to get this finished," Charlie replied, flipping through reams of notes without seeming to look at any of them. "I don't get paid until it's done. Can I owe you for this week?"

Alice had been expecting as much. Inventing was not a reliable trade, although Charlie could be depended upon to pay her debts. Eventually.

"I've made a pie," Alice said casually. "Got a bit carried away with it. Far too much for me and Temperance, and I'd hate to throw good food away. I don't suppose I could foist a bit of it off on you?"

Charlie flashed her a grateful, sheepish sort of smile. "You're too good to me, Granny," Charlie replied.

"I just don't like seeing perfectly good pies go to waste. I'll send the girl over later with a piece."

"I've no time to teach her today," Charlie said, apologetically.

"Don't worry, she's too keen on spying on the new neighbor to concentrate on anything else. I doubt you'll see her for long."

"The archaeologist?" Charlie commented.

"Did you know he's a woman?" Alice enquired. "I suppose we shouldn't be surprised by these things anymore, what with you inventing."

"I had no idea," Charlie said.

"Not far off your age," Alice added. She'd hoped there might be a friend in the offing for her young neighbor. Charlie could use some company of her own age, and someone with the right kind of mind to understand her.

However, Charlie didn't seem very interested, which was usually the problem. Alice supposed it went with a certain kind of cleverness, but it didn't make for much of a life.

After Granny had straightened the dishes, made a pot of tea and dealt with an unexpected mouse, Charlie was left alone to her more usual silence. Alice was the sort of grandmother everyone ought to have. She looked like a battleaxe, cleaned like a fairytale elf, smoked peculiar concoctions in her pipe and adopted stray girls whose families did not want them. Temperance was a proper grandchild, Charlie a waif who had washed up in her street a few years previously. Her own family did not approve of cleverness in girls, or of anything else much.

She turned her attention back to the job in hand. Mr. Trefidick had ordered "some kind of device that will stop my machines from exploding so often." It wasn't proper inventing, just patching up the insanities in other men's creations. Proper inventing had not proved very lucrative. No one wanted her handy table piece that kept toast warm for quite a long time, or anything else in that vein. The clockwork bird-scarer languished under a table, along with the shoe removing device and the pocket mathematics machine that hadn't turned out at all pocket sized. Other projects remained in the developmental stage, mostly because she could not yet picture a use for the ticking, whizzing innards. That kind of work required a lot of time. So did "some kind of thing that will make this thing a bit quieter," and those were always the paying jobs.

The thought of an archaeological neighbor did not excite Charlie's interest. She was not a sociable creature, so a new addition to life on Barker Street held no appeal. Furthermore, she had failed to notice all signs of the new arrival, including the unloading of the cart. Voices beyond the window had gone unheeded as she remained focused trying to beat an uncooperative bit of metal into place. And then she hadn't heard the cart leaving because her entirely faithful miniature reconstruction of a Trefidick machine and then dutifully exploded. Again. History people, of all the professionals, held little interest for her. They were, by definition, a backward looking set, and Charlie Rowcroft was all about the future.

Having unloaded her worldly possessions, the archaeologist stayed at number seven for one night, then disappeared again almost as quickly as she had come. The residents of Barker Street were disappointed, but peered around their curtains regularly, in the hopes of some new and gratifying development. Very little else had happened lately to entertain them. In the last few months the biggest dramas had been a chicken escape, the man who had fallen off his bicycle, and Temperance breaking a window. A person did not move to Barker Street in search of adventure, unless they were Temperance, but her case was very much the exception. Still, the occasional distraction was not unwelcome. A quiet life could become all too tedious after a while.

Chapter Two

The pernicious Welsh climate and its influence upon the development of historical sciences

Wales corresponded almost exactly to Justina's image of hell: Not so much fire and brimstone, more rain and mud. On arrival at the train station, she had been obliged to walk nearly two miles to a grubby little inn. She had been promised something decent; something worth bothering with, but from the moment of departing the train, and relative civilization, pessimism had set in. The landscape looked so empty, if one did not bother to count the sheep. Counting sheep did not seem an appropriate task for a woman of her class and distinction. Wales seemed to offer little else though. There were hardly any roads, much less the trappings necessary to decent, human existence. Only the lure of a compelling man and the promise of adventure had drawn her this far. There would have to be some dramatic improvements, or she would be on her way.

Chevalier had arrived at her inn late, but enthusiastic, whisking her off into a world of frenetic activity where she had no chance to really question anything he said, much less protest about it. A brisk walk, a dramatic plan, and a promise to meet again after dinner rapidly ensued.

"Where on earth are you staying?" she enquired as he tried to leave her. "Because really, if it is even slightly less depressing than the Wilting Bush, I demand that you escort me there at once. This place is like a relic from the Dark Ages."

"Dear lady, I fear I can offer you nothing more salubrious." He kissed her hand, and bowed. "So fair a flower should be protected from the rough winds, yes? But so courageous a heart will not baulk at the challenges of a great and noble quest, I feel certain."

Justina had every desire to baulk at the bed she had recently seen, but in face of such a compliment, could not quite work up the desire to confess her apathy for the whole business. She rather hoped that he was leading her on, that the evening would evolve into something far more pleasing.

Normally, she had a great deal of self-possession. "No," was a word that came naturally to her lips. And yet something about this man made it fiendishly difficult to maintain her usual sense of right and wrong. The inn was terribly wrong. Ill-furnished, damp-smelling and intermittently smoky. But she could not quite articulate her dislike of it to him. Once Chevalier had swanned off with all the same arrogant assuredness displayed by his arrival, she wondered what on earth she had agreed to.

"It will be worth it," she repeated, suffering her way through a monstrous bowl of stew made out of God alone knew what. "He will be worth it."

Wales proved even worse to observe from the position of being in an illicit trench by lantern light and unexpectedly alone. She blamed him entirely and had already decided what cutting and chastening words to bestow on Alain Chevalier if he did ever dare to show his face in her presence again. Although she chided herself for believing him, with his pendulum parlor tricks and his seductive voice. It was the kind of thing her mother would like, and she should have been more alert to the intellectual dangers. Chevalier claimed a secret, esoteric method for uncovering treasure, and offered her a share in it. He had arrived at a low point in her life, and she ascribed her own fleeting weakness to temporary vulnerability. She would not be so foolish again.

They had walked a most innocent-looking field together that afternoon. He had proffered extravagant compliments – not that she ever paid great attention to those. There were few things Justina had been told about the lusciousness of her lips, the radiance of her cheeks, the fine sparkle of her eyes, the dignity of her brow and the allure of her auburn tresses, that she had not heard a hundred times before. Then Monsieur Chevalier had waved his tool about and declared this to be the very spot for digging. They had marked it with a little pile of field stones. No matter that they had not conversed with the land owner. All would be well. Why had she believed him?

"Meet me here, dearest lady, in the middle of the futtering night," she grumbled aloud as the rain water seeped into her boots.

Calling this a 'trench' was a joke. What she had was a muddy hole, now an inch deep with water as the rain soaked through her clothes to chill her skin. Of course there was no sign of Alain Chevalier now, with his pristine white hands that had never dug into anything more challenging than a trifle. He had sounded so plausible when they first met at a lecture some weeks before. So charming. Having chosen to remain, in appearance at least an old maid, Justina was used to the purely academic interest of scholars even more aged than her own thirty years. Handsome young men did not normally frequent such gatherings in the hopes of finding lady archaeologists to flirt with. That had been part of the attraction in attending. Justina suffered agonizing ennui in the company of handsome young men and often contemplated murdering those who proposed to her.

It now occurred to her to wonder what he had really been after. No doubt her physical charms had enthralled him. He had seemed a promising rake, likely to mislead. Otherwise she would have ignored his attentions. However, the manner in which he had chosen to mislead was not remotely to her liking. Perhaps it was his idea of amusement.

She slammed down the shovel, meaning to get out of this ridiculous hole and depart with what little dignity she could still muster. Down in the mud, metal clunked on metal. She paused and tapped the shovel down again, less forcefully this time. The same dull clink cut through the patter of rain. Her heart skipped a little. A sudden sense of adventure clashed with her desire to be anywhere warmer and drier than the hole.

"Drat," she said, with feeling, because now of course he had to stay and dig. The find seemed to be calling to her, begging, demanding that she unearth it. They generally did. Or at least, the idea of how they would lift her to fame and accolades had that sort of effect.

It would probably be some worthless item of junk, planted by the nefarious Alain as part of the jest. Only the grass she'd lifted at twilight did not suggest recent digging. The thrill of the find acted upon her as any vice might upon the devoted addict. Her pulse raced, and she could think of nothing else but digging.

As she worked, an edge came clear, catching the lamplight. She pulled it free and could see the faint glint of something else beneath it. Heavy, filthy and slightly curved, the item did not look at all familiar. Justina forgot about pendulums and rotten jokes, her attention wholly focused on digging up whatever the Welsh mud concealed. The rain ceased to matter, the cold no longer registered in her mind. Only when the lamp faltered, threatening to run out of oil, did she struggle back to her temporary lodgings, barely able to carry what she had lifted from the ground. One thing to be said for the dingy place, was that the proprietor took little interest in her comings and goings.

Dawn was encouragingly devoid of rain and saw her frantically at work. There had been no sign of Chevalier, but she no longer cared a great deal about this. The young man clearly lacked staying power, or was a fool, or both. She had forgotten plenty of others before him and had every intention of forgetting a great deal more young men in the years to come. It was one of life's little pleasures.

Further pieces emerged from the ground and were loaded into a borrowed wheelbarrow. The hole did indeed look more like a respectable trench now. She made no notes or drawings of her progress though; nothing that would please a fellow antiquarian.

The damp conditions precluded any such efforts, and she did not feel inclined to waste time on sketching. Discovery had always interested her more than the banal elements of science, and on this occasion she had dug up a lot of things. Working out what came from where would have been tedious in the extreme. The delirium of discovery felt more important at that moment than the niceties of a thorough report. When an hour eventually passed with no further pieces, she conceded that might be the entire haul, and set about hiding the evidence of her theft.

She'd seen no one in this lonely spot since her meander with Alain on the previous day. Not even the otherwise ubiquitous sheep. Other fields where speckled with them, but this one appeared to have no function whatsoever. Nothing indicated human use at all. In fact, since arriving in this desolate landscape, the only evidence of people she'd seen outside the gloomy little inn, were the distant tents of some kind of circus, or freak show. She could only assume they were performing to the sheep, because human beings were in very short supply. There wasn't another building for a mile, but still she felt rather guilty. Technically, her find belonged in part to someone else. Technically. But she had no idea whom that might be, and they had no awareness of her.

In the light of day, her finds looked like a selection of metal things, but their precise nature eluded her. Still, she hoped it might make more sense once clean. She had the feeling that this was a valuable find, something of importance that she could take pride in. Even if the items did not resolve into coherent identities, there might still be enough here to impress the famous Doctor Melgrave. She still dreamed of earning a place on his next dig. Rumor had it that he was heading for the South of France to search for Noah's Ark. Chances to be that close to the great events of her era would not be numerous, she knew.

While Justina knew her powers of attraction were enormous when it came to young men, she had no such capacity for alluring Doctor Melgrave. He had been resolutely impervious to all her advances so far. It frustrated her, but she had not yet given up trying to win his approval.

She packed her bags, arranged transportation for the intriguing find, and headed to the sanctuary of her new abode. Justina Fairfax felt certain that, given a suitably quiet and dependable environment, her scholarly skills would develop to their natural apex. Life may have thwarted her ambitions thus far, but striking out alone encouraged her to think that great things would naturally follow from this brave and unconventional move. She had a small income left in her father's will, enabling her to live independently. Now that she had turned thirty, this choice would not seem so scandalous to others. A spinster of thirty might safely live alone, where a beautiful young heiress could not. Society expected things of beautiful young heiresses – most especially, matrimony. Much of her youth had been occupied with the laborious effort of avoiding this fate. As most of the inheriting would not happen until her mother's demise, she had little to help her escape the snares of convention. None the less, Justina remained free, and proudly independent.

Advancing age had not done much to defend her from advancing males though. Justina blamed her face, with its exquisite proportions, flawless skin and luminous eyes. She also blamed her swanlike neck, along with the perfection of her arms and the grace of her hands. At thirty she still had a stunning figure and a way of moving that drove men to distraction. It was hardly her fault. God had made her this way, and then given her a mind that did not appreciate the inevitable consequences of her body.

"That's a lot of metal you've got there," Temperance observed as she peered over the fence. She had borrowed a ladder from Charlie only that morning, and it was proving very helpful indeed for the spying business. This might be the direction her life should take. Already, Temperance could see her future in distant countries doing unspecified but dangerous things for the sake of Queen and country.

"Yes, it is," the woman beneath her replied, not even looking up.

"Is it a coffin?" the girl asked. "All those pieces. They look like you could make something out of them. Probably big enough to put a dead person in." The more she looked at the bits of metal, the more interesting they seemed. Hopefully there would be an invitation to take a closer look.

The archaeologist did not seem impressed with Temperance's inspired idea, which in turn disappointed the girl. In her experience, people were impressed by what she said. Charlie Rowcroft was always interested in her ideas for inventions and had agreed only yesterday that what the world really needed was her box for keeping butter just right. Warm enough to spread, but not so warm that it went rancid. All she had to do was get the weather on a mild afternoon into a box, and keep it there, and she would make her fortune.

Charlie took her seriously, because Charlie was a much better sort of person than this boring woman who didn't even have any dead people she'd dug up.

"Miss Rowcroft makes things out of metal all the time. Much better things than you've got. That's because she's cleverer than you." With this damming rebuke, Temperance climbed down the ladder and headed off in pursuit of lunch.

Chapter Three

A working person's guide on how to live a more virtuous life

According to the letter, a Mister F. B. Anderson, lately of Torquay, had recently come into the area for reasons of business and enterprise. He most sincerely wished that Miss Rowcroft would be so good as to create for him a recipe appropriate to the concept of Penance Biscuits. The packaging for said biscuits had already been designed and the factory that would make them had already been constructed. The biscuits themselves were to be healthful, but not over-stimulating to the senses. They should be modest in appearance, and eating one should cause the penitent individual to never again hanker after excess or to be gluttonous in their habits.

Charlie Rowcroft had never before felt moved to make a biscuit of any sort, but this did not strike her as being a natural obstacle to the task in hand. These biscuits would not merely be penitent, they would confer moral superiority with every bite. At least according to the empty box Mister Anderson had sent.

She'd experienced a few moments of disquiet, thinking about Lief's Chastity Sweets and Mrs. Pennyface's Responsible Buns. Charlie had tested these edible miracles and knew that they were at best, unreliable. On one hand, that meant her penitent biscuits couldn't be any worse than things people already bought. On the other hand, it felt a bit like stealing. Then there was the whole issue of her not actually starving, to consider. As she had only flour and tea leaves in the cupboard, these biscuits were going to be very penitent indeed.

The first batch were cooling and filling the air with a depressing sort of smell when someone knocked on her door. Having more creditors than debtors likely to call upon her just now, she considered sitting under the table in the hopes of not being noticed. Friends all came to the back door. It then occurred to her that it might be work, so she decided to risk answering.

"Good afternoon," said the unfamiliar woman at her door.

Charlie registered almost no details of dress or appearance, just a keen sense that this did not appear to be anyone she owed any money to. She exhaled sharply in relief.

"I have been told that you make things out of metal," the woman continued.

Work, then. Charlie put on her best smile and made an effort to stand up straight and look businesslike. "Repairs, improvements and innovations undertaken to your specifications." She couldn't rattle out that line now without thinking of Temperance, who had recently said, "I want a bicycle I can fold up so small that I can take it with me in my pocket."

"I have recently moved in across the road, and wondered if you might spare a moment to look at something for me." The stranger looked hopeful as she spoke.

"Of course!" Charlie stepped out at once, not even bothering to shut the door. The smell of Penance Biscuits would convince all but the insane or desperate that her home lacked anything worthy of theft. "You're the archaeologist then?" she observed as they past the side of number seven and plunged into the back garden.

"I am. Where are my manners? Justina Fairfax. Can I offer you a cup of tea while you look at this?" She gestured towards a pile of debris.

"Absolutely yes to tea, and biscuits if you have any?" She crouched down to look at the bits. Charlie knew a dismantling when she saw one.

"Cake?" the archaeologist replied. "Bread and butter perhaps, or a scone with jam?" There might have been sarcasm, but Charlie had long since mastered the art of selective deafness.

"That would be capital." She lifted up one of the large metal pieces. "What on earth was it?"

"That, is what I rather hoped you would be able to tell me." She left Charlie in the garden.

Snotty little madam, Charlie thought. You could hear the money in Miss Fairfax's accent. The private tutors and a fair helping of tennis, ponies and silk handkerchiefs. With a shudder, Charlie recognized that the new neighbor was probably one of those awful, moneyed enthusiasts who dabbled at work for entertainment. Half the inventors she had met were spoiled rich boys who enjoyed blowing up the family income. Not that she had any particular prejudice against blowing things up.

Charlie picked up two of the metal plates and looked at them. There was some kind of image on the side of each panel, but it looked more like decoration than fine art. Part of her mind focused on the important question of whether the rich dabbler would pay up, or take her for a fellow enthusiast who would be insulted by an offer of money. Despite time spent deliberately mimicking Granny Alice, Charlie still had a suggestion of ponies and silk handkerchiefs in her own voice. Sometimes, it had its uses. Possibly not today.

Fingers worked their own, illogical magic. For as long as Charlie could remember, she had been taking things apart and putting them back together again, not always in their originally intended shapes. It took her about five minutes to assemble the heap of metal into something that could have been a sundial.

"Is that it?" Justin enquired, returning with a pot of tea on a tray.

There were biscuits. Charlie took three of them. "It could be," she said.

Justina did a full circle of the new construct. "A sundial? Or a means of measuring the night sky, or perhaps a strange, round altar to previously unknown gods." She seemed pleased.

Looking at the longer, thinner bands, Charlie wasn't entirely convinced by her first attempt. The roundness seemed right, but there were grooves in the square plates, and that middle one suggested something else...

She laughed and started slotting the pieces together. They went around the base, and the long, thin lengths could have been riveted to the top and middle to turn the whole thing into a large, round cauldron. Only there were no rivets. It had been in one piece at some point, by the looks of it.

"And are we any more confident about this interpretation?" Miss Fairfax enquired.

Charlie reminded herself about possible income and bit back the impulse to insult. "How old is this?" she demanded instead.

"The designs have a primitive aspect that could suggest antiquity, but the condition of the metal suggests more recent origins to me."

"In other words, you don't really know," Charlie couldn't resist saying.

The metal showed no signs of corrosion, but Charlie wasn't sure exactly what the alloy was, and of course the soil itself would probably make a difference. She didn't really know either, but decided not to mention this. "I am confident it is an ornamental bucket or cauldron, the pieces have not fallen apart, they were deliberately separate, and I think it would be too impractical for everyday use."

"That doesn't make a great deal of sense, so I imagine it must have had religious significance. An offering, perhaps. Can you put it together?"

Charlie smiled. "For a fee, of course."

Justina rolled her eyes with the habitual distaste of the wealthy for spending their own money.

"I am a working woman, not someone intent purely on their own amusement," Charlie pointed out.

"I see. And I assume you charge by the hour?"

"Naturally."

By the time she left, Charlie had taken extreme dislike to the new inhabitant of number seven. Still, the woman was sufficiently lacking in sense to pay well over the odds, and putting the bucket back together would not take as long as she intended to claim. Something about the project made her fingers itch with anticipation. She had to assemble the item. The Penance Biscuits could wait.

She ferried the pieces home, and set up outside with the necessary gear. It was an easy job, and once she got started, the pieces fitted perfectly into place. She had plenty of rivets, enough of the right size to make the whole process embarrassingly easy. Why more jobs like this couldn't come her way, she didn't know. It was money for old rope, really.

Luck had it that Temperance was absent on an errand when the baker's cart ran over her cat. It was an old, half-blind and moth-eaten creature that had invited itself into their outhouse. There had been repeated efforts to bring it indoors. Temperance wanted to pet the cat, but Alice did not believe in having animals in the house. Despite this barrier, the girl had made considerable fuss of the ever-hungry visitor. Alice did not mind indulging the child, to a point.

She had seen the accident from the window, unable to intervene. Blind and foolish as it was, the cat just strolled out in front of the horse, and there wasn't much anyone could do about it. On closer inspection of the damage, the cat turned out to be exceedingly dead. Being a publically minded woman, Alice did not even consider leaving the furry corpse in the middle of the street to fester. However, she had nowhere suitable to bury it, and Temperance might return at any moment. Alice did not have time for the throes of youthful anguish. She picked up the sticky corpse, carried it across the road and pushed Charlie's side door open with her bottom.

"Morning, Alice," Charlie said from the table, not looking up.

"Sorry to be a bother, but the baker's run over a cat and you know how Temperance likes to go on about these things. Can you dispose of it for me?"

Charlie waved noncommittally, her mind clearly on other things. "Pop it down where there's a space. I can get shot of it later."

Alice looked around, not wanting to leave the dead cat on the small clear are of floor, where unspeakable things could so easily happen. There weren't a great many other options as all of the available surfaces appeared to be in use. She plumbed for the funny looking pail, which had evidently seen better days and would not suffer unduly from the blood.

Although it took over an hour to reach Cheltenham Spa by train, Justina had been determined to attend Doctor Melgrave's lecture on the instances of classical geometry in English antiquity. The technical aspects of his lectures tended to give her headaches and she often struggled to follow the logic of his progressions. However, she felt that only went to show what a very superior sort of mind he must have. By way of further attraction was the possibility that Monsieur Chevalier would put in an appearance. Justina had considered a number of rude and damning things she might say in front of him, but not to him. It would be the perfect opportunity to publically spurn the cad, a prospect she very much looked forward to.

She reassured herself that of course she had no personal desire to see the man, only to cause him discomfort. That he had lured her into a Welsh field and then failed to turn up and do anything of note, proved his unworthiness. Had she been absent from this important gathering, he might have taken it personally and assumed himself triumphant. No one humiliated Justina Fairfax, largely by dint of her complete inability to feel the relevant emotion. However, she very much enjoyed causing just that sensation in others when they irked her.

On arrival, she discreetly scanned the hall, observing a

number of familiar faces as well as a few new ones. There were polite conversations to enter into. By the time they were all seated, she felt certain the errant young man was not of their number. It disappointed her, but she refused to let this setback spoil the day. Putting on her most attentive and serious expression, she focused on appearing to be very interested in everything Doctor Melgrave might deign to say.

At the end of the lecture, she approached the great man, waiting her turn amongst the throng of eager admirers. Her own most recent paper, diligently copied, was clutched to her breast. "Observations on unusually placed stones in gateways that may be prehistoric remnants" had taken the previous summer to research and all winter to write. Even so, it was sadly lacking in any definite discoveries.

The room emptied as the famous Doctor condescended to read her humble effort. Eventually, he spoke. "You have clearly put a good deal of time and effort into this piece, dear child." His voice oozed generosity. "Solid thinking, dogged persistence, but I fear a lack of vision impairs you. I see only the pedestrian facts, devoid of illumination."

She nodded, recognizing the truth of this.

Doctor Melgrave continued. "To be great, one must have vision and imagination! Where are your unspeakable rites? Your tragic victims? Where are the insightfully and morally significant judgments upon a darker age? The work is too dry, too much like an exercise in housekeeping to make a stir in the world." He patted her arm. "But it was very brave of you to make the attempt. You must have a copy of my next book."

Justina knew then, with bitter resignation that there could be no talk of France now. She could not aspire to be part of that eminent adventure. With careful attention to maintaining proper manners and decorum, she made a seemly exit, determined that one day, she would make the leading men take her seriously. Perhaps the Welsh bucket, or whatever it turned out to be, would do the trick.

There was a weight on her chest. Charlie woke in a state of panic, half-remembered tales filling her mind with vague notions of nameless, midnight dread. For a few moments, she thought it might have just been the effect of a nightmare, but the weight shifted, pressing down upon her in a distinctly real sort of way. Normally, Charlie held a calm, pragmatic view of life. Alone in the depths of night with a real presence, nature unknown, on top of her, she didn't feel remotely sensible. She would have screamed, only she could not summon enough breath. Visions of death and horror swam through her mind. Every penny dreadful scenario read to her by Temperance, came rushing back. Unspeakable, indescribable things of darkness were very much a staple in the girl's reading. They might seem funning by daylight. Right now, they seemed very real. And very heavy.

Charlie wondered if she was going to die. The waiting was hideous. Where was the pain? The slow consumption by monsters from beyond the realms of human understanding? The weight shifted, and there followed a series of slurping, chewing noises. Perhaps it had brought its last victim here, to consume. Charlie pictured entrails. At least it wasn't eating her yet. Still she could not summon up the strength of mind to move. All of the courage had gone out of her.

Then, the purring began.

Chapter Four

Meditations on the various ethical implications of using dead animals for scientific experimentation

In the bit of yard beside the outhouse, Temperance was quietly tormenting her cat. This was a favorite activity of hers, involving bits of string, overenthusiastic petting, screams of adulation and other humiliations that only the most world weary of felines could endure. The old creature made every show of disinterest, intent only on sunbathing. It was a familiar scene, but today Alice watched with a feeling of profound discomfort. Three days ago that same cat had been most assuredly dead. Mashed in places. Alice had seen enough dead things in her life to be wholly confident in her ability to detect an absence of life. She had roasted chickens that were more lively than the unfortunate moggy had been. The only explanation she could come up with, was that she had found a different cat to this one in the road. At the time she had felt certain it was the child's pet, but given the squashing, there could have been room for error. Watching the two of them, she could only assume there had been a mistake. The dead cat had been a bit of a mess, and there were always stray kitties around.

Mystified, Alice wandered across the road to look in on Charlie. "How is the great biscuit adventure today?" Alice asked, wasting no time in moving dirty plates towards the kitchen sink.

Charlie shook her head. "I have the recipe. I'd offer you one to try, but they're horrible. Apparently my buyer is entirely happy with that. Now he wants a machine to cook the biscuits, print the packaging and put one into the other without so much as a human hand involved!"

"Can you do that?" Alice asked, firmly of the opinion that

Charlie could do anything, given enough time and cake.

"The trouble is," Charlie said, looking mournful, "people imagine machines should be able to do everything for them. It's not always that simple. I'm going to write back and explain that it would be far better to get some people to bake the biscuits, a regular printer for the boxes, and a boy to put one into the other. It would cost him less and be easier to run. Really, I don't see the point in making a machine that will do a task any eight-year-old could manage. Machines should do that which humans cannot, only most people fail to imagine what that might be. Understandably, I suppose."

Alice's mind was on less philosophical issues. "What did you do with the dead cat?"

Charlie frowned at her. "The one you brought round the other day?"

"That's right. I left it in your enormous bucket."

"Oh, I don't think it was dead. It woke me up in the middle of the night," Charlie said, able to laugh at herself in retrospect.

"That's queer," said Alice. "I could have sworn it was done for. I must have been mistaken." She turned, and nearly fell over Temperance who had wandered in behind her. "And what are you creeping about after my girl?"

Temperance produced what Alice knew was supposed to be her innocent look. "Can I have some bread and jam please, Granny?"

Alice glanced at Charlie. "I'd best be off then." She paused, then added, "Number seven, she's got a hired girl in there. I've never heard the like of it in this street. A maid of all work! What is the world coming to?"

"I think she's overestimated our gentility," Charlie replied. "And the better for us if she took her airs and graces somewhere people might have a use for them."

Somehow, Alice had not thought the two young women were going to get along with each other. Still she'd hoped it would be otherwise.

Having caught the entire conversation between her grandmother and the inventor, Temperance was out testing a theory of her own. Or at least looking for the means to commence a suitable study. It took the girl all morning to find a dead thing. Eventually, she discovered a waterlogged rat in the lane between Barker Street and the old tannery. When she lifted the corpse by its tail, it held together. That would do. Temperance thought about asking permission from Charlie before starting the little test, but knew the adults were all too fond of saying 'no'. Instead, she hid the rat in her large apron pocket, which invariably bulged with something, and invited herself round for a chat with the inventor.

Charlie was busily trying to screw something together, that anyone could see wasn't meant to go. The planned distraction that would enable her plan, involving designs for a device that would let you sweep the front path without leaving the house, turned out to be unnecessary. Charlie was too engrossed in her work to care about much else. It didn't take Temperance long to spot the big metal bucket Granny had mentioned. It was now serving as the bottom section in a pile of otherwise undistinguished objects.

When she felt sure Charlie wasn't looking, Temperance dropped the rat into the bucket. It made a soft 'plop' as it landed. Then, with all the skills of misdirection she could muster, she went to bombard her favorite neighbor with a series of difficult questions. Several times during this, she wandered, casually back, to see if there had been any progress. The rat remained resolutely still and dead looking. She could smell it a bit, and she wondered how long it would take Charlie to notice this. Possibly a while. There was quite often something going gently moldy somewhere in Charlie's kitchen. She was both untidy, and forgetful, Temperance had noticed. When she grew up, she was going to be a lot like Charlie.

At first the lack of rat-resuscitation demoralized her. She wanted it to leap back to life in an exciting way. But then, grownups were always alluding to things that sounded exciting when you hear about them, but turned out dull in practice. From mango chutney that was clearly made out of apples to the let down of mock turtle soup, Temperance knew adults were not to be trusted. However, not knowing how long it might take for the bucket to work, Temperance decided she should not abandon hope too soon. She had already reasoned out that the bucket had the power to bring things back to life. It was the only explanation for what she'd hear about the cat. Assuming the adults hadn't been overegging things again. They said overegging, but they never smeared eggs on anything, and didn't like it when others tried to do the job for them, she had found.

If today's experiment didn't work, she already had thoughts about how to give the rat a proper funeral, appropriate to its status as part of a scientific experiment. For some time now she'd been looking for a deceased candidate to send off in a burning boat. The glebe fields' pond was the ideal spot, and a raft made out of twigs would probably float. If she doused the rat in lamp oil, it should catch fire nicely. With this cheerful prospect in mind, Temperance decided not to worry about the outcome of her investigation. Either way, there would be something interesting to do tomorrow.

Some horrible person had built a new factory on the far side of town. There were shabby houses going up as well. Temperance did not like seeing her former haunts disappearing under bricks and dust. She couldn't think of any way to stop them though. Charlie said it was 'progress' and Granny said it wasn't worth the fight, and Friday Bob didn't care, which left her with nothing at all. The work made her curious though, and heading out that way gave her a long walk on which to keep an eye out for other dead things. She far she'd tried a dried frog, half a bird, and a bit of leftover bacon. All of these duly disappeared after being left in the bucket. However, Charlie hadn't mentioned it, so Temperance didn't know if the things she put in were coming to life and escaping, or whether Charlie was finding them and throwing them out. She'd hoped the bacon would come back as a whole pig, and rather thought that would have been obvious, even to the frequently oblivious Charlie. Not knowing how her experiment was going, frustrated her enormously.

Temperance did not think it was a good idea to ask outright. Either way, Charlie could be funny about it, and while she'd never invoked the inventor's anger, now didn't seem like a good time to start. Temperance had a fair inkling as to how far she could push people. Today, with no sign of anything much from her experiments, she was a lot less sure about the magical properties of the bucket. Nevertheless, she stuck with the finding and testing of dead things as a way of amusing herself. It would do until something better came along. Not that she could see anything very promising. The archaeologist woman had been very disappointing, being dull in person and usually somewhere else anyway. Temperance had climbed over the fence and explored her way through everything in the small garden. In that process she had found neither treasure troves nor dead people. To make it worse, Miss Fairfax had brought in a very silly girl to work for her. Temperance did not approve of silly girls. Especially not ones who chased her away with brooms.

Returning to Charlie's house with a dead cat rolled up in her apron, Temperance reflected that she might be getting too grown up for this sort of game. She wondered what came next. No one had told her, and she felt a long way from the things proper grownups did. Maybe it was obvious when you got there. She imagined that at a certain age, perhaps sixteen, the understanding of how to be an adult would magically descend upon her and all would become clear. You woke up one morning and knew, and then it was fine.

She found Charlie sat on her back step, eating Penance Biscuits.

"What's in your apron, Temperance?" The inventor asked, eyeing her suspiciously.

"Nothing," Temperance answered, trying her best to look innocent.

Charlie reached out a hand, wearing a facial expression that suggested it would be better to cooperate. "Why have you got a dead cat rolled up in your apron?" She enquired, as though it was a topic of only mild interest to her.

"I found it," Temperance said, which was entirely true.

"Yes, but why are you carrying it about?"

The girl thought frantically. She had not prepared an answer for this. "It's for science," she asserted, hoping that would cover it.

"Have you, by any chance, been leaving wild animals in my house a lot this week?" Charlie asked, still looking stern. "I've had a lot of little visitors, some of whom have been eating each other."

"Only dead ones," Temperance said, not thinking this through properly. "Not live ones at all." Her head was spinning with ideas. "You've not found any live ones, have you?"

"Lots of live ones, half a bird, and a piece of bacon that was a lot closer to being alive than would have been my preference."

"They were all dead when I brought them around. Especially the bacon!"

Charlie laughed at this. "You do come up with some things."

Temperance prickled. She hated being laughed at. "Let me prove it to you. Let me put this dead cat in your funny bucket and see what happens."

Charlie considered Miss Fairfax and her self-important manner, and rapidly concluded that adding a dead cat to the bucket would have a certain charm. She also enjoyed the funny ideas the child frequently saw fit to share with her. Indulging

Temperance would brighten an otherwise miserable day. "All right," she said. "Let's do it. For science."

"You're the best," said Temperance, handing over her pathetic find.

At four in the morning, just as the nearest church clock chimed the hour, Charlie stood in her nightdress, candle in hand. The small cat in her kitchen banged against the door, stumbled, and then repeated the motion. The bucket was entirely empty.

Charlie poked life into the ashes in her range and put the kettle on. She found a drop of milk for the cat, and tried very hard to come up with a reasonable explanation. Even once she had consumed several cups of steaming brown brain stimulant, she couldn't put together a line of reasoning less silly than 'the cat came back to life'.

By dawn, she felt a little more awake, and set about letting the sun in. Daylight always made her feel more sensible. The bucket remained empty, the cat continued to be disturbingly alive, even though it hadn't touched the milk. Penny dreadfuls might be full of stories about the returning dead, but one of the most essential principles of Charlie's world view, was that death did not change its mind. The most essential principle she had though, was to trust her own observations and to believe in good evidence. The cat in her kitchen could not be ignored.

Knowing Granny Alice always rose with the dawn, Charlie went to dress, and then crossed the road to consult with her neighbor. Alice might not know any science, but she had a considerable store of common sense. She considered talking to her honorary grandmother, and then realized that her young accomplice should be the one to hear what had happened. The idea of saying it to Alice made her realize just how mad her impressions seemed.

"You been working all night then?" Alice asked as Charlie pushed the door open.

"Not quite. I was wondering if I could talk to Temperance?"

Granny nodded sagely. "What's she been up to this time?"

Charlie decided not to try and explain. Her own mind was in far too much turmoil. "Oh, she's not done anything. I just need some extra hand for what I'm doing today, and she's usually very keen to get into my house. I thought it would make a change to invite her."

"I knew I was right," Temperance said, as soon as Charlie mentioned the condition of the cat. "It's because I'm a genius."

"I'm not sure what's happening here, or why," Charlie cautioned.

"You told me that the secret of good science is to keep testing things until you're sure," Temperance said.

Oddly, things she had stated always sounded cleverer when Temperance said them back to her. It wasn't an entirely comforting feeling. "True," she said. "So, do you want to help?"

"Of course! We're going to need more dead things, aren't we?"

Armed with an old coal scuttle with no known rejuvenating capacities, inventor and child set out in search of the aforementioned dead things. The day was warm and pleasant, ideal for poking around in rubbish heaps. Never before had Charlie felt so enthusiastic about the sticky-sweet aroma of decay. The local pond rewarded them with two drowned puppies, not too swollen. They found several rats in gutters, a bird with a broken neck that had flown into a window, one very large earthworm and most of a stoat. A small boy, who saw them pick up the stoat, offered to kill them a few rabbits.

"Much better eating, rabbits. Stoat like that, won't taste very good," he assured them.

"No thank you," said Charlie.

"Don't say I didn't warn you," said the boy.

After they'd escaped from him, Temperance started talking

29

enthusiastically again. "We should get a bone from the butcher. If we could bring a whole cow back to life from a bone, no one would ever be hungry again. Well, we wouldn't be hungry, and that's the main thing."

"I'm not sure what I'd do with a whole cow," Charlie observed. "Or quite where we'd put it, much less how to get it out of the bucket in the first place. It's too big, a cow."

"You'd just about fit," Temperance replied, poking her long stick into something that could have once been a hedgehog.

"Best leave that," Charlie told her, "I think it's falling apart. And I am not getting in that bucket, and neither are you. We don't know what it does, or how it does it. For all I know, it might kill anything that went in alive."

"I like dead things," Temperance said. "Dying is very sad though. I wouldn't want to try an alive thing in there either, if it could kill them." She sighed. "I wish we'd had that bucket when my little brother died."

Charlie shivered. Experiments with dead animals were one thing, but the idea of putting a human corpse in there made her feel queasy. She scrambled for something safer to talk about.

"The bacon!"

"What?" Temperance looked confused.

"You put bacon in there, and it went moldy. We didn't get a pig out of it, so the bone idea definitely wouldn't work. And the half a bird stayed dead. It has to be a whole creature. "

"Ah," said Temperance, "Could be. Although the bacon was cooked, I bet fried things don't come back. That's like being dead twice over, isn't it?"

Charlie agreed, glad to be on safer ground now.

Chapter Five

Illuminating observations on the perils of an indiscreet life

"If it were a more fashionable town, I could perhaps under-stand," Mrs. Fairfax pronounced over clotted cream and scones.

Justina smiled at her mother. "There is a train station. I get about perfectly well, and it suits me." Having said her piece, she sipped at her tea, unperturbed.

"But the whole affair seems so pointless. We have enough outbuildings. You might have had one of the cottages even. And then I would not have to spend quite so much of my time alone, and missing my little girl without even the likely consolation of grandchildren to contemplate!"

Justina kept smiling indulgently at her mother. It never paid to falter at all. "I have looked into it very thoroughly and it is a good arrangement. There really is no cause for concern on your part and I have hardly been negligent in visiting you."

"It smacks of seriousness. A little dabbling for one's own amusement is appropriate for a person of leisure. To take too much interest suggest professionalism." Mrs. Fairfax shuddered at the word, demonstrating the horror it inspired in her lace covered breast. "I suppose that a little knowledge of antiquities could be considered an accomplishment, they seem all the rage at present, but these things can be taken too far."

"Would it be so very terrible if I were successful and feted as an archaeologist?" Justina asked.

"It would be vile," her mother replied, smearing jam with a rare display of ferocity. "It would be uncouth and unseemly. A woman may be feted for her beauty, as you surely are. A woman may be valued socially for the wealth of her family or husband, but to be able to do anything well, is unspeakably common, and

I do not approve."

"The world is changing, Mother dear," Justina said, rescuing what little remained of the jam.

"Society does not change. The human condition does not change. You court scandal and you will ruin my twilight years with your sordid exploits!" Mrs. Fairfax protested. Despite the passion of her words, she kept her voice smooth and low so as not to attract attention to their dispute.

"I am not a lady whose means allow her to entirely please herself," Justina said, pointedly.

"When I die, it will be all yours and you may please yourself thoroughly, and dance upon my grave as well if you so desire, but you might refrain from such humiliating gestures while I live."

Justina resorted to sipping tea. Sometimes it took a lot of effort not to shout at her mother, but it was a public space and there were standards to maintain. She loathed a scene as much as anyone else. "I wish to make a name for myself as a scholar, and to be able to live independently. I do not see any great shame in that," she remarked.

"Men do not care greatly for independent women," Mrs. Fairfax commented. "Gentlemen of good breeding will not consider you as a potential wife or a suitable mother for their children."

Justina nodded, her fixed facial expression holding up well. "It is would be a great relief to me to find myself no longer sought after by ridiculous young men."

Mrs. Fairfax dabbed at her large, blue eyes with an immaculate handkerchief. "Sometimes, I almost imagine that you say such things purely to vex me."

"Of course not, Mother."

Mrs. Fairfax brightened dramatically at this. It would have been an unnerving shift for anyone unaccustomed to it. Justina did not flinch.

"This afternoon we are to visit my good friend Mrs. Easelfeet," Mrs. Fairfax declared.

Justina's heart sank. Her mother no doubt intended to introduce her to yet another abominable male of the species. "Who is he?" she enquired.

"He's quite a sensation, my dear, but I shall tell you no more for now."

They were all supposedly sensational if one believed Mrs. Fairfax. Brilliant of mind, successful of career, healthy of bank balance and wondrous with facial hair. Except in practice they all seemed so terribly dull and insipid to Justina's critical gaze. Then to make matters worse, the fools invariably threw themselves at her feet, begging for her hand in marriage. Not only was it disconcerting, it could put a person off her lunch entirely, just contemplating it. Justina had long since given up on the idea of marrying a man, and rather whished the men who entered her life would have the decency to come to a similar conclusion.

The parlor was overfull of familiar and overdressed women when Justina and her mother were shown in. She looked around despondently, taking in the grotesque excess of decoration on women far too old to carry such girlish extravagance. They clucked and preened like so many hens, the bulk of their skirts filling up the spaces between closely packed items of furniture. Why it was felt desirable to squeeze so many warmly dressed people into such a confined space, Justina had never understood. It was one of the features of her life that had greatly hampered her social development – she simply did not enjoy being pressed against a large number of other people in the confines of heavily furnished rooms.

A gentleman with exceptional moustaches leapt at once to his feet. He appeared to be wearing a white night gown with rather elaborate embroidery at the collar and cuffs. Seeing him only increased the terrible urge she had been feeling to scream, and run away. Before she could plan an escape, Mrs. Easlefeet hurried forwards to make introductions.

"Ah, my dear, I must present this young lady to you," she began.

Justina loathed her for that. The person of greater social status was asked first, and she could not, possibly, be of lesser consideration than a man who went about in public in a nightgown?

"This is Justina Fairfax, dear Elizobella's daughter. Justina, this is none other than the ArchDruid Henry Caractacus Morestrop Jones!"

As Mrs. Easelfeet continued with an incomprehensible list of further titles, ArchDruid Henry indulged in some complex hand maneuvering and offered her his services.

"Founder of the Brotherhood of Restrained Enlightenment, and current leader of the Truly Venerable Order of English Druids," he added.

Justina took a few careful steps backwards whilst saying, "How charming." She had only encountered Druids once before, at a meeting of the Society of Archaeology an Antiquities. A lecture about whether the Romans might have constructed on Stonehenge had been disrupted by a man, dressed entirely in clothes made from the skins of very small mammals. He had entered without invitation, stood upon a table, waved a sword about and made a wholly unfathomable speech about classical geometry at ancient sites.

Just as she as paused to flee this current scene of dismay, Mrs. Fairfax commenced exalting Justina's many virtues as an antiquarian scholar. With her reputation the new topic of conversation, escape seemed less appealing.

"I myself have a great interest in the ancient times," the strangely dressed man announced. He had the kind of voice that would even whisper loudly. "The Truly Venerable Order of English Druids has written records going back to before even the Roman invasion. Our oldest manuscripts are known to be the work of Taliesin himself."

He paused, and Justina knew she was supposed to be impressed by his claims. Certainly such documents had the power to re-write English history, and that made her very suspicious. It was amazing how many bored gentlemen and obscure vicars turned out to have ancient manuscripts stashed in their attics.

"I should very much like to see these documents," she acknowledged.

"Only the most trusted initiates of our order are permitted to look upon the most ancient and precious relics. You must understand that, as guardians, we have a duty to keep the writings safe."

"Then I suppose you had better initiate me," she said.

For a moment, the ArchDruid hesitated. "You are a woman, it would be most unsuitable." He smiled. "But fair maidens are always welcome as flower bearers and pourers of wine at our public solemnities, should you feel inspired to attend and celebrate with us as our priesthood has done from the very dawn of time."

"Perhaps not," Justina said. She wanted to ask what the order had been called before its name alluded so obviously to its ancientness. Looking around at the sea of enthusiastic faces, she decided not to bother. There were times in life when it did not pay to be reasonable, and she had a keen sense of this being just such a one.

Temperance perched comfortably on the outhouse roof, throwing small stones at anything within range, and several things that weren't. "Take that!" she shouted at the empty air around her.

Her airship, The Diligent Squid had finally emerged from the last of the clouds. Temperance could see now that they had left all the other airships far behind them. The crew were ecstatic, waving swords and pistols. She raised her fist and shouted out, "Three cheers for Black Alice," and they all cheered.

It was no small thing, being the granddaughter of the fiercest, most dangerous sky pirate in the world. No one could stop them, or catch them.

"Black Alice says tea is ready," Granny called from the yard, "And you'd better not have scuffed the toes off your shoes climbing up there."

Temperance climbed down from the rigging. No one risked angering Black Alice. Walking the plank from an airship did not tend to improve a person's health.

One of Ebenezer Smith's chickens had died during the night. From the top of the outhouse roof, Temperance could see and hear the Smiths debating in the garden over whether the bird might be safe to eat. From there she had apparently managed to procure the deceased one for herself. Charlie had no idea what had happened between roof and chicken delivery or how Temperance had persuaded the couple to give her the carcass. They were a kindly old pair though, and the girl could be charming when she wanted something. As with their other complete and recently dead things, the chicken had revived. Unlike previous experiments, this one had been returned to its confused owners on the following day. Charlie had a feeling the bucket had sped up with the process, but not having timed a re-animation, she wasn't sure.

"How?" Ebenezer asked, as Charlie handed the chicken over.

"Science," she said. It had taken her a while beforehand to decide on the best strategy for handling such questions.

"Oh, well, if it's science, that must be alright then, I suppose," said Ebenezer, taking his chicken from her hands.

There were so many variables to consider and investigate so as to enable a proper understanding of the resurrection business. The creature had to be viable in terms of having enough component parts. A dried frog would come back, half a rat wouldn't. Bacon did not turn into pigs, it just smelled worse. At least that made a kind of mechanical sense.

Word of Charlie's new and remarkable resurrection skills got around, as she knew must happen after the chicken. A slow but steady stream of departed creatures appeared at her door. Often accompanied by eager children who wanted to watch, and pouted when told that they couldn't. Having dead animals in the house overnight was one thing, but she drew the line at living children. After the first day, Charlie constructed a cage around the bucket, so that those returning to life did not go wandering around the room or come visiting up the stairs any more. People left her coins and other small offerings, which felt odd. It was as though her house had turned into some sort of saintly shrine.

Try as she might to think about experiments, the whole process felt less and less like proper science. There was something uncanny about the cauldron, and she became increasingly conscious of it as a presence in her house, as though it were a living thing with a mind of its own. Sometimes, when working, she found herself talking to it, and that didn't seem like a good sign. To her relief, it never proffered any audible answers.

"What are we going to do with you though, that's the question," she asked the cauldron as it worked upon a recently departed dog.

Eventually, Miss Fairfax was bound to come back and demand the return of her find. Despite much consideration of the issue, Charlie had no idea what she would do, or say, when the moment came. Her current strategy rested entirely on the hope that she wouldn't get to that point. Somehow, magically, the archaeologist would fail to return, or fail to remember, and all would be uncomplicated. Insofar as a life spent putting dead things in a rejuvenating bucket could ever be said to be uncomplicated. If things carried on in this vein, she would become a full-time resurrectionist, with a bit of science on the side by way of a hobby. That future did not entirely charm her.

As it happened, Miss Fairfax had temporarily forgotten about her cauldron. A scholarly acquaintance had helped her to a place on a dig at a stately home in Oxfordshire. A planned extension to the house, which had been growing steadily since 1746, resulted in some objects being discovered. Convinced that a glorious family history would be revealed, taking them back to the Norman conquest, the house had been thrown open to any enthusiastic and well-bred Digger who might feel inclined to lend assistance. Due to a slight error in the posting of this news, a confused group of Diggers were now camped on the lawn. This caused no small amount of disruption, not least because none of the family, or the archaeologists thought that Diggers existed. The Diggers, on the other hand were entirely convinced of their own reality, denied all suggestions of being several hundred years out of date, and insisted that they should be allowed to dig. They rather fancied the lawn for this enterprise, and a stalemate had rapidly been achieved.

Between the Diggers, archaeologists, lawyers, constables, family members and an increasing number of sightseers, Miss Fairfax found herself entirely occupied.

On the day after Miss Fairfax's hired help was picked up by the police, her pockets full of tableware, Barker Street talked of little else. It was not an area prone to great excitement, in a town which had steadfastly ignored as many great events as it possibly could. Evidently the mistress-free establishment had proved too great a temptation for the solitary servant. Either that, or sheer boredom had prompted her to run away.

Granny Alice leaned against the fence, puffing on her pipe and sharing wild, unfounded speculations with Charlie Rowcroft. The fate of hired help and the absent archaeologist featured heavily.

Edith Smith hobbled down the street to join them. "We ate that chicken, in the end," she said by way of a greeting. "Didn't lay any more eggs after it died the first time."

"Must have been a shock to it, the dying," Alice said. "And the coming back, almost bound to put it off a bit I reckon."

"Well, I said a word to our minister about it on Sunday and he said that while resurrection was all well and good for Lazarus, it didn't seem right in a chicken. He thinks it is ungodly!"

The Smiths were chapel folk, and about as close as Bromstone had ever come to having citizens who publically advertised themselves as radically unconventional.

"How can it be ungodly" Charlie enquired. "Surely, if God thought they shouldn't come back, they wouldn't." Charlie's relationship with faith had a warm, hazy quality to it. The idea of asking the kinds of questions of God that she would ask of the material world had always seemed disrespectful. Best to keep God out of the messier details, she felt. For the greater part, she left him alone, and he'd shown no signs of any personal interest in her. It all seemed very reasonable, and most of the time she gave it no thought at all.

"Tasted all right with a nice bit of rosemary stuffing, mind you. I don't know what the minister's position on stuffing is. I haven't dared to ask," Edith added.

The three of them watched in curious silence as the postman entered the far end of Barker Street. Very few of the inhabitants were ever troubled by items that came by post. Usually, if the postman came at all it was as a shortcut to somewhere else. Still, there was no knowing where fate, or letters, might strike, so they studied his progress with interest.

None of them spoke as the envelope was deposited through Charlie's letter box. The postman passed on under their silent gazed.

"Best go and see what it is then," Granny said.

Charlie knew she'd get no peace until she divulged the contents of the delivery, so she brought the mystery envelope back outside. Hopefully, it was another commission.

"Dear sir, we have heard that you are the possessor of a metal cauldron. We wish to purchase this, and offer you the sum of five hundred pounds."

There was an address in Bromstone for her to reply to.

"Must be some kind of a joke," Alice said. "That's silly money."

"It's also not mine to sell," Charlie pointed out.

"I'd take it as a sign from God," Edith added, confidently. "I'd take the money, give up resurrection, go somewhere nice and make a donation to a church. If it was me."

Charlie scratched her head. "I'm going to have to sleep on this, at the very least."

Stood in the ramshackle room that served as both kitchen and workshop, Charlie looked around. It wasn't a very large space. Considering her work, it barely counted as 'adequate' and then only because she couldn't cook and lived mostly on cake. Right now her provisions consisted of the stale end of a loaf in the cupboard, and a whole box of Penance Biscuits. Five hundred pounds. A person of modest tastes could live on that for a fair while. A person with five hundred pounds could afford a proper workshop and the time to really invent something. On the other hand, it wasn't her cauldron to sell. But…she had put it together, and discovered the strange properties that gave it such worth. Without her work, there would have been no such offer. She could pay the archaeologist later, if the woman came back. Some of the money. Something fair.

She looked at the cauldron – currently empty – and wondered what to do for the best. It made her uneasy, and felt like a responsibility ill-suited to her particular shoulders. And at the same time this offer of money was a fairy tale blessing, and hardly to be ignored.

"You don't make life easy for people, do you?" she said. She could imagine the cauldron nodding agreement to this, although not what it might nod with. Imagining responses was worse than talking to it. "I don't think we're good for each other," she added, conscious of sounding like someone from a bad romance.

The longer Charlie thought about it, stomach rumbling as she softened stale bread in her tea, the more convinced she became. Why not take the money? She could work out the details with Miss Fairfax if the need ever arose.

Chapter Six

On the proper employment of females

A week into the great Chaveny Manor dig, the weather turned for the worse. Damp and dreary mornings replaced the previous congenial sun. The sightseers vanished, as though dissolved by the persistent moisture. Two of the hobbyists were unexpectedly called back to somewhere no doubt warm and dry. With fewer people under foot, the real work increased dramatically. On the lawn, the Diggers sat about dolefully, their part in the dwindling carnival ever less certain. Justina hadn't devoted much time to them, not least because they seemed an indolent lot, including far too many young men in their ranks. She wished to dig, not fend off unfortunate marriage proposals.

"Why is no one paying them any attention, do you imagine?" Clarissa Bentley-Smythe asked as they worked together.

Clarissa was the kind of archaeologist Mrs. Fairfax would approve of. Her spotless, white gloves never touched soil. She made careful notes, and charming remarks, called herself a 'happy amateur' and was clearly looking for a suitable husband.

"The Diggers?" Justina replied, whilst poking about with her trowel. "I have no idea. They can hardly be considered decorative."

"I believe retro-politics are the height of fashion in Paris at present," Clarissa added dreamily. "All the pleasant distractions, but no one expecting you will actually do anything."

"They aren't serious then?" Justina asked.

"Oh, of course not. It is a sport to them, I have been told."

"Perhaps they would like it if you took interest in them," Justina observed.

Her immaculate companion flashed a glance at the party on the lawn. "I do believe there are some interesting gentlemen amongst them. The fourth son of the Duke of Monmouthshire. The third son of Lord Entwhistle, and at least three... oh, it is hardly polite to say what they are, but perhaps I might observe that their fathers are also great gentlemen." She sighed. "I can hardly approach them alone, it would be indecent! Would you not chaperone me, Miss Fairfax? You are quite old enough to be safe from them, I think."

Although she had every intention of being safe from them, she could have happily gouged the girl's eyes out for the remark. "I can spare a moment," she said. "Let us walk in their general direction and see if we know any of them. It is such a nuisance to have to find an appropriate person to make introductions."

Within the hour, she was entirely free of Clarissa Bentley-Smythe and confident that archaeology would be none the poorer for having married off another feeble dabbler.

One of the chaps found what everyone agreed must be mediaeval pottery, in very small pieces. It clearly demonstrated a longstanding noble presence at the site. There was also a sizeable pit that contained a wholly different kind of earth. It had a bluish tinge, and no one could make any sense of this at all. Mindful of Doctor Melgrave's advice, Justina had been trying to find a better suggestion than that it might be left over from cloth dyeing. But what else could it be, so smooth in texture, and in such vast quantity? It must have been widely available and of no great worth. She surmised that the blueness may have been due to the passage of time, but could not think what might have become blue. She had no idea.

"We should be careful, in case it is poisonous," she said.

Almost at once, three young men proposed to send samples to one eminent gentleman or another, taking the opportunity to advertise excellent connections. They had all been vying for her attention for a while now, although she had been doing her best to ignore it. It was just matter of time before one of them proposed. While it was gratifying having them listen to her opinions and take her seriously, the fear that it all came down to matrimonial desires rather ruined the pleasure for her.

It felt as though a flash of magic had illuminated her brain. "It might be the remnant of some mediaeval torture method," she pronounced. "The skeletons of ravaged victims might, even now, lie waiting for us somewhere in the depths if this sinister substance has not dissolved them entirely."

Disprove that, Doctor Melgrave.

Her three admirers threw down their trowels and hurried for shovels.

Four feet into the deposit of blue sludge, work ceased because Justina had found a small, bronze item in another location. It could have been almost anything, but they were hungry for success. One young man declared it to be a Roman bathing implement, another swore it must be medical in application while the third assure them that it had to be the sacrificial bade from an ancient pagan shrine, further evidence of which, they would surely find. Justina had not bothered to remember the names of the enthusiastic trio. There were always such fellows, and they had long since blurred into one another in her perceptions. They were like a plague and to be treated with disdain.

Yet more urgent letters were sent to gentlemen whose great repute meant that they were not at Chaveny Manor already. An expert in Roman remains appeared for precisely an hour, lured by descriptions of a mosaic that, once clean, turned out to be the floor of an old pig sty, a feature the resident family had forgotten to mention.

None of the three shiny-faced boys claimed to have invited ArchDruid Henry Caractacus Morestrop Jones, but he came none the less.

"I see where you are in error," he announced, as soon as he was in earshot of the bemused archaeologists. He did not even have the decency to wait upon introductions. "You are digging in quite the wrong place. The temple, plainly, would have been to the east of the complex, in the direction of the rising sun. Here would have been the sacred grove and there, no doubt, the pool wherein great treasures were deposited as offerings." He raised a finger and indicated the sprawling mass of Chaveny Manor. "There is no helping it, the building must be destroyed if any valuable work is to be done here."

His booming voice carried with ease not only to the archaeologists, but also to the ignored and unwanted Diggers. In the midst of more intellectual challenges, no one had found the time to evict this small and melancholy band, although a few had departed of their own volition. They might be the sons of great men, but they were not dressed in a way that enabled anyone to invite them inside, or even offer them tea on the lawn. It was most embarrassing. On hearing the ArchDruid, they rose up as one man, spades at the ready. It looked as though they were entirely willing to set about demolition work at once.

Justina foresaw potential embarrassment if things got out of hand. She felt, as the highest socially ranking person currently standing in a hole, morally obliged to act. "Should we not consult the owners first?" she enquired.

"Ownership is theft," one of the Diggers pronounced.

"The owners will understand that we serve a higher purpose," the ArchDruid claimed.

"I realize I have an urgent funeral to attend," one of the admirers added, creating his own cue for a swift exit.

Justina felt all too alone as she tried to calm the chaotic situation. "Surely we should not commence before afternoon tea has been taken?" she tried, in desperation.

"Oh, that is a great statement of wisdom," one of her remaining admirers piped up. He didn't look like the sort to demolish another man's seat without at least having had a cucumber sandwich first.

"Just one small thing," the other admirer said, his young voice tinged with unmanly squeaks. "It is my house, after all. One doesn't suppose the parents would be amused by its deconstruction. They were intending to make it larger, not smaller." He gazed thoughtfully at the Diggers before continuing. "Why don't you chaps take up Chartism instead? Digging is dreadfully out of date. Do you not keep up with the niceties of political objection?"

"It's retro-objection," one of the Digging gentlemen responded. "It's far more fashionable than Chartism. We don't dirty our hands with the sordid details of contemporary politics!"

"I'm sure that must be very pleasant for you, but kindly do it somewhere other than on my lawn!" The young man of the house concluded. "There will be no cake for you, and no demolition work either."

By the looks on his face, Justina knew the youth had no sense at all of political fashion, much less what one might do with a chart. The idea of retro-objection had come as a surprise to them all, only Miss Bentley-Smythe seemed to have a prior awareness. Fashion could occupy so much of a person's attention, it seemed. Politics was not Justina's sphere, be it actual or leisurely, and she thought organized prejudice against charts seemed rather extreme. Charts could be rather useful, she supposed, for people who did things on paper. Didn't these foolish young men have anything better to do? From their shoes alone she could tell they were not utterly impoverished. Several of them had quite decent coats, and shirts that might have been smart, had it not been for days spent on other people's lawns. She suspected them all of being youngest sons, a pernicious tribe, who would not inherit, and whose older brothers had already been allocated to church, doctoring, lawyers work and the army. What remained for them but the ignoble fate of politics? It only showed the importance of keeping young people gainfully occupied, if they did not have proper fortunes of their own.

That evening, between the fish course and a rather disappointing sorbet, the young man of the house challenged his rival to a duel, at dawn. This would be the fifth duel she had knowingly been the cause of, although Justina went to considerable lengths to avoid these embarrassments. Thus far there had only been one fatality. She thought longingly of her little retreat in Barker Street, and determined to get out of this tiresome place the very next day. The street had no male inhabitants under the age of fifty, and as a consequence her brief time there had been free from proposals of any kind. She could rest, regain her strength, and see if her find had turned into anything interesting.

Her reflections were disturbed as one of the admirers banged his fork handle upon the table in a most unbecoming way. He rose to leave. Justina followed her instinct for etiquette by carefully undertaking to see and hear nothing of his departure.

A large hand clasped her shoulder. Warm breath annoyed her tender ear.

"You do cause a stir, don't you?" said Henry Caractacus Morestrop Jones.

His perfectly loud whisper was audible to all of the other diners. To Justina's relief, the mistress of Chaveny promptly suggested that the ladies should withdraw. Rising with all the grace she could muster, Justina was determined not to show her discomfort. Even when the ArchDruid patted her bottom. Her small bustle saved her from feeling more than a tremor of contact, but it did not please her.

She had only just finished undressing and brushing out her long hair when a firm knock reverberated against her bedroom door. The eternal stream of proposing devotees had not previously produced a late-night door knocker. Intrigued, she went to see which one of them had found his courage. Through the inch of open door, she was surprised to identify the unmistakable, candle-lit moustache of Henry Jones.

"I thought you could use a good rogering," he said.

Justina smiled. Apparently the age of chivalry wasn't dead after all.

Before there was any risk of seeing which dueler triumphed, Justina made good her escape from Chaveny Manor, by the insalubrious means of a farmer's cart. Henry Jones might be entertaining bedroom company for one night, but when it came to matters historical, the man was barking mad. He had, between bouts of feverish passion, explained far too much of his personal philosophy.

Quoting assorted equally mad Welshman, he built a picture of a world that had nothing to do with this one. A world full of ancient survivals and rivalries. Possessed by a vision from no lesser a person than God Almighty, he was clearly one conversation away from being gently recommended to an asylum. She supposed that while he remained able to afford fine shirts and well-cut waistcoats, and continued capable of remembering how to wear them, he would be safe. Poverty would see him incarcerated if an embarrassed family did not. With their tryst already fading from memory, she felt quite indifferent to his likely future.

As the farmer's wagon bumped cheerfully down the uneven lane, Justina listened to the birds singing and smiled to herself. The Chaveny Manor dig was fast becoming a disaster, and she felt relieved to have departed from it. Fond recollections of Barker Street filled her thoughts. She should have a few days of respite there, at least. Sooner or later her mother would demand attention. And then? Some new adventure, perhaps. She was bored with the dubious spoils of muddy, English fields. Somewhere in the world there might be a place with a pleasant dry climate, likely treasure and men who eschewed marriage proposals in favor of far less honorable and far more entertaining alternatives.

Number seven turned out to be cold and damp on arrival.

There were no fires lit. Closer inspection revealed no trace of the girl she had hired, and also showed the absence of certain valuable household items. It meant she had no choice but to fend for herself. How hard could it be to make a fire and boil a kettle? One employed twelve-year-old girls whose education had been rudimentary, and they managed such tasks. Clearly a superior mind would not struggle to locate the kettle. An educated woman would know what one did to commence a fire, surely? Justina wracked her brains for inspiration. Normally, one walked into a room on a chilly day, and there the fire would be, burning cheerfully in the hearth. Servants, were how one lit fires. But still, one did not expect servants to be in possession of any great intellect, and therefore...

"She knows some very rude words," Temperance announced as she climbed down from her spying place. "She's just thrown a kettle right across the garden, and her face is all dirty and it was ever so funny."

Granny Alice pondered this assessment of the neighbor for a little while. "She's come back then?"

Temperance nodded. "I wonder where she went? Maybe she was kidnapped by pirates and sold into slavery and it's taken her these last two weeks to escape and get back and I bet there were fights and guns and..."

"Temperance Perry, have you been reading penny dreadfuls again?"

"Sorry, Granny."

"Filling your head with nonsense! If she'd been sold into slavery, she'd never have got all the way back here in just two week, would she? Foolish girl."

"Maybe it was slavery in Yorkshire, that's close enough," Temperance said, defensively.

"I wouldn't like to say what goes on in Yorkshire," Granny answered, darkly.

After some deliberation, she went round to number seven. A rich young woman in pursuit of a cup of tea might very easily set the whole street on fire if someone didn't keep an eye on her.

After Granny Alice had put out the fire in the bread bin and commenced one in the range, it did not take very long to retrieve and fill the kettle. A great deal of work needed doing, but Miss Fairfax was a different order of person entirely, and Granny had standards.

"There's not a bite of food in the house, your best bet would be The Coach House down on the main road." Other disadvantaged neighbors she would have taken in and fed, but Miss Fairfax had a mouth that sneered too often and furthermore, Granny did not want to get into any awkward conversations just now, about missing buckets.

Everything it crossed her mind to say seemed to allude to the item. 'Dug up anything good lately?' 'Did that girl of yours steal much?' Better by far to send the young lady down to the inn for her supper. A woman like Miss Fairfax had no business at all living somewhere like Barker Street, where no one else had maids or went gadding about for weeks at a time. Once you moved somewhere like this, Alice felt, your gadding days should be safely historical.

"What about that girl of yours? She is of the right age. Can she work?" Miss Fairfax demanded.

Alice bridled. "My Temperance is not going to be anybody's maid. I've not been bringing her up all this time just to put her in service, thank you very much." She huffed. "Kettle's almost boiled. I'm sure you can manage on your own now. I'll see myself out, thank you."

Justina over-stewed the tea, the result so bitter and tepid that it offended both the throat and the stomach. It was no good, she could not possibly continue in such barbarous circumstances. How anyone survived without servants was a mystery to her.

Evidently there were two kinds of people in the world, and she belonged to the sort that could not reasonably be expected to deal with the sordid details of life. She would have to try her luck with the inn for the night and then retreat to her mother's little place in the country until help could be secured. Someone must run a bath for her. She could hardly live without having her shoes polished and her dress brushed. Mother had a cook, several maids, footmen, a butler and a chap who did...whatever it was that one employed outdoors chaps to do. She would be safe there.

The family home looked as though it had been the recent scene of a small-scale peasant's uprising. On approaching, Justina half-expected to see some new manifestation of retro-objection. Familiar items of furniture were strewn, forlorn-looking across the front garden, depriving innocent flowers of sunlight. Alongside the usual servants, new creatures bustled, labored, fetched and carried. For a moment, Justina feared that the house had been sold in her absence, and the new occupants were, even now, redecorating. Fortuitously, her mother stepped out of the front door at that very instant. Even with the style-disaster of a shapeless dress and eccentric veil, her presence did a good deal to allay fears.

"This is not the best time, my dear. You will have to make do with whatever can be managed," Mrs. Fairfax said.

"What on earth has happened?" Justina hoped for a simple explanation, like a parlor ruined by water damage, a fire in the sun room and other such natural disasters.

"I have been inspired. We are constructing an altar in the drawing room, which catches the sunrise to best effect. It will be just like the sacred places of the ancients!"

"Only, in the drawing room?" Justina wondered if this could be an especially unreasonable dream which would soon dissipate and leave her in a far nicer reality.

"We're going to have a splendid mural on the wall, and we must have a tree, somehow. Do you think a tree in a pot might create the right impression?"

It took Justina a little while to locate the critical detail that had been troubling her. "To whom do you refer, mother, when you say 'we'?"

"Oh, my dear." The matron blushed. "It has all happened so quickly. A whirlwind, a wonder. Such energy, such inspiration, such..." She smiled in a way that did not improve her daughter's mood at all.

For all her many eccentricities, Justina's mother had never before converted perfectly sensible drawing rooms into pagan shrines. Nor did she blush, and that kind of smiling was positively indecent.

"Your room is as you left it. I shall be back before supper." With that, Mrs. Fairfax departed.

Justina reflected that she preferred it when her mother played at being a quiet and retiring widow. These rushes of enthusiasm never boded well. But at least there would be supper, without the indignity of having no cutlery to speak of.

As Temperance Perry, pirate queen of the seven seas waved her cutlass, the soldiers all stepped back. Three of them fell in the sea because of this. All of the other pirates were dead, the boat sinking under brutal cannon fire.

It was just her, and Archduke Albert Nose left now.

"I am the granddaughter of Black Alice. You will never take me alive!"

In her head she could hear Black Alice herself saying, "That's not a very good battle cry, and if you wave a real blade about like that, you'll probably cut your own leg off."

"I reckon we ought to hang you," said Archduke Albert Nose.

"You did that yesterday and it was very dull," the pirate queen pointed out. "I'm going to kill myself heroically instead."

The archduke folded his arms. "Go on then."

Temperance Perry fell over, making a point of not rolling around dramatically. It was going to be a more dignified sort of death this time.

Chapter Seven

Lessons in remembering our civic duty towards our neighbors

On Tuesday mornings, Alice liked to take a gentle stroll into town, to make a few purchases and arrange her orders for the week. Mondays were wash day, and she preferred to be wholly traditional about that. After Tuesday, the week was entirely at liberty to surprise her. Usually, it didn't. The Tuesday of this particular week threatened drizzle through breakfast, but promised to clear up by the return journey. She felt hopeful about the prospect of getting the laundry dry. The downside to taking in other people's washing, was what to do when the sun chose not to cooperate with the process. Ever since Charlie's arrival she'd been saying that the girl should make an indoor wind machine. It would solve a lot of problems. As yet, no miraculous laundry solution had arrived.

Baskets of damp clothes and linens cluttered her otherwise neat kitchen. Later would come the weekly wrestling match of ironing. Getting the creases out of linen required tactics that an army commander would have taken pride in, and persistence enough to fuel several martyrs. Alice liked a challenge. It wasn't that she needed the modest sums laundry brought in. It just gave her something easy to get angry with. So long as there was creased linen to do battle with, she probably wouldn't end up killing anyone.

Walking past the front door, she noticed a funny box on her step. Granny Alice paused, and cast a cautious eye up and down the street. Aside from herself, there was only an escaped chicken in view. She picked up the box.

Anderson's Penance Biscuits, salvation from your sins. Leave behind the false life of gluttony and rejoice in the foodstuffs sent to purify your soul and save you from damnation.

Alice gave the box a very dark look. It struck her as a nasty sort of thing to leave lying around. She wondered if someone wanted to send her a message.

In the baker's, Mrs. Waterbottom sidled up to her. "Have you seen the new road they've made, just beyond mine?"

Alice hadn't, and confessed as much. The small town of Bromstone had doubled in size of late. She didn't like it at all, but what could a person do?

"Ugly things," Mrs. Waterbottom continued. "Not so much space as would let a mouse get between them. I've been watching them go up. Awful sad-looking. I don't see who would want to live there."

"I suppose if you're poor enough, and kind of roof will do," Alice observed.

"That's as maybe," Mrs. Watterbottom responded at once. "I've never known anyone that poor in all my life, but you not being from around here, you might know different, I suppose."

Alice had lived in Bromstone for the best part of thirty years, but that still made her a foreigner. "That's all a very long time ago," she said. "Aren't they all fearfully poor in the cities now, and out in the colonies, for that matter?"

"That's no reason to come and be poor round here," Mrs. Waterbottom pronounced. "Although I did hear these are for workers, for the new factory, so I suppose they must be from away. Do you think they'll talk funny?"

"If they're from away, I've no doubt of it," Alice said. Thirty years of residency gave her that much authority, at least.

There was something unwholesome about eating breakfast with a man whose carnal acquaintance one had recently made. Justina normally avoided such socially troubling experiences by departing from the scene of her adventure with all haste.

Although the kind of fellow she preferred usually had the decency to make a swift exit himself and spare her all discomfort. Only once had she and her companion in debauchery fled in error to the same train. That had not been disastrous, she recalled. However, the poor ticket inspector had been quite put out.

Sitting opposite a recent conquest at breakfast might put a woman of heightened sensibilities off her kedgeree. When that same chap had clearly done something unthinkable with one's own mother...recently...perhaps more than once...Justina found it quite impossible to eat her toast, much less contemplate nibbling anything more robust. It was a most distasteful, disgraceful situation and she could not possibly continue under this roof in the presence of this man. The speed of it! To have come almost directly from her bed, to her mother's! Or had he been a guest here before, and taken a slight detour into her company? Justina could hardly bear to imagine it.

Indiscretions carried out tactfully in the privacy of other people's residences were one thing. Even the suggestion that one's mother might undertake a liaison, seemed dreadfully crass. Of course a person knew these things in a broad, and general sense, but it was quite another to be unavoidably, and specifically aware of what had happened. That her parent had so little self-regard as to entertain the man at home, offended Justina's sense of social dignity. But where to go?

Barker Street without a servant was unthinkable. The whole business of hiring help perturbed her. Really one needed to hire someone with the right outlook who could then sift through the array of potential girls and discover which one would suffice. In the current circumstances, appealing to her mother for aid would not solve the quandary. Justina packed her bags. She would have to stay at a hotel and sort the wretched hiring issue out herself. It seemed most unfair. Why had all her childhood lessons involved French, and piano music? Surely someone could have taught her how to manage staff? Or was it supposed to come to one naturally, as an inevitable consequence of the right breeding? Justina feared to mention her difficulty in case this turned out to be true, and marked her as a pariah. On the whole she did not respect natural things. Artifice seemed much more refined, more civilized. Poor people did things naturally, because they knew no better. Artifice had to be learned, and paid for. Servants did not fit into the scheme tidily at all.

Charlie had always imagined it would be easy. With space to work in and money enough for food, the whole inventing business would naturally follow. She had always wanted to be an inventor, ever since she'd seen a threshing machine in action. The noise and smell of it haunted her imagination. Realizing someone had created that extravagant beast set her on a quest to be able to make one of her own. Well, not necessarily a thrashing machine, but something that banged, chugged and emitted smoke, at any rate. Childhood had involved a great deal of clandestine dismantling, from grandfather clocks to unfortunate mice. She wanted to know how the insides of everything worked. In time, she became able to reassemble the clock such that they functioned once more. Until this curious business with the bucket, she'd not managed the same trick with the mice.

So far that morning, Charlie had cleaned all of her dishes, sorted through her cupboards and emptied the entire kitchen table of notes and detritus, in readiness for The Big Invention. Since then, she had consumed three cups of tea, made innumerable trips to the window, and eaten her entire supply of biscuits. On the table, a solitary sheet of paper gazed up at her. Its blankness felt like an accusation. Everything was perfect, ready and in place. She just couldn't think of anything to invent.

"Bugger!"

In all those years of dreaming about this moment, she had been picturing herself *as* an inventor. Not actually inventing something. The realization that she didn't really have any ideas just now, depressed her enormously.

In the last few days, she'd been over every project she'd half formed in the past, and come up with a grand total of no ideas for taking any of them forwards. Yesterday, Temperance had been round with a list of impossible suggestions – from machines that would make sure you never got lost, to spectacles for short-sighted felines. The cat they had most recently revived kept walking into things. It didn't care for anything much, as far as they could tell, but who knew what effects resurrection might have on a creature's mind? Or for that matter, how it had been before death.

There was no inspiration to be found in staring at the blank page. Charlie deposited a shapeless hat on her head, and picked up her decrepit shopping basket. At least she could pretend to be doing something, and walking might help her think. She stepped outside.

"You've forgotten it's the Lord's day then?" Edith Smith called out from her front garden.

Charlie frequently lost track of days, sleeping entirely through some of them, and occasionally dreaming extra ones into existence. She shrugged and walked across to where Edith stood. "I might find something."

"Ah, it would be best for you if you found Jesus," Edith sighed.

Charlie resisted the temptation to note out loud that he probably wouldn't fit in her basket anyway. She'd never been very good about going to church, but had the impression from her infrequent visits that she wasn't alone in this. God didn't seem to put in a personal appearance every week either. All things considered, that was probably as well.

It apparently being a Sunday, no one was working on the new road, and Charlie walked through its eerie silence alone. She had never before seen a road like it. The nearly completed buildings on one side had no gaps between them at all. There were no gardens. Not so much as a square of dirt to dangle the washing over. More troubling yet, there were no windows whatsoever. The scene made her shiver. What kind of life would a person live here, in the darkness, deprived of a view, deprived even a scrubby corner of grass to call their own? The row was close to the externally complete factory building, so that workers would need mere minutes to go from the newly built hovels to the gates. It wouldn't be much of a life.

As yet, no painted boards announced what kind of production would take place inside those unhappy looking walls. Generally, Charlie undertook not to think about the relationship between her efforts and actual industry. She'd always imagined that inventing would make the world a better place. Today, she felt far less certain. Between this observation and her previous lack of creativity, Charlie started to wonder about her whole life. What was it for? What was she doing? Her dreams had been big, and vague. The need to earn money had kept them that way. One day she would have time. One day she would work on an amazing project destined to change the world. Time and money she now had, but inspiration remained sadly lacking. What did the world need? More machines? Faster machines? Or something else? Looking at the melancholy development around her, the only thing she felt certain of was that progress did not look like this.

Her mother had warned that she must eventually come to crisis as a consequence of the life she had chosen. Unwed, childless, dried up and dissatisfied, was her mother's prophecy, meant to shock her into matrimony. Charlie had fought long and hard not to conform to other people's expectations. Especially that one. This was no time for regrets. She just needed to fine tune the grand plan a little.

"You look like you've lost a guinea and found a shilling," Alice commented as Charlie let herself in.

"Oh, I'm not too bad, just wondering what I should do next."

At this point, Temperance climbed out from beneath the table. "You could be a highwayman. That would be exciting and you'd make lots of money. You probably need to steal a horse first, and you'll be hanged when they catch you, but it'll be fun until then. Definitely."

"Oddly enough, the prospect of certain death never struck me as being a good feature in a job," Charlie said.

"You've got to be willing to accidentally blow yourself to bits, if you want to be an inventor," Temperance replied, defiantly.

Charlie smiled. "Perhaps that's where I've been going wrong."

"Temperance, go and sweep the front path," Granny ordered.

With sullen noises sufficient to make clear a whole multitude of grievances, Temperance departed.

Granny Alice looked Charlie up and down. "You've got this far. Now all you have to do is keep going."

Not wanting to sound like Temperance, Charlie managed not to heave a self-pitying sigh. "I don't know what I'm doing anymore."

"I'd think about it this way," said Granny. "There's folks who set their minds on making money, and folks who want to do some good in the world. Most of us don't get a lot of choice, beyond trying to make ends meet. But you get to choose. There's money and fame on one hand, good deeds on the other. Not many people get to do both together, so don't go counting on that for an easy answer."

Charlie considered this. "I'd never thought about it that way."

"Well, think about it. And have a chew on one of these, if you want." Alice pushed a box across the table.

Eat your way towards a better eternity announced the packaging. Charlie recognized the familiar, smug descriptions of the Penance Biscuits. There had been a pamphlet through her door that morning suggesting them as a suitable gift for family, friends or neighbors who needed guiding back onto the path of right-eousness. It made her feel a bit queasy.

"Second lot I've had turn up on my doorstep. Someone's idea of a joke maybe," Alice explained.

Charlie took a Penance Biscuit, and wondered if it was some sort of sign.

The new girl had the kind of unspellable Old Testament name that sounded ridiculous when applied to a plain-faced fourteen-year-old. Justina decided that the help would instead answer to Mary, a decision to which Mary acquiesced in a most encour-aging manner. They established that Mary, although not quick in her speech, grasped the mysteries of range and kettle, the details of cleaning and the importance of a nice fire in the sitting room. She showed a pleasing lack of interest in her employer's personal life and work, promising to stay entirely out of the small garden except when drying clothes or disposing of unmentionable things. Justina felt that she had matured considerably in her household management skills and thus felt able to devote the entire afternoon to work.

The finds she had left outside where unharmed, her larcenous former employee oblivious to their potential value. Justina had no idea about their worth either. She had not reached a stage in her research where that would be relevant. About this time it occurred to her that her find from Wales might be reconstructed. She hastened to the inventor's door.

"Ah," said Charlie, poking her head round the side of the house.

Justina nodded. "Good afternoon Miss... Miss..." She could not recall the name.

"Rowcroft. I see you're back in residence."

The inventor had never been one for small talk during their previous conversations, so this bluntness came as no surprise.

"Have you made any progress with my pieces?" As Justina

voiced the enquiry, she had the distinct impression that her words had caused some discomfort.

"Umm," Miss Rowcroft said. "I was about to go out, as it happens."

"Might I see your progress, at the very least?" Justina watched as her words caused the other woman to wilt, visibly. Clearly something was amiss. "Have you damaged it? Broken it? You may as well say so, madam, we shall make no progress with this dithering of yours." That straightened the inventor out, and caused a dramatic shift in her facial expression.

"I have sold it."

"To whom?" Justina was too amazed to be angry, yet.

"I don't really know."

"As a completed item, or in pieces?" She could not imagine who would have wanted it, either way. "Or as scrap metal?"

"Whole," confessed the inventor. "I made it into a kind of large, round bucket, in the end."

"So, where is it now? A private collection, a museum, or a university?" She kept wondering how anyone could have found out about it, unless Miss Rowcroft was not at all as she seemed, and had significant connections in society.

"I assume it was a private buyer. I can furnish you with the address, if you like?"

Justina nodded. "Yes, as a matter of some urgency. I must know what has become of it."

"And the money?" Charlie asked.

"Oh, hang the money! I don't care a jot about that, but if it makes someone else unjustly famous I shall... I'll... I warn you...it won't be nice."

She would write at once. It might yet be possible to get her name associated with the find. Not that unearthing a large metal bucket sounded terribly auspicious, but one couldn't be too careful. The money made her wince. The inheritance from her father did not allow the kind of life Justina preferred, but to argue over shillings with a creature like Miss Rowcroft was entirely beneath her dignity. And for the sake of a handful of shillings, it hardly seemed worth the effort. The foolish chit would not have received much for the piece; that was certain.

As Miss Fairfax departed, clutching the address like a talisman, Charlie pondered this new development. Clearly the woman wasn't interested in wealth at all, which came as a great relief. Charlie's whole perspective of rich, amateur dabblers improved dramatically with that observation. Such people might have some benefits to offer the world after all. She also felt a good deal lighter for no longer needing to fret about her ill-gotten gains. On the whole it seemed like the bucket business had finally come to an end, and with it the termination of all her responsibility in the matter. Tomorrow, she was going to sit down and invent something that would make the world a better place for people.

Chapter Eight

Practical methods for supporting our friends in times of moral peril

The postman brought a rather peculiar design request; a means of harnessing the treadmills popular in prisons. Charlie knew nothing at all about prison life, but the correspondent helpfully included a few diagrams.

Water wheels have long powered the grinding of good corn. We send men to hard labor for their punishment and improvement, yet no gain is made from the countless footfalls upon the treadmills across our noble country. Surely the methods of water mills and treadmills might be combined so as to create a process by which the energy of a toiling man upon the wheel might be transformed into some benefit for the wider brotherhood of mankind?

It seemed providential that an idea with such high-minded intentions behind it should come to her at just this moment. Charlie got her tools out, and set to work making some very small treadmills so as to better see what might be done. Later in the day it occurred to her that she lacked very small men to run inside them. Temperance was duly commissioned to see if a few live mice could be found, and soon the small house buzzed once more with the energy of invention, and squeaked occasionally with the complaints of disgruntled rodents.

Do you fear that friends or family members lack certain moral attributes? Enquired a new poster in the baker's window.

Granny Alice stepped a little closer to it, squinting to make out the rest of the words.

Do you worry about falling standards and indecent behavior? Give them Penance Biscuits, the miracle food with the power to redeem lost souls.

She snorted, and hurried away, not wanting anyone to think she might buy something like that. Alice had standards, but did not appreciate moralizing lectures, especially not from people who made exceptionally depressing biscuits.

It was possible Friday Bob had another name, but it had never occurred to Temperance to ask him about it or enquire where the Friday came from. In some matters, she could take things on faith. Friday Bob was very much a faith issue. Challenge him with questions, and he might answer. Or he might pelt you with mud, or shout incomprehensible words that could be gypsy curses. Apparently, Friday Bob knew a lot of gypsy curses, including ones that means you would only get dry bread for breakfast for the rest of your life. Only the previous week, he had called her a paleontologist, and Temperance was still trying to work out whether to be pleased, or violent, in response.

While Friday Bob demanded the absolute belief of his various followers, he did not reciprocate. He entirely refused to believe that Granny Alice was a famous pirate who had retired and gone into hiding. Nor did he think that Temperance was really going to build an airship and fly to Brighton. This being the most distant and exotic place she could think of when describing her plans. Charlie's refusal to have strange children in her house overnight meant that Friday Bob had not been allowed to see the magical bucket in action. Consequently, he didn't believe that was real either. If Friday Bob hadn't been so funny and clever, Temperance felt certain she would have shot him in the head years ago.

"I've seen them of course, when I've been out late at night," Friday Bob announced to the assembly of wide-eyed, grass-stained children. "They come with special carts that are oiled and stuff, and silent, and they put slippers on the horses so no one ever hears them clopping. They go to all the orphanages, for miles around and they take all the children nobody wants and then they kill them, and they bring all the bodies back to that new road and hide them there and no one can ever see inside at what's happening because they ain't got windows!"

Any other child would have been interrogated over the details. Minor issues such as how he had seen inside the windowless houses were not open to discussion. Friday Bob did not stand for such treatment of his person, and they all knew better than to ask about small things. Such as how on earth he could have known anything like this. Friday Bob was a force of nature to whom the usual rules of law and logic could not be realistically applied.

"Stands to reason," said one of the twins, who usually had sweets in his mouth. "They're going to grind up the bodies in that new factory and... and..." Imagination had apparently failed him.

"Make them into Penance Biscuits," his identical brother suggested.

Temperance had to agree. Penance Biscuits tasted like dead people. Rapunzel wasn't having any of that, so they pinned her down, fed her one and waited for a half-chocked agreement. For now, they were just practicing their evil skills on each other, but when Friday Bob said it was time, they were going to do some really bad things. Things so bad that he wasn't even going to tell them what they were yet, in case anyone's head fell off just from the shock of hearing it.

"It isn't right at all," announced Mr. Fullberry as he served flour and sugar to a selection of customers. "We don't know a thing about them, these new people. Haven't seen so much as a face, but that factory bangs away all hours of the day and night. T'aint natural!"

Charlie didn't venture out for supplies more often than was necessary. Unless she couldn't solve a problem and wanted to distract herself. Shops always seemed to feature this kind of talk.

You couldn't buy a sausage without a political lecture. The baker had opinions on salvation, the fishmonger majored in vice and indecency while the greengrocer most usually gave vent to issues of road maintenance and the misbehavior of other people's chickens.

"I'm so glad to see you aren't stocking any of those miserable biscuits," announced a fellow shopper.

"You won't catch me doing that, rest assured. Religion's for the pulpit and the vicar, and not for my shop. It's not what it used to be in these parts, and no denying it."

Charlie reflected that had Bromstone been a university, Mr. Fullberry would have held the chair for Nostalgia Studies.

"It would be a crying shame if those Penance Biscuits got well known and the name of our good town linked to them in the public mind," the grocer added. "Why couldn't we have something decent and respectable, like a Chelsea bun or a Melton Mowbray pie?"

"Eccles cakes," agreed one of the other shoppers. "Not something awful and dry that makes you feel sad when you eat it. No, something with a bit of fat and sugar to brighten up your day."

Charlie wondered if it might be her calling to invent a Bromstone cake. The trouble was, with 'stone' in the name you were never going to get a famous food. People would hear it and think about gravel and broken teeth, and buy a lardy cake instead. Bromstone bicycles had a good ring to it though. Only she didn't know much about bicycles. How hard could it be, really? Two wheels, something to sit on, something to steer with, the means to unite these various parts and some inspired extra that would trump all previous bicycles. Perhaps improving existing ideas was the way to progress as n inventor. She'd had more practice at it, and it cut down on the thinking time. Bicycles with inbuilt clocks perhaps? Bicycles that would play a cheerful tune as you pedaled them?

"Were you going to buy something, Miss Rowcroft?" Mr. Fullberry asked.

Charlie realized she was the only customer left. She'd been waiting so long that she had forgotten what she came in for. "I'll come back tomorrow," she announced, hoping it hadn't been important.

"Ah the youth of today," Mr. Fullberry observed to her departing back. "Young ladies are not at all like they used to be."

As Edith didn't normally bother to knock before popping her head round the door, Alice knew something was afoot and so she launched the conversation by asking, "What have you gone and done this time?"

Edith looked guilty as she hobbled in and found a chair. "It's not all my fault. It's this new minister we have and he's dreadful serious. Not like old Mr. Lilly, who didn't think it any of his business what anyone did outside of the church." She shook her head. "I expect he's going to call on you."

"Well, he can call as much as he likes but I doubt it will do him any good."

"And I may have said something about our Miss Rowcroft. She doesn't go to services at any of the chapels, does she?"

Granny Alice smiled. "Hard to say, there's so many, but you can tell him she probably does, when she remembers."

Edith nodded. "I suppose that's what happens when you're clever, the not being able to manage the regular things too well," she said, charitably.

"Charlie gets the important things right," Alice replied. "She just has some different ideas from most of us about what matters most in life. You won't catch her scrubbing her front step of a morning."

"Nor you, either. Not once in all these years," Edith said. "But you do a fine wash."

"I've never seen much joy to be gained from going through

life in dirty knickers," Alice conceded, "But there is more to life than cleaning things."

"I've never see you when you weren't working," Edith said.

Alice took this as a cue to poke a few dry twists of tobacco into her pipe. Edith spent a lot of time watching other people's lives go by and no doubt thought she knew a good deal about the ways of the world. Alice didn't feel any need to disillusion her well-meaning neighbor. "Tell you new minister not to waste any time on me. I'm not going to be saved."

Edith made a decent stab at looking shocked, but Alice suspected the other woman was rather enjoying the potential impropriety of it all.

No one warned Charlie about potential visits, so the serious-faced young man on her doorstep made no initial sense to her.

"I wish to help you," he announced, hat in hands, brow furrowed.

Charlie blinked a few times, considering this. She hadn't asked anyone to help, had she? Temperance wouldn't have found him somewhere? He didn't look like the things the girl normally retrieved from under hedges. "That's very nice of you, but I don't need any help. The wheels are turning perfectly well now and I have all the mice I need, thank you."

When her mind was on a job, Charlie often struggled to change track.

"The wheels of eternity are not turning perfectly for you if you live without the true comfort of faith."

It occurred to her that she may have missed something. "What do you actually want? Are you trying to sell me something?"

The young man shook his head gravely. "What I offer cannot be sold. It has no price and is yet the most valuable treasure a man can possess."

He was obviously a bit confused. Thinking that her visitor

might be suffering from a touch of the sun, or that his undernourished form meant sickness or near starvation, Charlie took pity on him. "I think you'd better come inside for a bit."

He followed her in. "Do you live quite alone, Miss Rowcroft?"

That comment rang a small bell of disquiet in her mind. He might be a thief, not that she had much worth stealing, but a desperate person might pawn old linen, or anything of that ilk. "There are always friends and neighbors dropping by," she said, hoping that would discourage any larcenous ideas he might have. "Sorry, did you tell me your name? I'm not good at names."

"There is no one close by to guide you? No father or husband? No one?"

Charlie had encountered plenty of this sort of thing before. She supposed even robbers might indulge in it: The idea that a woman of her background and age could survive alone was beyond some people. She'd noticed that working women did it all the time. Apparently no one worried about how they were being guided or whether their delicate brains could handle small wages and perpetually hungry children. Biting her lip, Charlie managed not to launch into a full-blown rant. Just a little one.

"Look at me closely. I am clothed, fed, and able to keep this roof over my head. What kind of guidance can you possibly imagine me to need?"

"Spiritual sustenance, Miss Rowcroft. A guidance in faith."

"Who are you, anyway?" Charlie demanded, hands on hips. "I thought you were feeling ill, that's why I invited you into my home. But you aren't ill, you've got religion."

"I am the minister at Bromstone's Chapel of Quiet Independence, my name is Edward Edwards, and my business is the saving of souls from sin."

"You don't look old enough for that! You can't be any more than fifteen!" She supposed it could be a prank.

"Madam, I am twenty-three years old!" Surprise opened his eyes in wonder, adding to the impression of extreme youth.

"Have one of these."

Alice had given her a box of Penance Biscuits, which she now offered to the minister.

His eyes lit up. "These are truly a blessing in the world. They are spiritual nourishment for the sinful body. I have eaten nothing else for more than a week now." He took one.

Knowing exactly what the biscuits were made of, Charlie winced. "I'm not sure they are that good for a person, actually."

"Of course they are! It says so on the box. And you have them under your roof and so I must conclude there is hope for you yet."

Edward Edwards had a far shorter conversation with Granny Alice. As she never normally had strange gentleman callers to contend with, she identified him at once and did not give him chance to speak.

"Go away, young man. God and I have a very clear under-standing and you are not a part of it." She emphasized this point by shutting the door again.

They buried Augustus Neville at the Chapel of Quiet Independence on Thursday morning. He had passed into the next life at the impressive age of seventy-two, with not a tooth inside his head and not a single hair upon it. While Alice normally had nothing to do with churches, she made an exception for the funerals of old neighbors. Not least because it was a gesture of support to his widow, Myrtle, who was a dear old girl. There was also the issue of Temperance and her delight in all things morbid. The child loved funerals and took great pride in her special mourning dress. It seemed an innocent enough enthusiasm, far less dangerous to a girl's future prospects than boys or an obsession with baby dolls. As they didn't have a great many treats or outings, it would be cruel to deprive the child of a good burial.

The young minister did a decent enough job. At least, his soft voice took very little ignoring, and that amounted to very much the same thing, for Alice. Afterwards, they all went back to Myrtle's house, the various neighbors all having brought little offerings of food. It was a cheerful sending off, as these things usually were in Barker Street. Not much to grieve over in a long life lived well, Alice felt.

Myrtle's rooms were still crowded with Mr. Neville's many attempts at finding cures for his many illnesses. There weren't any chairs that didn't vibrate or bounce, or remonstrate at the touch of a button. One of the older devices operated itself on whim, having broken years before. The 'tables' all had edifying purposes as well. Even the pot plants were supposed to have remedial properties, according to their faded labels. Temperance sat on top of the Electronic Strengthening Machine and poked its knobs, but could not get it to do anything of note.

"What are you going to do with all of these now?" Alice asked Myrtle.

"I don't rightly know. He was very fond of them, and they will always remind me of my Augustus, so I may just keep them. You know, as soon as a new curing device came out, he'd go right ahead and get the sickness. He was very dedicated, was my Augustus." She sniffed. "I suppose if I did let them go, I'd only have to go and find some normal furniture, and that seems like far too much bother at my age."

"True enough," said Alice. "Sometimes it's best to stick with what you know. There's a comfort to be had from the company of familiar things."

"Oh, do be careful Mr. Jones!" Myrtle called out. "That chair..." She was too late. It had already bounced the elderly man into the air.

Some minutes later when Mr. Jones had been rescued and the Therapeutic Chair for Sufferers of Inert Blood had been tamed, Edith Jones presented her own contribution to the feast. She had a large, black box, which she presented with a flourish. Alice watched as Myrtle squinted helplessly at the item, trying to read its discreet label. Now her eyesight had gone, the poor woman couldn't manage writing at all, and Edith wasn't very much better.

Alice piled in to resolve the mystery. "Lacrimous cakes, to ease the grieving heart and comfort the sorrowing mind," she read aloud.

"That's a funny sort of name, now you say it," Edith observed. "I wouldn't have bought them if I'd known. It was the box, see, I thought it was appropriate, and tasteful. You know."

"That's all right my dear, very kind of you, and no matter about the funny name." Myrtle opened the black box. The cakes inside looked plain, aside from the dark band each one sported across its center. She lifted one and wrapped her soft gums around it. "Mmmm," she said through the cake, then, "Very nice. Warming. You have one Edith."

It was the first suggestion anyone in Bromstone had of the great patisserie war to come.

Chapter nine

Studies in the science of human abnormalities and their role in educational public entertainments

Ever since Friday Bob had issued his description of the new road and its dead children, Temperance had been itching to go there and look. A quiet afternoon with no one free to play afforded her the perfect opportunity. Charlie had spent the morning helping her with numbers, and now she could please herself. First she wandered the whole length of the street, and established that Friday Bob's windowless buildings were entirely real. The road itself was empty, not so much as a stray dog wandered its length. Not far away, the factory ground and grumbled, miserable smells emerging from its twin chimneys.

The sign at the gate read: *Anderson's Penance Biscuits, redemptive snacks to alleviate every human ill.* Temperance was trying to decide what that meant, when a cheerful, red-faced man with exciting-looking whiskers approached her.

"Can I help you at all young missy?"

Temperance gave him a long, thoughtful look as she considered her option. "Are the biscuits made out of dead people?"

He laughed. "What a silly idea! Of course not. They are good and wholesome."

"Friday Bob said they were." In certain circles, that would have settled the matter, but evidently the gate man didn't know about Friday Bob.

"You don't look like the sort of girl who would want to spend any time in a dull place like this. Why don't you run off and find somewhere better to play?"

"I might want to work here," Temperance said. "How would I

74

go about getting a job with Mister Anderson?"

The gate man never once stopped smiling. "I don't think Mister Anderson is taking anyone on right now. No, there's nothing for you here. Nothing at all. Best run along now."

"Who lives in those houses?" Unperturbed, she pointed at the windowless buildings of the new road.

"Why, Mister Anderson's workers of course."

"So, where are they?" She still had pictures of tragically dead children in her head.

"Working, naturally."

Then she saw something that put Friday Bob's dead children story to shame. There were two figures coming out of a door right at the far end of the factory yard. They looked like a woman and an older boy. Temperance knew at once that something was desperately wrong with them. She couldn't quite decide what it was though. Still, that could be worked on later.

"Time to go now," said the gate man. "Nothing to see, nothing at all. Very boring, just a big factory full of people who are working very hard to make biscuits." A bead of sweat made its way down his brow.

Temperance could see she wasn't going to get past him today. "Maybe there will be a job for me another time," she said, and skipped off. She knew from experience that skipping was one of those activities which encouraged adults not to take you too seriously. A person who was not being taken seriously could, in certain circumstances, get away with a great deal.

There was no point telling Granny, because Granny never believed her about anything and always said she was far too fanciful. As she didn't know more than he did, talking to Friday Bob or the rest of the gang would be pointless. That left Charlie, who always listened even if she didn't seem to have answers very often. And Charlie knew about the bucket, and had mostly believed her over that, too.

However, whilst going the long way home, she noticed people setting up a big tent on the Lost Monk's Meadow. Big tents could be depended upon to mean something good. And the kind of food Granny claimed not to approve of but ate in great quantities when she thought no one was looking. There were painted wagons on the field, too. Normally Temperance would have run over to look, but then, a normal day did not have quite as many dead people in it. Or possible dead people. Temperance still hadn't quite decided what to believe about any of it.

She found Charlie leafing through a pile of pictures.

"Are you going to make me a clockwork horse?" Temperance asked, hopefully. That had been on her wish-list for some time now.

Charlie didn't smile, which was not a good sign. Especially not on the horse making front.

"What's the word for dead people who have become alive again?" Temperance demanded.

"No idea," Charlie said. "I think there is a word for it though. One of those awkward composites. The paraliving? The unalive?" She frowned with concentration. "Maybe it's French... Mortless!"

"Mortless is a good word," Temperance decided. "It sounds right. So, I walked ought to Mister Anderson's biscuit factory because Friday Bob said he made penance out of dead orphans and I wanted to see."

Charlie nodded, still looking at her notes. "Is there a Thursday Bob as well?"

"I don't know. And anyway, this is important, don't side thingy me. I didn't even get distracted by the big tent, that's how important it is!"

"What big tent?"

"In Lost Monk's Meadow. Charlie! You keep doing it." Temperance scratched her grimy brow, train of thought wholly derailed. It took her a few seconds to remember what she'd wanted to say. "I saw them."

"Saw who?"

"Mortless people. At the biscuit factory. They were moving, but they were all wrong. You remember how the cats went, after the bucket and they didn't eat and they walked into things and I saw these two.... Well, they didn't walk into anything but they weren't right and Friday Bob says New Road is full of dead people, so it stands to reason, doesn't it?"

Charlie put the pages down and looked at Temperance. "Do that again, only slower and with more words, because I'm fairly certain I didn't understand any of what you just told me."

By the end of the afternoon, Temperance lost count of how many times she'd retold the events of the day. She didn't mind. Charlie believed her, that was the main thing.

"So is he putting dead people in the bucket?" Temperance demanded.

"Could be," Charlie conceded. "I didn't have a name for the bucket buyer. It would be an odd coincidence if it was Mister Anderson though."

"Why?" Temperance asked.

"Oh, just, it would be," Charlie said evasively.

Although she suspected there was more to that, Temperance didn't want to get distracted from the main issue again. "What are we going to do about it then? It's not right, messing with dead people like that."

Charlie looked somewhere behind Temperance, which usually indicated she was thinking hard. "We put a lot of dead animals in that bucket."

Temperance sighed. "That was different. That was us, and it was science."

"I'm not sure it's any of our business now," Charlie said.

"But I want it to be!"

Charlie smiled benevolently. "Why don't you and I take a little stroll and look at the tent?"

Temperance thought about this, and decided that maybe she should be distracted after all. It was a big problem she'd uncovered, probably too big to fix in one afternoon. Charlie would need time to figure it out, and the tent wouldn't be with them forever. She agreed to go.

Booths and stands clustered around the big tent, with caravans providing an outer ring. The freak show had a festive air, and already plenty of people were sampling its gruesome delights. There was a great deal of fun to be had trying to guess which ones were real, and which were clever frauds. Charlie and Temperance passed a happy hour peering into darkened booths, murky jars, miserable cages and the big mermaid tank. This freak show had gone all out to impress, having a lady who sported both a luxuriant, auburn beard, and a profusion of colorful tattoos. They had no doubts about her. Equally convincing was the strong man, lifting a barrel full of delighted and squealing children.

"Why is he wearing so little?" Temperance asked, far too loudly.

"Same reason as the tattooed lady," Charlie replied, blushing. Even approaching the subject from a calm and scientific perspective, it did unsettle her seeing that much flesh on display.

"What reason?" Temperance demanded.

"Well, it's the same with the mermaid, the cannibal savage and the dog-headed boy. They're all freaks, so the usual rules of human decency cannot be applied to them." She was also aware that their making good exhibits depended on showing as much as they could of their biological deviance, but wasn't sure what Temperance would make of that.

"Oh." Temperance paused in an ominous way that suggested another, even more tricky question would soon follow. "So if I got all covered in tattoos, could I go around with my unmentionable parts showing?"

"Your grandmother would kill you," Charlie pointed out, not quite seriously.

"She's got a tattoo. It's on her back and it's like a map with all little writing on it. I expect it's a treasure map."

Charlie imagined a birthmark, or horrible scarring from being caught in a fire.

They went back to look at the mermaid, who was resting both arms on the edge of her tank and splashing her tail about. Fish scales glinted in the sunlight as she moved. They studied the tail together, trying to spot an obvious seam or other evidence of theatrical costume.

"Are you really a mermaid?" Temperance asked.

The mermaid smiled at her, raised both eyebrows, then plunged beneath the water. Charlie drew in her breath at the same time, and held it. Years of guarding against discomfort whilst setting fire to things had given her an excellent lung capacity. Eventually she had to breathe out. On the other side of the glass, the mermaid blew casual bubbles into her waters and gave them a cheerful little wave. Charlie wanted to believe it was all a trick, like the creature last year – supposedly a demon, but when you looked closely it was bits of fish, lizard, half a bird and a collection of bones all cleverly strung together. The mermaid must have really big lungs, or a secret breathing tube up her nose, perhaps.

To Charlie's dismay, they ran into Miss Fairfax as they all entered the big tent. She acknowledged them with a dismissive nod, so Charlie saw no obligation to be sociable. That was a relief, but the mere fact of the other woman's presence dampened her mood.

A little way into the gloom realms beneath the canvas, they found a plinth, which on closer inspection turned out to be an old table. On this wooden remnant lay a large, transparent block, with what appeared to be a man inside it.

"Behold, the famous Russian demon Astra-la-la-lakalovicov," announced a small man sporting a disproportionately large hat. "Touch his temporary grave, feel the deadly chill that surrounds him."

Charlie reached out, ready to be entertained with this latest nonsense. Her fingers found the surprising chill of ice. In this warm tent, it should surely, be melting a little? She could see no hint of thawing, and no means of maintaining its low temperature.

"How do you keep him frozen?" she asked.

The little man beamed at her words as though he had been waiting for someone to ask. "Dear lady, it is a mystery! You can see that this ice block rests upon a mere kitchen table, and yet it does not melt. Except, if the demon chooses to wake and wishes to go forth into the world. Then the ice will fall from him, life will return to those strange limbs, and terror will stalk amongst us!"

"He's not dead then?" Temperance asked, sounding disappointed.

"Not at all, but we would all sleep a little easier, a little safer, if he were indeed no more than a harmless corpse," said the showman. "It is the demon himself who conjures forth the ice, so that his body is protected and he may sleep untroubled."

Temperance squealed with delight, and the showman continued with enthusiasm; clearly a man who loved his work. "He wakes for beautiful women, and, when he seeks a mortal, he will hunt her and devour her entirely. It might be dangerous for three such beauties as yourselves to come too close. He might wake up for any one of you."

Temperance went right up and leaned her head over the alleged demon's face. She stuck her tongue out, then, when nothing at all happened, she retreated in obvious disappointment. "Your turn, Charlie."

Charlie didn't believe a word of the demon story. The question of how it had all been achieved deserved more consideration though, so she too leaned over the ice block for a closer look. The man inside it appeared young, was vaguely attractive and did not look like a waxwork. He appeared to be in peaceful repose, but she assumed he must be dead. Could it be a glass case with some chemical applied to the surface so that it felt icy to the touch?

As she pulled away, Miss Fairfax took her turn in coming closer, leaning across to look from the other side. Charlie saw the eyelids beneath them flick open. She was pondering the mechanical arrangement this might call for, when Miss Fairfax screamed, and dropped in a dead faint.

The ice did not melt. The demon did not rise up, and, Charlie noticed with no small amount of satisfaction, she felt no terror at all. The strong man and a couple of other chaps got into an almost instant fist fight over who should carry the wilting maiden out, and by the time some bold matron waded in with smelling salts, Miss Fairfax was beginning to recover.

"That was fun," Temperance said as they headed for home. "The demon trick was ever so clever. Could you make me a demon in ice?"

"Probably," said Charlie. She had worked out some plausible mechanisms and felt sure a little chemical research would account for the rest.

Justina did the only sensible thing a woman could do in her circumstances: She fled back to her mother's house that very night, having hired emergency transportation. On arrival, and no more calm than she had been when departing, Justina found her mother conducting a meeting. It looked exactly like the kind of thing she had once put on for the local church, and later on behalf of local séances. The same group of women were now decked out in white headdresses, with nightgowns over their regular attire.

"Hello," said her mother. "We've got some entrails from the butcher, it's for divination. Are you going to join us? Tea and cake later."

Justina did not ask what they were doing. After the incident with the Eastern mystic and the spittoon, she never thought it prudent to enquire. Her mother's little coterie changed obsession every six months or so, but when it came to matters beyond the bounds of science and reason, these were the only people Justina knew who might help her.

"You look as though you've soon a ghost, dear," Mrs. Spifull declared, enthusiastically.

"It wasn't the phantom duck hunter in the lane again, was it?" another enquired.

"Oh, a good ghost story would be charming just now. Was it very dreadful? Or was it a man? The fellow with the long coat and no trousers again? He's always so… unexpected. Was there anything indecent?" One of the older crones asked, gleefully.

Justina collapsed into the nearest empty chair. "It may have been a demon," she announced. From that moment onwards, the entrails ceased to exert any fascination upon the assembled party.

Having described her experience at the freak show, Justina concluded, "The worst thing was, I had seen his face before!"

There followed a chorus of suitable, and rather gratifying gasps. Beyond retelling the day's adventure she had not planned what to say about the wider context of these events. Of course they all wanted to know precise details about her circumstances. She took a deep breath and launched into the second round of explanations. It had all begun innocently enough; a chance meeting at a talk on primate art, followed by a stroll and a cup of tea. He had amused her with sleight of hand tricks, culminating in a more vulgar finale in which a series of little mice had dropped out of her skirt. From this, she had assessed him as being less than perfectly honorable in his intentions. Justina skated over that surmising and made no mention of her fondness for being led astray. It was not an interest in buried treasure that had tempted her into a distant Welsh field, but the hopes of a little sport.

In the end she had dug just to ward off humiliation. Up until that moment, there had been only three kinds or men in her life; scholars, men who proposed, and men who seduced. Not that she ever taxed the ingenuity of men who wished to lead her astray. Men who suggested trysts in dark fields and then failed to present themselves, clearly had something wrong with them. Such a man was Alain Chevalier. Furthermore, he was French, which should have been warning enough that he might prove unreliable.

The circle of currently Druidical women picked over the details of her case with relish. They had more questions than she could keep up with and more wild theories than she could hope to remember.

"Reincarnation," one of them asserted.

"Did we not speak, only the other day, of ancient, nameless ones, worshipped in olden times who might yet return to torment the earth and destroy the human race?" said one of her mother's cronies, with joyful enthusiasm.

They took such delight in the prospect of death and mayhem. It gave her a warm, reassured feeling, listening to their funny ideas. In a room full of women with table decorations on their heads, it was hard to stay apprehensive for long.

"ArchDruid Henry will know what to make of it," Mrs. Fairfax announced. "We shall ask him in the morning."

Normally, mere mention of the man would have sent her running. At that moment, Justina would very happily visit every one of her former lovers if it might spare her from the uncomfortable mystery of Alain Chevalier.

After her experiences during the bucket period, Charlie had grown used to hearing odd sounds from the kitchen early in the morning. At first she rolled over, pulling the blankets over her head as she tried to work out which day it was, and whether she was supposed to be doing anything. The noise sounded like someone rattling about in a cutlery drawer. At this point, Charlie remembered that she was no longer resurrecting dead animals in a bucket of uncertain provenance. She grabbed the pistol from underneath her bed and tiptoed down the stairs, carefully dodging the creaky spots.

As she pulled her kitchen door open, she saw the dog-headed boy, standing a matter of feet away from her. For quite some time, the pair of them remained still, just staring at each other. She wondered why he was there, and then found herself thinking it was more of a doggish face, than a proper dog's head. In a minute he'd start singing hymns, and then mice would dance across the work surfaces and the walls would melt. It would just turn out to be another dream.

"Please shoot me," the dog-faced boy said. "Don't make me go back. Just kill me now. Please."

He had big sad eyes like a puppy, but the ears she'd last seen him sporting were apparently fake, and now absent. He still had distinctive the coating of fur though.

Charlie put down her pistol. No mice, no melting wall. She had to assume this might be real. Either way, it felt like far too early an hour for making decisions. "It's not loaded," she confessed. "Sorry."

The dog-faced boy looked even more miserable. "I wondered if any of the jars were poison, but I can't read. Are you a witch?" he asked.

"Inventor," Charlie said. Which might amount to much the same thing. "You've run away from the freak show, then?"

"Awful hard life," said the dog-faced boy. "And the new freak scared me. I couldn't take it no more. But what else is there? No one hires a dog face and I don't know how to do anything except sniff and bark and stuff."

Charlie felt sorry for him. Where indeed could a dog-faced boy go, other than some different freak show or circus? There was begging, or course. "How about the army? They're always glad of new recruits."

"I tried that for a bit, but I don't really have a nose like a blood hound, and when they realized I'm not good for much... well, it seemed like the freak show might get me less kickings."

Charlie tried to picture him in the red jacket, standing to attention. She couldn't do it. Nor could she think of anywhere at all to send him. She couldn't take him in. Bad enough being a young woman alone. The presence of a dog-faced boy would scandalize people. She would be ruined.

Big, puppy eyes looked up at her, full of hope.

"Buggarit," said Charlie. "Great piles of heaving arse."

Dog boy smiled at her, which revealed his canine teeth in an unsettling way. "I answer to most things," he said, "But I always thought Nigel was a good sort of name."

"You'll have to sleep down here somewhere," she said.

If dog boy had a tail, she knew he would have wagged it.

"And I'm not saying this is permanent, we'll have to see how it goes."

He placed furry hands on her shoulders, and licked her face.

Chapter Ten

Between civic duty and vigilantism: Dilemmas of modern citizenship discussed

"They say he eats children," Friday Bob announced. "He ate his own family, and that's why he had to run away and join the freak show. He was the most dangerous one of them all. Only the bearded lady wasn't afraid of him, and that's because her tattoos give her magical protection, and she can't be killed by anything."

"Where is he now then, do you think?" one of the chubby twins enquired.

Temperance had never been able to tell the twins apart, and as they did and said much the same things, discrimination had not seemed very important.

Friday Bob appeared to be thinking. "I bet we'd get a reward if we found him."

"We could be eaten," Temperance pointed out. It seemed like a significant flaw in the scheme.

"We could be bait," said Rapunzel, the only other girl who frequented their circle. It wasn't her real name, she just had very long hair.

Actual names did not count for much. Temperance kept trying to persuade them to rename her as Tempest, which had piratical potential. However, for historical reasons she'd been stuck with the far less impressive title of 'Pie Face' for several years.

"We have to prepare," Friday Bob decided for the gang. "We need weapons, rope, or string at a pinch. Don't tell your parents. Meet me here in an hour."

And so it was that the least methodical children in Bromstone began to hunt for the dog-faced boy.

After the morale boost of an excellent breakfast, Justina and her mother went down to The Hermitage. It was a small cleft in the rock down at the bottom of the garden. The location's colorful history included cheese storage, a brief flirtation with smuggling and a short stint as a replica of St Francis of Assisi's retreat, based more on imagination than insight. Several of Justina's early trysts had occurred there. Since the death of her father, The Hermitage had seen a number of enlightened visitors and acquired its current name. Currently imprisoned behind the metal gate was Henry Caractacus Morestrop Jones, his moustaches wilting mournfully.

"You two have a nice little talk now, and I'll just arrange for some breakfast, Henry my dear." Mrs. Fairfax pottered off, singing to herself.

"Please, let me out," the fallen ArchDruid implored.

He did look much reduced, the kind of diet Mrs. Fairfax considered appropriate for mystics, was not consistent with the maintenance of girth. Justina rather felt he deserved a stint as the resident spiritual guru.

"That would rather spoil my mother's fun," she observed. "But if you can advise me, I'll make sure you have a decent lunch."

"I've eaten nothing but flowers and leaves this week," he replied, clearly feeling very sorry for himself. "She will be the death of me. I would gladly barter my knowledge for a slice or two of beef, and perhaps some bread, or potatoes."

Justina settled in the comfortable visitor's chair outside the gate, and recounted her tale.

During the first phase of the hunt, they discovered Bodger Snots trying to hide under a bridge and had the brief, but pleasant distraction of pushing their old rival into the river. Later, they discovered a dead dog in a hedge, and a broken bicycle, which Temperance took for Charlie to fix. In Fish Street, they found a remarkably hairy man, but on interrogation, he turned out to be an Irish navvie, and not very dog-like at all.

"Maybe he left," Rapunzel said, as they scuffed their boots through the dust of Haypenny Road.

"Are you saying I've got it wrong?" Friday Bob demanded.

"No," Rapunzel returned. "Only maybe we were too slow, with the looking."

"Maybe he's taken sanctuary in a church, like the highwayman in that book Pie Face got last week," Friday Bob said. "Let's try there."

The parish church was entirely empty of dog-faced boys. They even made it up to the belfry before the churchwarden threw them out. The little Methodist chapel was closed, so too the Quivering Chapel and the Church of Latter Day Martyrs, which very seldom opened. For some reason, it had never attracted a large congregation. Eventually they ambled round to the Chapel of Quiet Independence.

"Do independents give sanctuary?" Temperance asked.

As the only dissenting children in the gang, the butcher's boys had no idea. "But Lanky Edwards is funny anyway," they promised.

There were boxes of Penance Biscuits stacked up by the chapel door. Temperance spotted Redemption Rations, and Salvation Sticks as well. A glance at the contents did not tempt her to try them, and she prided herself on a willingness to eat most things.

A pale, skeleton-like creature lurched towards them, crooked teeth on display, eyes too bright and hands shaking.

"Children! What a delight. Can I give you food for your souls?"

"Hello, Mister Edwards," chorused the twins. "We were looking for the dog-faced boy."

"He is a false idol! Better spend your tender years searching for Jesus."

"He ran away from the freak show," Friday Bob explained.

"Jesus?" Rapunzel asked.

Temperance kicked her in the ankle for being stupid.

"There's only me here," Edward Edwards confessed. "Me, and this manna from heaven, this edible absolution from all the sins of the flesh." He gestured towards the stack of boxes.

"He's mad," Friday Bob assessed once they were safely back outside.

"Comes from eating dead people," Temperance replied.

Both of the twins kicked her. "We eat The Host, at communion," one of them said. "Jesus isn't dead people."

Being a bit vague about how the resurrection fitted in with being mortless, Temperance decided not to invite more violence by getting into a proper argument. "I meant the Penance Biscuits," she said.

"Well, that would be bound to drive you mad, in the end." Friday Bob paused to consider the two possible streets before them. "Odds are the dog-faced boy has heard we're looking for him, and he's lying low. I reckon we should take the bicycle round to Pie Face's friend instead."

"I think you will find it all comes down to your mystery object," ArchDruid Henry suggested. "And it did come from Wales, after all. That is of great consequence."

"Pray continue," Justina said.

"Wales is a most ancient and magical land. It is the source of ancient Druidry as practiced by my Order. The fount of all wisdom, home to heroes, legends and miracles."

"Wales?" Justina repeated, puzzled. "I thought it consisted mostly of rain, Welshmen and sheep."

"You only see the mundane surface, dear girl. No, I believe you were sent to find this artifact for a reason. It has a purpose, and whether you have encountered a man, or a demon, I feel confident that the object you so diligently disinterred is the key to all of this mystery. Understand the item, and the rest will follow, I have no doubt."

"While I am not prone to flights of fancy, I cannot help but feel there is something sinister in all of this. Some dark malevolent force that means me ill."

Henry Jones shook his head. "The lurid tales of Druidical human sacrifice are much exaggerated," he said.

Later, when she brought him the promised plate of beef and potatoes, the ArchDruid asked if she would consider marrying him.

"You are the second fellow to ask me today. The other chap dropped to his knees in the street when I went out for a stroll."

"Shall I take that as a refusal, dear girl?" When she nodded, he continued, "How do you rate my chances with your mother? Do you think she'd let me out if I offered to make an honest woman of her?"

Justina smiled. "Considering my father's experience, I suspect not. But give her a few months and she will probably replace you."

"In a few months, I shall be able to escape by sliding between these wretched bars."

Justina nodded. "I gather our friend the Eastern mystic did just that thing."

The gang were not subtle. Although Charlie hadn't met them all before, she knew them all from Temperance's stories. By the sounds of it, they had only just turned into Barker Street. She wasted precious moments wondering if there was any risk to her new lodger. Temperance never brought her friends round, although there had been an enquiry during the bucket period. Charlie took a peek out of the window, saw the mortal remains of a bicycle, and panicked.

"Dogboy! Nigel. Off the table!" She hurried him out of the door and into the tiny sitting room here he slept in the company of spare parts and broken things.

"What are you up to then?" Temperance demanded as she strolled in, flanked by other grubby youths.

"I've been working on the treadmill machines," Charlie said, gesturing to the piles of cogs and contraptions on the table. One of her mice had escaped and took this opportunity to plummet gracefully from the table and dash under a cupboard. She felt sure they were becoming cleverer. It was the third mouse escape this week.

"We found this," Temperance said, "And I knew you could fix it."

Charlie cast a professional eye over the warped frame and buckled front wheel, and shook her head.

One of the boys made a dismissive noise. "Charlie can fix anything, that's what you said, Pie Face." He had a weasel set of features and hair that could easily have had something living in it.

The look on Temperance's face conveyed to her that this was all very important to the child. Charlie thought frantically in the hopes of finding some pride-saving solution for the dead bicycle. "But there's quite a few of you. One bicycle wouldn't be a great deal of use to you. Fixing this isn't the answer. It need turning into something better." Social disaster had been averted.

"And you can do that?" Weasel face asked.

"Of course it would help no end if you could find me more wheels," Charlie said, designing furiously in her mind.

"We can look while we're hunting for the dog-faced boy," suggested Temperance.

Charlie kept smiling and waved them out. "No had any luck then?" she asked.

"Not yet," said Temperance.

She stayed at the door until they all disappeared from sight, the false smile rigid on her lips. Shutting the door, she called out "It's safe now."

Silence.

"You can come out, Nigel."

Only with some coaxing would her guest return to the kitchen. He wasn't just a freak, he was an extremely sensitive, easily offended freak with extra helpings of paranoia and a side dish of self-pity. Charlie wondered what she had done to deserve him.

"They are looking for me, then," he said, puppy eyes despondent.

"Oh, they'll forget in a day or two. A couple of days ago I gather they were all hunting for the living dead, and I don't know what else. They read a lot of novels. It's probably not very good for them."

The dog-faced boy went back to sitting on the table. "They should stay away from dead people." He shivered and reached for the device he'd been working on before. His furry fingers grappled with the set of rusted gears. He had a useful talent for dismantling, but Charlie could see it would take a while to get him properly house-trained.

The two old women dissected the fruit cake with all of the care and skill of expensive surgeons, only without the blood, or the screams of pain. Dried fruits were skewered and inspected before passing into mouths. When it came to teeth, Granny Alice had the advantage over Edith, but then, she'd never been one for sweets. Only cake.

"Good consistency," Edith said. "I think you've got it perfect this time." She took another slice, just to be on the safe side. "I wish I could get our Mister Edwards to take a bite of this."

"Him no better then?" Alice enquired, just to be conversational.

"Penance Biscuits, Salvation Sticks and I don't know what, but nothing as would put a scrap of meat on a man's bones. I've nothing against being holy, but a person can take these things too far."

"Cakes and biscuits should be a bit sinful, or you aren't baking them right," Alice said.

The kitchen door opened, and Hephzibah leaned round it to smile at them both. "Got any more cake, Granny? I could smell you baking it all morning."

"Sneaking out of work, eh?" Granny asked, with a conspiratorial smile as she loaded another plate with fruit cake for the maid from number seven.

"I can't think what else to clean." Hephzibah sighed and sat down. "Don't know when she's coming back, and no money to get food in."

"You come straight round here if you're hungry," Alice ordered. "I'm not having hungry people on my doorstep. T'isn't right."

Hephzibah laughed. "I'll get fat on all this cake."

"Wouldn't do you any harm. I don't hold with being thin," Edith said.

"Did you see the man who came round earlier?" Hephzibah asked. Neither of the older women had, so she carried on with the gossip. "He was looking for Miss Fairfax. Wouldn't say why. Got angry when I wouldn't say where she'd gone or when she'd be back. "

"I saw one yesterday, looking up at her windows," Alice said.

"She gets a lot of gentlemen callers. Too many, I'd say." Edith put on her most disapproving face.

Alice nodded. "I'm no prude, but I've seen a few more men than I like the look of. It does make me wonder who she is and what she's about."

"I can't see why they all like her," Hephzibah chimed in. "She's not very nice."

"Men don't worry so much about nice as they do other things," Alice said darkly. She watched Hephzibah consider this. The girl was fifteen and from a large family, but it occurred to Alice that she might not have grasped some of life's basic details.

"One of these days, you and me should have a little chat," Alice added.

Hephzibah's face was a blank mask of perfect, dangerous innocence. "Right you are then, Granny. Well, thanks for the cake. I'd best be off."

The two old women waited until she'd gone before indulging in a long bout of melodramatic sighs. "The young folk of today," Alice said, summing it up neatly for both of them.

"We were never that young, surely? Or that dim." Edith sighed one last time for good measure.

"Don't be too hard on her. She means well."

"We've got to get the Minister off Penance Biscuits and onto worldly things before he starves to death," Edith said, plunging back into their former conversation.

Alice started to clear away the tea things. "Bring him round to save me some day when Miss Fairfax is in. Given the effect she seems to have on men, that might do it."

"You're a very unchristian woman, Alice Perry!"

"I'll burn in hell, and no doubting it," Alice chuckled.

Chapter Eleven

The dreadful implications of laxity in moral conduct

The obvious thing to do would involve talking to the wretched inventor woman again, but Justina couldn't face it. There were far too many details she didn't want to explain. Being a clever woman was one thing, dealing with a woman who might be clever, quite another. It didn't help that she could not pin Miss Rowcroft down to a precise class designation. Who were her people? She might be anyone, and uncertainty as to whether she should defer, or patronize left Justina quite unable to converse at all.

However, she did have the address of the cauldron buyer, and while writing had not been fruitful, a personal visit might enlighten her. Sitting in the comfort of her mother's drawing room, with its new, plush couches and elaborate altar, she tried to plan ahead. Picturing herself at an unfamiliar address, asking questions of a stranger was distasteful enough, without having to actually do it. What choice did she have? There were no brothers or friendly uncles to hand who could smooth over such delicate business for her.

"Mother, can I borrow your carriage and a footman or the day, do you think?" she asked.

Mrs. Fairfax looked up from her needlework. "Of course, dear, but please don't roll him in anything unpleasant, I've just fitted him with a new livery."

"I shall return him in good repair."

Justina could see it was a new embroidery project that had her mother engrossed enough not to ask questions. With a bit of luck, those were mystical symbols in the making, and not, as she had first thought, complex copulatory arrangements.

The footman did indeed have a new livery, although it looked quite a lot like his attire during her mother's nine-month Roman period: White, shapeless, and showing far too much leg for public decency. He also had the fixed smile of a man accustomed to dealing with both raging insanity, and a very pleasing wage.

"Do you have any trousers?" Justina asked him.

Having checked that there was no one close by, he nodded.

"Put them on then, if you please. We are going out."

His face showed relief.

"Does the coachman also have trousers at his disposal?"

"Yes Miss Fairfax. I'll see to it."

At least, through all her fads and phases, Mrs. Fairfax had never dispensed with the actual coach in favor of greater authenticity. It reassured Justina that her mother knew when to stop. Toys, costumes and occasional prisoners were one thing, but the basic dignity of genteel life must be maintained. In this regard, her mother never faltered.

She sent the footman off to bang on this most inauspicious of doors. Observation from her window inclined Justina to think Linden Road a willfully unremarkable place. It would attract the kind of wealthy tradesman who intended to marry his daughter up a degree in society. No one with real breeding would choose such a road, nor did it suggest the charming Bohemianism of Barker Street. Linden Road plodded insipid, full of plump children and unoriginal aspirations. Justina felt offended by the very idea of her find coming to rest in such a dreary spot.

The footman returned with an invitation to enter the property. Justina shuddered at the prospect. Already it seemed that the cold hand of fate meant to throttle the aesthetic sensibilities out of her.

Once within, the house confirmed her darkest suspicions. From the choice of rug to the displays of china and glass, the house spoke of a shameless desire to demonstrate wealth, coupled with appallingly bad taste. A round, over-decorated woman sailed towards her. The dress wafted with a monstrous profusion of frills and bows. Justina shuddered again.

"Miss Fairfax? Do please step into my little parlor. I am Mrs. Futtercluck, although I do not think that we have met before."

Justina said, very politely, that they had not been introduced, but that an item of hers had been mistakenly sold by a third party to someone at this address, obliging her to make a few, delicate enquiries.

"Perhaps you should go to one of those great detective gentlemen I'm always reading about, because I very much doubt I shall be able to help you, Miss Fairfax."

"If only they were not all fictional," Justina replied, reminding herself that to sharp a tongue would not help her at all."I don't suppose your husband might have made the purchase?"

Mrs. Futtercluck eyed her suspiciously. "My husband has been dead these last four years. I'd be very surprised if he's bought anything at all. I myself only make acquisitions through the dealers in town and I have no doubt they would not have relinquished my address. I mean no offence," the rotund matron added, "I'm sure you're a very nice young lady, to be making business enquiries on your own account."

Justina sat very still, her spine perfectly straight, chin held in exactly the right position. She had no idea what to say, and resorted to frigid silence whilst collecting her thoughts. "Is there perhaps some other gentlemen who might feel entitled to give this as his correspondence address?" she said, tone sweet to the point of malevolence.

Mrs. Futtercluck went a most enlightening shade of crimson, and stuttered for several seconds before any identifiable words emerged. "Of course not!"

"In which case I may have to broaden my search and be less discreet in my methods. As your address is my only lead at present, you will forgive me if I find myself obliged to mention it. Perhaps to the local press? I fear publicity may be the only solution for me. How terribly inconvenient for us both."

Mrs. Futtercluck achieved new intensities of crimson that suggested the potential for bursting blood vessels, if not the first spasms of a convulsive fit. "I'll kill the little bastard," she said.

"I implore you, madam, at least furnish me with his usual address before you resort to violence."

Mrs. Futtercluck huffed, making the bows and ribbons on her dress rise and fall in a most disconcerting fashion. "You'll find him on the far side of town, under the name of Mister Anderson."

Justina blinked frantically in disbelief. "Not the biscuit man?"

"The very same."

She rose. "Thank you for your time, Mrs. Futtercluck. I shall not trouble you further."

"I'm very glad to hear it."

Justina wondered what a biscuit man could possibly want with her find. Perhaps he imagined that a collection of antiquities would enhance his social standing. Needing to ponder the implications of all this, she had the footman drop her in Barker Street, before he headed back to her mother's Druidic debaucheries.

"I shall require tea at once, Mary, and supper within the hour, Mary, and a hot bath," she called out, then threw herself inelegantly into a chair. She had no idea what any of today's discoveries meant or how this would help explain events at the freak show, much less throw the light of reason upon the dark face of Alain Chevalier.

Temperance banged on the door. Something was wrong. Charlie never locked her door. Fear and frustration had the girl on the brink of tears.

"Why won't you let me in?" she wailed. "Is it because I've been so busy? I didn't mean to slight you, Charlie! I'm sorry if I've done something to make you cross. I didn't mean it, I promise!

Please open the door. Please..."

Temperance ceased her outpouring of grief instantaneously as the door opened, asking, "What are you up to?"

"Just work," Charlie said.

"So I can come in, yes?" Temperance rested her hand on the door and found it did not open further for her. She looked up, confused.

"All right." Charlie stepped back. "Just don't fiddle with anything."

She couldn't see anything special about Charlie's kitchen. There were the usual piles of unwashed dishes. The same piles of notes as always, the same pen and inkwell were all in view. Two pale mice gazed up at her from inside a large glass jar. Even so, she had the impression something had changed, and Charlie was acting funny. Being one of a horde of siblings, Temperance had developed a necessary sixth sense for detecting attempts at deceit.

"So, what have you been up to?" Charlie asked as she fed biscuit crumbs to the mice.

"We're having a go at being archaeologists, like Miss Snot Face over at number seven, only much better," Temperance announced. "We've dug lots of holes. We've found bones and bits of blue china and Friday Bob says those come from the time of Jesus and we're all going to be famous and go to London to do a show." She nodded to herself. They'd been very busy indeed.

"No luck finding me any wheels then?"

Temperance had forgotten all about the thing that would be better than a bicycle, but covered for this by asking about progress on the mechanical horse.

"I made a really small one, but the weight of the key made it fall over. You'd think, having four legs, that horses would be inherently stable, like tables. They apparently are not. I think it's because of the neck."

"Real horses don't fall over all the time," Temperance pointed out.

"Real horses aren't full of cogs and seldom need to be wound up, as I understand it," Charlie replied.

Temperance took another considering glance around the room, trying to work out what was wrong. Something had changed. "So you aren't doing anything exciting then?"

"Oh, I think so. Mouse-powered machines, for use in the home," Charlie said. "Small, neat, useful devices to make daily life easier."

"Do they sweep front paths?" Temperance asked.

"They might. Although most of the problem is stopping the mice from escaping. Some of them are awfully clever."

There was a scuffling noise from the next room.

"What was that?" Temperance asked.

"I've had a lot of mouse escapes," Charlie explained.

As she headed back to the latest archaeological hole, Temperance realized the smell in Charlie's house had been different. There had been a sort of animal smell. She supposed it was probably because of all the mice.

It wasn't a case of charity, piety or even civic duty. Alice had just discovered very early on in life that it paid to be liked. People who owe you favors sometimes proved to be a handy resource in a tight spot. Neighbors who thought well of you were more likely to defend, than assault. Following this philosophy, she had carefully cultivated the good will of Barker Street. Even so, there were times when being a good neighbor stretched her thin capacity for patience to breaking point. As Granny Alice listened to the almost incoherent rapture of Mister Edward Edwards, she reconsidered that assessment. She could be very patient indeed, for the right reasons. What she lacked, was any capacity for tolerating idiots. Mister Edwards had spoken nothing but foolishness for some twenty minutes now, and showed no signs of letting up.

To her great relief, Edith gave her secret signal, which

consisted of sticking a finger in her ear. Miss Fairfax was clearly in view.

Granny rose. "I'm quite overcome by your talking, Mister Edwards. I must step outside for some air and try to compose myself."

"Take these Penance Biscuits with you, dear sister," Edith said in a stilted, monotone voice.

Alice did not think anyone could be taken in by this lackluster performance. It sounded so planned, so false. She waited for the young man to ask what on earth was going on, but he didn't. Instead, the habit of politeness brought Edwards to his feet, and the lure of Penance Biscuits did the rest. He looked just like an opium addict, Alice reflected, as the pale young man staggered out after her. Miss Fairfax had reached the street. There was no time to waste.

"Miss Fairfax!" Alice called out.

The archaeologist paused and looked around.

Alice continued. "I am glad to see you safe and well. We were all quite worried about you, what with these funny callers you've had. I do hope there's not been any trouble?"

"I am perfectly well, I thank you," Miss Fairfax replied. Her gaze slid over Alice as though she couldn't quite bring herself to look properly. "If you'll excuse me," she added, and set off without waiting for a reply.

Behind Alice, something thumped ominously. She turned to discover the young minister on his knees.

"A vision!" he proclaimed. "I would call her a goddess, but I fear that might be pagan, or heretical. But might I not say she is an angel? Such grace! Such beauty shows the hand of God at work."

Edith stood beside him. "She's a very rich and clever young lady," she explained. "If you even want to kneel in the dirt in front of her, you will have to sort yourself out."

"I am not fit to seek her hand," Edward Edwards said, mournfully. "And yet, I must. I must. She shall hear of my overwhelming love for her, my absolute adoration and perhaps her sweet, angelic heart will be moved to pity me."

Alice resisted the temptation to say something about Miss Fairfax's heart and its likely capacity for sweetness.

"You will have to stop starving yourself," Edith instructed. "If you want to court such a fine young lady, you will have to eat proper food, and decent meals. There's nothing else for it."

"Ah, the Penance Biscuits!" Edwards cried out, a man in utter torment.

"Man cannot live by biscuits alone. Jesus said so. A man needs meat and cheese, and a few pints of beer to keep him strong." Edith was on a roll now, and needed no further help.

Alice watched the pair of them depart. The young man still had that unhealthy gleam of fanaticism in his eyes, but a few square meals might be enough to settle that down into something more respectable. Her neighborly duties discharged, Alice took out her pipe and set to the happy job of filling its bowl with good tobacco.

Despite much careful thinking, Justina could devise no better plan than "Go to Mister Anderson's factory and talk to him." No longer able to take easy advantage of her mother's considerable affluence, she had to walk. Living with mother had its advantages in terms of carriages, servants and not having to run one's own household. However, one could be required to live as a Roman priestess of Vesta for a week, then be overwhelmed with burning spices from the orient and surrounded by foreigners. Not to mention having to tolerate her mother's devoted following, each of whom seemed intent on marrying her to one of their dumpling-faced, perspiration-laden offspring. Justina knew a lady should not be aware of perspiration, but some young men made it difficult to maintain a façade of polite obliviousness.

It wasn't that she minded walking, but a lady who arrives by coach is bound to command more respect than one obliged to use her own two feet. Barker Street was too small for a coach house and she suspected it would be at odds with the Bohemian air she had meant to cultivate, all issues of cost aside. All proper scholars had their eccentricities, and she assumed these to be necessary for garnering proper respect. She just hoped people assumed hers to be a deliberate choice and not the consequence of limited funds.

Justina had never really looked at a factory building before. She knew such places existed, but, belonging to the spheres of poor people and tradespersons, they were normally quite beneath her. Miser Anderson's factory entirely lived up to her expectations as being exactly the sort of establishment she did not wish to be associated with. Still, Mister Anderson might have her find. Alain Chevalier seemed an ever more distant threat, but claiming the fruits of her labor was a different matter.

An impertinent little man stopped her at the gate. "You can't go in there, miss, begging your pardon."

She glared at him. "I have business with Mister Anderson."

"Very sorry, miss, but Mister Anderson does not conduct any business at this factory, saving," the man paused to snort out a laugh, "saving for the making of his most excellent biscuits."

"If I cannot go in, then you must go and fetch him for me."

Still the man hesitated. What kind of a servant was he? She intensified the glare.

"All right, miss, you stay exactly there. You don't want to dirty your hems with factory grime."

The yard looked pristine and the dust of Bromstone already clung to her hems but Justina said nothing and waited patiently for the odious little man to do his work.

Mister Anderson had a pinched, folded in sort of face, but an impeccable, if austere dress sense. Age-wise he might have been anything from thirty to seventy, with his silky looking silver hair, clear eyes and domineering presence.

"Forgive my gate man, we are not in the habit of receiving guests such as yourself in this place. I cannot offer you any appropriate space in which to refresh yourself even. I am rather Spartan in my habits."

"I quite understand. It is most forward of me, I know, to present myself to you in this unusual manner, but I must confess, that I am an unusual woman." She paused for dramatic effect. "I am an archaeologist." He blinked, once, but it was enough to satisfy her. "Miss Fairfax." She extended an elegantly gloved hand.

"Frederick Benevolent Anderson at your service." He kissed her fingers, lingering no longer than was absolutely proper to convey admiration. "It is difficult to imagine that such fine hands could ever have toiled in the earth."

"But it is so," she said. "The day is fair, might we remain here for a little while and converse?"

He smiled with lips entirely closed, and barely moved them to speak. "I am yours to command."

Justina explained the essence of her inquiries, during which time Mister Anderson listened with careful attention.

"Miss Fairfax, I have bought a cauldron in good faith. Do you in fact desire its return?"

"I would like to ascertain that it is my find, if you would indulge me?" she hesitated. "There is some mystery around it which I need to clarify for...personal reasons."

Mr. Anderson frowned. "You are aware of its nature and purpose?"

"I believed it to be either a bucket, or a sundial when I saw it last."

"Ah."

There was a long period of silence between them, during which she wondered what on earth he meant by 'nature and purpose'.

"I promise you that I do not wish to reclaim my find, but I do need to comprehend it."

"This is a most sensitive matter, Miss Fairfax, and intrinsic to my business," Mister Anderson said carefully.

"Mister Anderson, I am a gentlewoman and a scholar, this alone should assure you that I have absolutely no interest in your business arrangements whatsoever."

"I can rely on your discretion?"

"Consider that I have not even described to you the means by which I learned your name."

He bowed in recognition of this evidence of character. "I will show you. Would you be willing to wait until Friday?"

"Of course.

It was, she decided later, a rather peculiar interview, but an encouraging one. She supposed there must be complexities to business that had never entered her imagination. It seemed wholly reasonable that she should have no idea of the useful applications of the bucket, but hoped that lowering herself to such insights would be useful for her other problems.

Chapter twelve

A genteel novice's guide to
uncovering remains

When Temperance at last realized the bits of china looked a lot like one of Alice's tea cups, she was initially despondent. Granny's cups were merely old, and not worth anything at all. All that archaeological enthusiasm might have been for nothing. The bones they had unearthed looked an awful lot like the ones you could get from the butcher. She questioned the twins relentlessly until they confessed the remains probably had come from pigs and sheep, not ancient Britons. Friday Bob had gone down in her estimation considerably. She'd started to think the nails they had found weren't from Druids nailing people to trees, either. Although Friday Bob had been suspiciously vague on the topic of why anyone might want to do such a thing in the first place. All that left from their heroic excavation was the bottom of an old shoe, a couple of coins and what might have been a bucket. In an act of desperate optimism, Temperance tried a few dead things in the aforementioned pail. Either is was an unremarkable piece of hardware, or it had a magical nature she couldn't guess at.

Archaeology wasn't as rewarding as she had imagined. This development was as disappointing as the failed attempt to take up highway robbery had been. The only thing they'd managed to steal during that adventure was an old, ill-tempered donkey who had no desire to be ridden. Rapunzel ended up in the mud, Albert Nose got a bruise that lasted nearly a month, the donkey made a successful bid for freedom and somehow they lost Granny Alice's pistol. It wasn't her only one. It wasn't even one of the good ones, it didn't fire reliably or shoot straight, but she was furious just the same.

As a consequence of losing the pistol, Temperance had been

threatened with the awful fate of being sent back to her mother. That meant a life revolving around looking after all of her horrible little brothers, instead. Having nine younger brothers that she knew of, and perhaps more by now, this was a punishment to inspire both alarm, and abject apology.

"Why did you teach me to shoot, if you don't want me shooting people?" Temperance had eventually worked up the courage to enquire.

"I want you to have options," Granny said.

"Being a highwayman is an option!" Temperance protested.

"Not at your age, it isn't."

A great many things passed through Temperance's mind, leaving no trace of their journey. That conversation had stayed with her. Every time she remembered it, she had the uncomfortable feeling of having missed something important.

The failed archaeology scheme brought back memories of all the other wild and wonderful plans that had never amounted to much. Temperance felt she was getting too old to just be playing at pirates, detective or freak shows. She wanted to do something real. Digging up treasure seemed like a very sensible, and feasible sort of job, even taking the recent setback into account. Maybe she'd been going about it the wrong way. Maybe if she started following Miss Snot Face around, she could learn how to do it properly. Friday Bob was history, for now at least.

Charlie caught the dog-faced boy trying to put wheels on one of the mice.

"So it can go faster," he explained.

"But mice aren't supposed to have wheels!" She felt exceedingly uncomfortable. "Where are its feet?"

"I took them off, first, or they'd have got in the way." In his furry hands, the mouse barely moved. Little whiskers quivered, but it showed no signs of trying to escape. "Think what we could do if the mice all had wheels, not feet!"

She thought. Wheeled mice had potential, but the idea troubled her.

Nigel continued. "Then we could move on, to other animals. Think how much easier it would be, getting cows to market if they had wheels! And what horses could do."

"They'd need brakes," she said, imagining what would otherwise happen on slopes. Free-rolling cows did not seem like a good addition to the world.

"I always wanted wheels," Nigel added. He let the wheeled mouse go. It careered noisily across the table, dropped alarmingly to the floor and, faster for the wheels, escaped under the cupboard before Charlie had chance to even think about catching it.

She shook her head. "That's the fifth mouse this week. We'll have to get some more somehow."

"They'll come back," Nigel pronounced. "Once the ones under the cupboard have seen the wheels."

"How have you managed to put wheels on mice?" Charlie asked. He didn't have any tools out.

"It's pretty easy, once you've unscrewed their feet."

Charlie thought about this. Biology had not been a serious focus of study at any time in her history as a student of science. Her brief, childish foray into the messy world of animal dissection had taught her a few things though: Normal mice were not designed to be unscrewed.

On Friday morning, there were two gentleman callers who left cards. Justina instructed Mary to decline all gifts on her behalf, and to resist giving out personal information. As neither of the gentlemen were known to her, she did not want to grant either of them an interview. She couldn't imagine where they had come from. It was always possible they had seen her around town, and made enquiries. None had been so crass as to follow her home, but it may be just a matter of time. She despaired of the male half of the race.

The help had her uses, but Justina missed the polished grace of more senior and experienced servants. Her personal income did not even cover the basic necessities, like butlers. It was a case of suffering her restricted lot, or submitting either to a husband, or her deranged mother. Still, she missed living well. Strange men at the door could be fended off if needs be, but nothing quite matched the pleasure of having a manservant throw an unwelcome suitor into the street. Independent though she was, Justina would never consider it her business to undertake such bodily evictions.

She arrived promptly in the new road at one in the afternoon, having survived both drizzle and the terrible, intrusive questions her neighbors felt entitled to ask. The little gate man doffed his cap in a much more promising fashion, and asked her to wait. Moments later, Mister Anderson himself appeared, and offered her his arm.

"Good day, Miss Fairfax. Shall we commence? I must warn you that these are to be uncommon sights that would shock more delicate persons."

"I pride myself on delicate tastes and a robust constitution," Justina replied.

"I did not take you for an exotic flower, raised in a hothouse. You are an English rose, fair of form but possessed of fortitude."

Justina had heard far too many compliments in her life to be impressed by this, but it pleased her nonetheless. "You are very kind, sir."

He led her across the road to a curious row of buildings. In shape they were much like houses, but they lacked windows, or other evidence of habitation. She supposed these must be for storage.

Anderson produced a key, and let them in. They came at once into a fairly bare room, lit by gaslight to overcome the absence of natural illumination. At the center of the space stood a large, ornately decorated cauldron. She recognized the panels at once. Moving into the room, Justina left the door slightly ajar. The air felt oppressive and she did not want to be shut in.

"This is indeed my cauldron, or at least, I was its original discoverer," she said.

"You wish to learn its nature and purpose?" He did not smile.

Justina experience a moment of unease. It was not her habit to suffer from timidity, and so she pushed the sensation from her mind.

Anderson gave her a curt nod, then called out, "Hemming, Smith, we are ready."

A plain little door opened on the opposite side of the room. Two equally unremarkable men came through it, bearing between them a simple stretcher. Upon this crude pall, lay a stiff and lifeless form. From the sunken face, she had no doubt that the person had entirely expired. To her relief, Justina soon realized the corpse was fresh enough not to render the air putrid. Her natural fortitude might not have been equal to the influence of a festering aroma.

"We soon discovered that only the most recently departed will serve," Mister Anderson said.

The corpse was duly lowered into the cauldron. Mr. Anderson took a tin from his pocket, opened it, and removed a pinch of something dry.

"I am a great believer in science, and nothing if not thorough in my methods. This mix is not essential, but it speeds the process. One must otherwise wait some hours, which is most inefficient."

"How did you come by the mix?" Justina asked, trying to sound more composed than she felt.

"I have other sources," he said. "Now, observe."

She stepped close enough to be able to see inside the cauldron. Most of it was full of tangled fabric and limbs, but at once she could see signs of movement. The corpse climbed to its feet, eyes somewhat glazed. As if used to this occurrence, the two workmen helped it out of the cauldron and stood it beside the wall before fetching another deceased person and beginning the process again.

"I have found we can source and enliven between ten and twenty such creatures a day. We store the surplus here until needed. The rest are in use at my factory."

Justina's head swam. "In use? I do not understand."

"Then come and see." He led her back, across the road. Head reeling, she drew in great gulps of fresh air. There was no time to pause or think. They passed through the gate, crossed the yard and entered one of the ugly buildings.

"In use," Mister Anderson repeated, gesturing to his factory floor.

In a dimly lit room, workers filled great bowls with flour, water and other ingredients. No one spoke. Only the rustling of cloth and the slurp of mixing filled the air.

"All factories must derive their power from somewhere," Anderson explained. "The conditions in which many poor people are forced to work, are terrible. I merely utilize the recovered energy of the dead. These are not thinking, feeling beings. They are like steam engines that call for neither coal nor water. When the energy within them is used, they fall apart and are replaced." He looked tremendously pleased with himself. "I had been searching for the means to do this very thing for years before I chanced upon the cauldron. It is a marvel indeed."

Justina looked round at the grey, expressionless faces of the working dead. "They feel no pain?"

"None at all. It is all very humane and for the best, I can assure you."

"I am a little overwhelmed." She wanted to sit down, and not to be looking at dead people.

"Allow me to take you for afternoon tea. The company of the dead grows tiresome all too quickly and I am afraid I have wearied you."

He was glad to leave, but being outside in daylight, quickly turned her thoughts to other things. She chatted happily of very little, trading empty witticisms. Anderson was pleasant enough company. Years of experience told Justina to expect a marriage proposal, but they parted after scones and cream without the faintest allusion to matrimony.

"I hope that today will help you in solving your personal mystery," Anderson said, when the time came to part.

"I must confess to being more perplexed than ever, but thank you for your time, it will no doubt help me to fathom these matters in the future."

"If there is anything I can do to assist, then please do not hesitate to call upon me."

She promised to do so. On the journey back, Justina noticed that the large tent had finally gone from Lost Monk's Meadow. She could only hope that the frozen likeness of Alain Chevalier had gone with it. How the cauldron, with its uncanny properties, could possibly connect to him, she had no idea. A frozen demon, and means for resuscitation might have some plausible links between them, but it all seemed a little farfetched. Had she not seen the various developments with her own eyes, she would have dismissed them as superstitious nonsense.

Sitting along in number seven, she picked over the facts. Alain Chevalier had led her to the cauldron. The cauldron was now in Mister Anderson's hands, and brought dead people back to something like life. The frozen demon exhibit at the freak show had, in poor light, looked like Chevalier, and had winked at her. Such circuses traded on the credulity of the foolish poor, or the humor of the wiser rich. They were not to be trusted. Had she imagined the whole thing, letting a gothic fantasy take hold of her mind? She had meant to be a student of reason, not an upholder of the incredulous.

"I was overwrought," she told herself out loud. "I have

suffered too many afflictions and trials of late, it is entirely understandable. It will not happen again. The cauldron is a curiosity, I'm sure there is sound science underpinning what Mister Anderson does, and Chevalier is long gone. That is the end of it." She closed her eyes, and tried to feel better about things.

Temperance, meanwhile, was so busy imagining Friday Bob's disbelief at her discoveries, that she did not realize her escape route had been closed and barred.

It was only when Granny Alice said, "Well blow me," rather unexpectedly, that Charlie realized she had not locked the back door.

Nigel whined, jumped off the table and fled for the relative safety of the other room. Granny looked worried, but remained stationary.

"He's harmless," Charlie said.

"Temperance isn't here then?" Granny asked, still frowning.

"I haven't seen her in a couple of days," Charlie said. "Last I heard she was taking up archaeology, which is probably safer than some of the things she's tried, at any rate."

Granny looked around the kitchen as though she half expected Temperance to be hiding somewhere. "I can't think she'd have gone round to number seven."

"Temperance is full of surprises," Charlie said. "I wouldn't put anything passed her. Umm, Granny? She doesn't know about Nigel."

"Nigel?"

"The dog-faced boy. He ran away from the freak show. I felt sorry for him, but no one else knows he's here, and he's afraid they'll make him go back."

"I won't say anything, if he's harmless," Granny said.

"If Temperance isn't back by nightfall, let me know. I'll go and look for her."

Granny nodded. "You're a good girl, Charlie. I expect she'll get hungry sooner or later. It's just not like her to miss lunch."

Nightfall came, and Temperance did not return. Charlie left Nigel hiding in the second room, the back door unlocked in case the girl appeared. Several other neighbors came out to help, but no one in Barker Street had seen her since morning. Charlie walked to the butcher's, having heard mention of his twins in Temperance's various stories. The twins claimed not to have seen her all day either. They had no idea where Friday Bob lived, and their list of places Temperance might go was so long as to be useless. Charlie wrote all the spots down anyway. She could start on them in the morning, if needs be.

As she set out, one of the twins said, "Maybe the freak show took her to replace the dog boy."

"Pie Face isn't a freak," the other twin said.

"She could be, by now," the first twin replied. "Maybe that's where all of them came from."

Charlie left, trying hard not to let her imagination run away from her.

Even though Alice didn't sleep much, gone were the days when she could stay awake all night without consequences. The absence of Temperance made rest impossible. There had been a time in her life when she would have known exactly what to do. She remembered having that sort of energy. The brash confidence and certainties of youth all seemed rather distant now. Rheumatism and short-sightedness had slowed her down. Cake had done its worst to her once lively form. Her mind was not as sharp as it had been. Or possibly, she knew too much to be able to find simple solutions any more. Alice did not like being old, but she liked the only cure for it even less.

Rather than try to sleep, she sat in her big chair by the fire, and waited, fretting, remembering and chaffing with frustration. She wanted to be up and doing something. But, what could she do? What would possibly make any difference to the missing child? She didn't have any clues, or good ideas, or wild insight even.

Early in the morning, someone banged on her door. Swaying from tiredness, she went to answer, knowing that nothing good ever presented itself at the front. On her doorstep stood a funny little urchin with squashy little nose, pinched, triangular face and clothes that appeared to have been made for someone of an entirely different shape.

"I heard Temperance had gone missing," he said.

"Have you seen her?" Alice asked, hardly daring to hope.

"Not in a couple of days. But I know all the places she goes. I know everything that goes on around here."

Alice nodded. "Do you now? Have you got a name, my lad?"

"Friday Bob." He paused, head tilted slightly to one side as he stared up at her. "You don't look anything like a pirate."

Despite her current woes, Alice managed a small smile. "You don't look anything like a Friday."

She sent him off to help Charlie search, and tried to think of something useful to be doing.

In other circumstances, it would have been an entertaining morning. The previously mythical Friday Bob had a remarkable wealth of stories, coupled with unsurpassed confidence in the truth of everything he said. Thus far, Charlie had seen the place where Noah's ark came ashore, the crossroads grave of a highwayman, the place where Albert Nose had seen a ghost, the place a pig had died, and countless other sights of interest. She'd also been told that the lost monk of Lost Monk's Meadow wasn't really a monk at all. He'd apparently been escaping is disguise. Friday Bob was unclear around the details but claimed the meadow as the site of a gruesome and exceedingly detailed execution. By all accounts, the lost monk had a live eel forced into his throat somewhere between the thumbscrews and the being danced over by morris men. Charlie didn't believe any of it, but it spared her from having to say much.

"Maybe Mister Anderson had her killed," Friday Bob suggested.

They'd tried all of the halfway sensible ideas already. Charlie was ready to consider anything. "Why would he do that?"

"He catches orphans and kills then and hides the bodies in those weird houses on new road. Everyone knows that."

"Temperance isn't an orphan."

"Mister Anderson doesn't know that, though, does he? And she was probably wandering about on her own like a sad urchin. I reckon he's getting careless."

Charlie's feet were a throbbing mass of pain, but they headed towards the new road anyway. The street stood empty, silent and unsettling. The biscuit factory looked equally devoid of life, except for the man at the gate. Charlie remembered stories about mortless people.

"Maybe she did come here."

Friday Bob nodded agreement.

She tried the gate man, who recalled seeing Temperance before, but not in the last few days.

"Funny," he said. "We get so few visitors, especially not young ladies, but here's you today, and that Miss Fairfax yesterday. I suppose lots of girls would like to marry Mister Anderson, now he's got a big factory and is making his fortune. I'd marry him. If I wasn't a man."

"Right you are then," said Charlie. "I suppose there's no chance our girl could have got in yesterday? She's very much the sort of girl who would have a look around, if the opportunity presented itself."

"It's possible," the gatekeeper admitted. "But she'd stick out. I'll keep my eye open."

Friday Bob grinned. "The biscuits are made out dead people,

aren't they?"

The gatekeeper responded with an indulgent smile. "You children do get some queer ideas."

Chapter thirteen

Spiritual dilemmas in the shadow of Darwin: A case study

At some point, she must have fallen asleep, but Temperance couldn't remember it happening. When she woke, four hairy faces were regarding her with great interest. She had no idea who they were, where she was, or what any of it signified. For a moment, she remembered stories of bears and stolen porridge, not her own recent history, and felt certain they would eat her.

"What are you doing here, little girl?" one of the bears asked.

The light was dim, her eyes still bleary. She blinked a few times and the bear-face resolved into something a bit more human, if overgrown with a feral-looking beard.

"I didn't mean to," she began, using her most trusted line of defense. "The door was open, and I was looking for someone, then, before I knew it, the door was shut, and here I am." She shrugged. Recollections of the previous day bubbled up in her memory. "Then it was all warm in here and I got sleepy," she added.

"Who were you looking for?" another beard-laden face enquired.

What had she been doing? She tried to recall, but had the impression it had been one of those sudden whims. As a defense, 'sudden whim' never usually helped at all, so she tried a bit of lying instead. "Oh, just a friend of mine, Friday Bob."

The bearded faces showed no signs of recognizing the name. Evidently they'd never heard of him. Clearly the bears were from somewhere else.

"Who are you?" the original bear demanded.

"Temperance Rosemary Felicitations Esmeralda Perry," she said. Some of the names were more recent additions.

"She's just a curious child," the fourth man said, from further away. "I don't think she means any harm."

"I'm just nosy," Temperance agreed, wondering just how much trouble she was in. "Granny always says it'll be the death of me. But I promise, I'm quite harmless, I wasn't really doing anything and I won't give you any more bother if you let me go."

"We have had no premonitions about her, no guidance. I do not know what this means," one of them said.

Temperance couldn't really tell them apart. They were all dressed in much the same way and between the white clothes and the huge beards, there wasn't a lot to go on. They all looked ancient, but for Temperance, that meant anyone over the age of about thirty.

"I imagine it means she is of no great significance," one of the beards said.

While Temperance liked to be significant, this seemed a situation in which total irrelevance might be her friend. "Nothing interesting about me. Can I go home now?" Temperance asked.

They looked at her in silence for a while. Eventually, one of them said, "We do not know. We need a sign."

"I'm good at writing. What do you need the sign to say?" she offered.

Apparently, none of them knew.

Charlie turned the mouse over in her hand. It offered no resistance, but waved its little wheels in the air. Aside from the absence of normal feet, it looked entirely like a real mouse, with fur, ears, and whiskers. However, it felt quite heavy, and not very soft. She suspected it of not being what it seemed. Her taste for dismantling small mammals had departed years before, and she felt no desire to open it up and see if anything made it tick.

"Once the feet are off, you can peel them," Nigel said. "Putting the skin back's harder."

"Let's not," said Charlie. She put the mouse down and watched it speed across the floor.

"We're out of entrails. I could fry some bacon instead."

"How about reading her palm?"

"I'm not very good at palms. I'm good at entrails, but if we read hers, that will reduce our options considerably, so if it's all the same to you, I'd rather not."

"The statues are silent."

"One of us could drink a potion and seek a vision."

"Are you volunteering then?"

"That wasn't my intention. I was going to make lunch."

"I've never tried using lunch as a form of divination. I suppose we could."

"Or have her pull a card from the tarot and decide based upon that?"

"I should prefer to use the I-Ching."

"I have already doused her for malevolent energies and found nothing."

"Lunch is a good idea," Temperance said, hopefully.

The four men regarded her thoughtfully.

"The oracle has spoken," one of them pronounced.

The Subscription Room was packed and uncomfortably hot, but no one made the slightest sound as Doctor Melgrave gave sonorous voice to his lecture. Justina had been looking forward to this Saturday for some weeks, and even the disquieting evens of the previous day had not prevented her from attending.

"We live in an age that has its eyes firmly upon the future. There are many who ask, what can our ancient past possibly say that will be of any significance for the era to come? I say that the subject of history has never been more vital than it is today. We expose the roots of civilization so that the tree of progress can better grow. We expose ourselves, as men, we lay bare the innate qualities of our humanity."

Justina managed to keep her face entirely composed. It would not do to show amusement over an ill-conceived turn of phrase, and would reveal a vulgar capacity for innuendo. With some considerable effort, she managed not to envisage any exposure at all.

"And yet, we must not allow romantic ideas of the past to be made comical by the foolish actions of the uneducated. Our beloved country is rife with such foolishness. I myself have seen men who dare to call themselves Druids, prancing about at sites of scientific interest and claiming both ownership and insight! Archaeology and antiquarianism are serious subjects that should be kept in the hands of serious men. We cannot allow these fraudsters and fantasists to steal history from us. These are men who would surely cut down the great tree of progress. We must expose them!"

An image of ArchDruid Henry Jones popped spontaneously into her mind. For a while it took her attention entirely from Doctor Melgrave's energetic lecture. When focus returned, he had moved to the subject of his own quest for the final resting place of Noah's Ark.

Afterwards there were cups of tea, accompanied by buns. Justina perambulated slowly through the crowd, looking for familiar faces and exchanging a few words here and there. She found herself invited to a private dig at a residence in Bath – which sounded promising – and a more rough-and-ready expedition to the wilds of Lincolnshire. The latter offered no guarantees of hot running water, and no suggestion of social occasions, and so she politely declined. The thought of sleeping in a tent, and doing all of her own digging, smacked too much of hard labor. For all that she had defended her possible career to her mother, Justina had an aversion to bodily suffering that kept her archaeological exploits confined to genteel surroundings. The aberrant visit to Wales confirmed her impression that she did not belong in muddy fields, far from the comforts of dining room and bath tub.

Of all the faces she studied after the lecture, none belonged to the man she most feared to see. The absence of Alain Chevalier disappointed her enormously. Surely he should sweep back into her life now, with some even more momentous treasure hunt, dark request, or dubious secret? His brief presence and departure made no sense at all, surely it must lead to more? It seemed incredible that he could have forgotten her so easily. Men did not forget her. They pined for her, wrote tedious letters, made outlandish promises and went on to be eaten by tigers, imprisoned by foreign powers or otherwise rendered heroic in the hopes of impressing her. However dull she might find them, Justina felt very clear that it was not her position in life to be forgotten by her suitors, merely because she rejected them.

None of her acquaintances had seen the Frenchman in months. They speculated that perhaps he had returned to his native soil. No one rated him as a scholar, no one had ever seen him even lift a trowel, or heard him offer a paper. He was not serious, they assumed, moving on to give careful allusion to their own recent finds and writings for comparison. Justina noticed a veritable rash of ancient cauldrons being mentioned. Mister Prestwick of Leamington Spa had unearthed one in the Cotswolds, although his was missing its bottom. Mister Scuddle of Malvern had dug up a very small one not ten miles from his own front door. Mister Preswick's brother, is transpired, had been in Wales only a week before, and had seen no fewer than three, with his own eyes.

Justina could not think of a discreet way of asking if anyone had tried putting dead things into theirs. She wondered, but did not say aloud, whether Alain Chevalier had any hand in the discovery of these other ones. He could have remained in Wales. But what would that explain? It could all be coincidence of course. The urge she had to seek him out struck her as both unhealthy, and undignified. To distract herself, she instead presented herself to the second Mister Prestwick, telling herself it was just professional curiosity.

Plump, middle-aged and overdressed, Mister Prestwick the younger was delighted to find he had an audience. "How did I happen to find a cauldron? I must, in no small part ascribe that to years of careful study, and good strategy."

She nodded enthusiastically, knowing full well that what he really meant was 'blind luck'.

"Once the field had been suggested to me, it was merely a matter of applying good, scientific reasoning to the procedure."

"Ah, you were prompted by some nugget of local folklore, perhaps? Or some traditional memory the working people have kept alive for centuries with their quaint oral histories?" she said.

"Something like that," Mister Prestwick conceded. "I met a chap in the pub. I'm sure he must have been local. Absolutely. The folk memory, laden with seeds from our ancient past, waiting for we blessed and learned few to unravel the threads of mystery and untangle the truth."

Even with the mixed metaphors, she had no doubt it had been Chevalier. But why? Perhaps he had buried these cauldrons himself and meant to make fools of them all in the eyes of the world! That would be very French of him. She supposed he must be a gentleman of considerable wealth and leisure to indulge in such a scheme, and felt relieved that her own cauldron had not drawn public attention. Were it not for the small matter of the resurrections, it would have been an entirely satisfactory theory.

After lunch, Temperance felt a good deal more comfortable and set about barraging the four men with questions. Having had years of practice on Granny and Charlie – neither of whom were naturally talkative people – Temperance was surprised at how easily the quartet were persuaded to divulge information. They were Druids, but apparently had never tried to nail anyone to a tree. They were on a quest, although none of them seemed to know what it was for, but they relied on portents and visions to guide them. Temperance assumed they had made do with the portents in the beginning, and then bought the caravan to live in when they had saved up for it. They all considered themselves to be very important and doing essential work. However, as there were only four of them and a dog, they didn't have anyone to be important at.

Once they started talking, she had a sense that it made a nice change for them to have an audience. There words were so strange that she listened happily. It was better than reading a book. She discovered that they wanted a suitably grand name, but could not agree upon one. The Universal Ancient, Terribly Important Order of Visionary and Learned Druids was just too longwinded, but was the only thing they'd agreed upon. Unity of opinion was their only rule, they told her, with some pride. As a consequence, they lived on porridge, bacon and potatoes boiled with mutton and cabbage. Looking around the inside of their caravan, she guessed that the rule of unity probably made life hard for them in other ways too. Did they all have to go to the toilet at the same time?

"You remind me a bit of bears," she said. "All growly and beardy. I saw a bear once. A dancing bear. It was very big."

The four Druid bears looked at each other. "The Druidic Order of the Bear," one of them said.

"Shouldn't it at least be ancient, or venerable? No one will take us seriously otherwise."

"It's a sign," said the third.

"It's only a sign if we see another bear in the next day," another protested.

"I should really go home now," Temperance said, thinking about Granny.

"We never go back! The only way is forwards."

"I thought that was a metaphysical proposition, not a matter of geographical direction," came the reply.

Temperance could see they would be straight back into another really interesting argument that didn't go anywhere, if she wasn't careful. "Yes," she said, thinking they really were quite mad, but harmless. "Can I just point out that I'm not a Druid? I've got an important job to do, involving dead people and a bucket."

"Oh! Why did you not say so?"

Temperance shrugged. "You were busy, and you didn't ask."

They all studied her through their facial hair. "She's just a child," one of them said.

"I think my Granny will be worrying," she reiterated. "I've never been away over night before, and she doesn't know where I am." There were sage nods to this. "Where am I?" Temperance asked.

It was the first Sunday in months that Alice had not cooked a proper Sunday lunch. These routines of normal life mattered to her. They were the stitches holding the fabric of her existence together. None of that seemed to amount to very much now. There was no one to cook lunch for.

Three different sets of neighbors had invited her to eat with them, but she had declined them all. Not that she had anything to do instead but wait and hope. Or at least, there were things around the house that needed doing, but she couldn't find any enthusiasm for them either. Sooner or later, she would have to tell the girl's parents and that did not cheer her. Technically, Temperance's mother was Alice's daughter, but it had never worked well in practice.

When the kitchen door opened, she assumed it would be Charlie again, as Hephzibah had not long been round.

"Isn't there any lunch?" Temperance asked, looking sorely disappointed by the barren state of the kitchen table.

Alice considered shouting at the wicked child, who appeared every inch her usual, disheveled and unconcerned self. Words of accusation couched in sarcastic questions sprang to mind, but were never voiced. Instead, very much to her surprise, Alice found she was crying.

"I didn't mean to!" Temperance said, running to give her a hug. "It was all a mistake, I got muddled up with some Druids and we travelled for hours and hours but it turned out we were only in the next village after all, so I walked back today. They were very funny."

Alice held Temperance's face between her hands. "Did they hurt you?"

"Oh no. They looked at my hands and asked me a lot of funny question. They did make me drink tea. Without any milk in it even." She burbled on, but Alice wasn't really following any more.

Relief surged through her, but all the images of what could have happened remained present in her head. All she wanted to do was keep hugging this reprobate of a granddaughter to make sure she was still there. Temperance squirmed a bit, but did not complain.

"Don't ever scare me like that again," Alice said.

"I promise," said Temperance. "I will scare you by new and surprising ways and not repeat the old ones ever."

Alice shook her head. "You're incorrigible."

"Does that mean the same as 'ravenous'?"

"No," Alice said. She managed to pull away, and started thinking about lunch. Life as usual. The little threads of normality holding her days together. How easily those threads could be torn away! She put the thought aside. This was not the time to be maudlin, the child needed feeding.

After disembarking, when the train pulled out of the station, Justina felt certain she saw the infamous Alain Chevalier smiling at her from one of the windows. She stared back, frozen and confused. Why would he be on her train? Why had he waited until she alighted on the platform to make his presence known? Was he following her? Or had it just been someone who looked a lot like him?

She had no answers, and a fast-developing headache.

Chapter fourteen

Discourse on the social impact of advertisements and the danger of unregulated pamphleteering

Charlie was contemplating the colorful array of dry pulses in the grocers when Mrs. Smith asked her about the factory, and whether she had heard anything.

"Which factory do you mean?" Charlie asked, not very interested but feeling obliged to say something.

"My Agatha's married to Bob, and his brother Arthur lives next door to a chap who makes deliveries to Mister Anderson. That's how we came to hear," Mrs. Smith explained in a peeved tone of voice. "Really, it's shocking, and unchristian, and should not be allowed!"

Mrs. Smith was not excessively prone to bouts of moralizing, so Charlie assumed this probably wasn't a minor act of impropriety that had her riled. The Anderson connection made her decidedly uncomfortable, so to be one the safe side, she feigned ignorance. "I don't hear a great deal about anything, Mrs. Smith."

"Oh my dear, you have to keep up with the times, a girl of your profession! I'd better tell you. As I heard it, Mister Anderson has got dead people working for him. Bits dropping off them and everything. That's why not a decent soul in this town knows anyone who works at the biscuit factory. It's a disgrace."

"I've never sold so much as a pinch of flour to a dead person," chimed in the grocer. "Oh, this town is not what it used to be, I can tell you."

"I suppose dead people don't eat," Charlie said, thinking of her mortless animals.

"Taking jobs from proper folks, too," the grocer said. "And I can't say the biscuits are any good. It makes me shudder, to remember once having eaten them, thinking of those dead hands in the biscuit mix. It quite turns me up."

"The church is getting up a petition against it," Mrs. Smith said, whilst arranging her small parcels in her basket. "I'm sure you two will put your names to it. There's to be a rally, and a protest on Thursday as well."

Charlie wondered if she ought to go. She'd known all along what might, theoretically happen to the cauldron. For the sum of money involved, it had been very easy to imagine there would be nothing of the kind. She hoped it was all a terrible mistake. Of course Mister Anderson wanted the item as a decoration, or at the very worst, to resurrect working horses. Not people. She'd very carefully pictured the biscuit factory as a model of normality, and had only been there that one time, with Friday Bob. They hadn't seen anything untoward. Really speaking, they hadn't seen anything at all.

Charlie kept telling herself that none of this was her responsibility. All she'd done was accepted a commission to reassemble someone else's item. No one had told her what the consequences would be. Admittedly, she had figured out the shape, and then thanks to Temperance, had discovered exactly what the object was able to do and how it could be persuaded to work is uncanny tricks. Then, admittedly, she had sold the cauldron, even though it wasn't technically hers, to someone she didn't know, and had accepted an embarrassingly large sum of money in exchange. She had not put any dead people in it, or even told Mister Anderson how it worked.

When you put it like that, it doesn't look very good... Charlie shook her head, not wanting any of these thoughts. Laid out plain, she had a lot of trouble justifying her recent actions.

A lot of other people had known though. Enough dead animals had been brought to her door for there to be no doubt on that subject. Bromstone being a small place, she supposed word had got round, and prompted the request to purchase. Of course

Mister Anderson was using the cauldron to bring back dead people. It made perfect sense. Half the commissions in her history had been for machines to reduce the cost of human labor. Mortless people would be the ultimate solution to the cost of a workforce. Dead people had no rights at all, and it the cats were anything to go by, no minds and no appetites. You wouldn't need to pay them. She wondered briefly, how he had persuaded them to work, but moral revulsion soon got the better of scientific curiosity.

At no point had she really known what would happen next. *Yes, but no one knows, so that's not a tremendous excuse in the scheme of things.* She had carefully undertaken not to wonder about the consequences of her efforts at all the critical points in the proceedings. The more she tried to defend her actions, the more persistent that other little voice inside her head became. *So this is all fine, is it?* The line of consequences that could be drawn from her choices to a factory full of dead people making biscuits, was hard to deny, and even harder to justify. But what could she possibly do about it now? It was, she decided, not the cleverest time to become squeamish about things.

If there had been a simple answer, she might have willingly acted upon it. Charlie had a mind for problem solving, but her bent was wholly mechanical. There hadn't been any significant ethical dilemmas in her past before, or at least, nothing more challenging than whether to dismantle any of her sibling's pets. She felt tremendously guilty about the entire biscuit factory arrangement, from the presence of the dead, to the contents of their hideous biscuits. She had made these things possible. But was any of it, technically speaking, wrong? How did you tell? Was it more wrong than working a living horse to death? She'd seen a bit of that along the way. How about the living people who became dead people in other factories? It had to be less wrong than that, surely? The business left an unpleasant taste in her mouth, but there were no easy solutions here. She couldn't just march in, take the cauldron, bury the dead and wait for the audience to applaud.

It's not my problem. I can't do anything. I'm not responsible.

She kept saying it in the hope that, after a while, she would start to feel it as well.

The first skirmish of the Great Biscuit War seemed heady by the usual standards of Bromstone life. Through its long history, the town had been relentlessly apathetic in face of a great many things. Political movements had entirely passed it by. While it had a profusion of chapels, it had not endured the effects of serious religious schism. People converted to whichever faith resulted in a person not being burned for heresy, and all the drama occurred somewhere 'away'.

Against all the odds, Bromstone had remained wholly oblivious to the progress of the Civil War, and had been untouched by revolting peasants. Even the Norman invasion had largely passed it by, with the Doomsday book recording it as Broomtown, offering a few additional measurements alongside, that no one since then had ever managed to decipher. Possibly they had something to do with goats. It just wasn't the kind of town that history tended to bother with. No important roads passed through it, the river was too small for significant traffic, it had never been on anyone's border, nor had it inspired rebellion or controversial thinking. The inhabitants seldom felt the urge to leave, and new arrivals were equally few, because there was nothing to come for. Even the railway line had not seemed fit to approach the town too closely, requiring local citizens to walk down the road in search of modern convenience.

As a consequence, a protest by even seven locals was an unheard of event. No fewer than twenty other people came along out of curiosity, to be diverted by the spectacle of six elderly citizens and one independent minister making their displeasure known. The walls of Anderson's Biscuit Factory did not tremble.

Intelligent Designing for Amateurs

The dead did not rise from either their graves or their workplace. After a while it started to rain, and everyone decided it might be best to retire home for afternoon tea.

"This is just the beginning," Mister Edwards told Alice. In this, he was entirely correct.

Alice noted that there was a good deal more color in the young man's cheeks now, and a deal more cheek to have color in. He looked far younger, as a consequence.

"Are you keeping well, Mister Edwards?" she asked.

"I am indeed, Mrs. Perry, thank you." He smiled. "I still haven't seen you at our gatherings, though. It's never too late to seek redemption."

Alice smiled back. "Nor will you see me there. I don't do church. I don't mind stepping out to raise a bit of noise and do a bit of work in the world, but I'm not the sort for chapel and that's all there is to it."

"The chapel is for everyone," Edward Edwards said, with utter sincerity.

"Well, it's a nice outlook, but don't expect folk to share it," Alice told him.

He glanced around, a little furtive. "Does Miss Fairfax attend a church, or other gathering, do you know?"

So her influence remained. Alice had a fair idea what men liked, but even so, the effects Miss Fairfax had took some explaining. Oh, the form of the woman was pleasing enough to the eye, but she could have been carved out of ice, for all the symptoms of humanity that she showed. "We don't see her so very much, I couldn't say where she goes or what she does."

He did not seem surprised by this, which might be as well. "I have not seen her at all in a long while," Edwards confessed.

"Let me give you a word of advice, young man, speaking as a woman who has been around for a few years. There are better girls than her in the world, for a chap like you."

"There is no one else!"

"Give it time. She's no better for your soul than Penance Biscuits are for your body. Trust me, I know a thing or two. Your heart's in the right place, young man, it would be a crying shame to waste it on a woman like her. Find someone with a bit more…warmth. You're young yet, you've got plenty of time."

Although he didn't say anything by way of a reply, Alice had the impression she'd been heard. Whatever Edith might think about the importance of getting flesh on a young man's bones, there wasn't much to be gained replacing one kind of madness with another.

They were all crammed in under the bridge, invisible form the road, and unlikely to be troubled by adults. It was one of Temperance's favorite hiding places, but with this many children, you did have to squeeze. Still, it felt a bit like a cave, and that created a suitable setting for revealing her plan. So long as no one slipped and pushed her in the river. They were all looking at her now, waiting for her to speak. She cleared her throat. This was the big moment, and she'd waited a long time for it.

"We're all going to be Druids." There was silence. She waited, letting the words sink in. It was a very new idea and not to be hurried. "I've met some real Druids, so I know all about how you do it. I've travelled with them, and learned their secret ways." By now, her audience was enthralled. Not even Friday Bob had further objections to her taking command. Feeling bolder, she continued. "First we've got to have all the right clothes and whatnot. It's no good being a Druid if people can't tell you're a Druid just by looking at you. So you've got to get white night dresses. You've all got sisters, that bit should be easy. And rope, to tie round your waist like a belt. I've got some sheep's fleece I found in the lane and we can make beards out of that."

"Have we all got to have beards?" Rapunzel asked, sounding a bit worried.

Temperance was not put off by this challenge. "Even us. The beards are important. It'll be fine if we all have them, no one will be able to tell who's who anyway. They'll just see our Druidness, and be really impressed. "

"All right," said Rapunzel, reluctantly.

"Right, we are also going to need a name, because Druids always go around in groups and we have to be able to tell people which Druids we are. And we need magical things for telling the future with."

"What sort of a name?"

"What sort of magical things?"

"I've got some gobstoppers."

"Can I wear a hat?"

"We're going to nail people to trees, right?"

"Does it matter if there's lace on the nightdress?"

"We could sacrifice my brother; that would be a good place to start."

"Why do we need a name?"

Temperance raised her hand for silence, and then did her best to explain what qualities the name of a Druid organization required, what kinds of objects would enable magical divination, and what the role of hats might be in their futures. She avoided the topic of sacrifice for now. Obviously, they'd have to tie someone to a tree, but you could take these things too far.

"We need big, impressive words in our name that make us sound important and like we've been a Druid order for ever so many years," she said.

"Constantinople," said a little voice, and then added, into the stunned silence, "It's the biggest word I know."

By the end of the afternoon, The Most Beardy and Redeemed Order of Old Druids was ready to make itself known to the world. Most of the Druids had whitish robes, apart from Rapunzel, who could only find a nightdress with a floral print, but had put her regular white apron over it. All of the Druids had tufts of sheep's wool tuck to their faces with honey. Several of the Druids were already attracting the attention of insects as a consequence of this. The Order had, by way of magical items, a wooden spoon, some nails for attaching people to trees, a few bits of bone, the abandoned old shoe from their archaeological period, and a tin pail. They had also decided that they would be getting at least some of their mystical omens by looking at the sky.

"Now what do we do?" asked Friday Bob, sounding just a little bit skeptical.

Temperance looked at the sky. There were a few pale clouds, some darker ones. They all had a blobby look and didn't suggest any obvious adventures or wonders. She let her mind empty, and waited for inspiration to strike.

"The wind is telling me that we should go out into the world, and look for cake."

The Druids cheered, and set off for Barker Street with all the haste that could reasonable be adopted by a newly formed old Order in unfamiliar attire.

In the days that followed, pamphlets went through ever letter box across the town. They were unlike anything anyone in the town had seen before, and as a consequence were much discussed in all the places where the people of Bromstone liked to gather.

The first page read,

Mister Anderson wishes to reassure his friends that, despite the impression recent protests may have given, there is no cause for alarm. Mister Anderson's biscuit factory is run along a truly modern and innovative design that will bring prosperity to the town. Other factories may be full of men, women and even children who toil for long hours in grime and misery, but the Bromstone biscuit factory will never cause such shameful suffering. Mister Anderson wishes to convey to his friends the comforting truth that no human life will ever be blighted by his business.

The rest of the pamphlet contained encouragements to purchase Penance Biscuits, Salvation Sticks and the new line of Righteous Crackerbreads. There were many dramatic suggestions as to the kind of benefits such consumables could be expected to bestow.

Then came: *Lacrimous cakes, rich, nourishing comfort made by good, warm, human hands. What better could there be for times of hardship and dismay? Replace tears with Lacrimous cakes, that the burden of your life be lighter.* Pictures, testimonials and advertisements filled the remainder of the sheet.

A third printing encouraged readers not to be lured into sinful, gluttonous cake eating when their immortal souls might be imperiled by such wanton acts of spiritual carelessness. *Eat your way to a better life without indulging the sinful flesh in acts of wanton indulgence! Penance Biscuits will save you from hell fire.*

On the day that Miss Fairfax departed for the private dig in Bath, Temperance led the Most Beardy and Reformed Order of Old Druids along to the second biscuit factory demonstration. By this time, they had added a flatulent dog to their number, given each other titles, had three separate fights about the titles, lost the wooden spoon of destiny and given up on the beards. They'd also changed their name twice and nearly had a fight about that.

However, their arrival at the factory was not quite the public triumph Temperance had been aiming for. The dozen or so people who had been inspired to rally around Mister Edwards, took their presence as an insult. They were called ungodly, heathen, and accused of making a joke at the expense of upstanding religious people. Angry words were spoken about the deficiencies of their parents. Friday Bob handled this in the traditional manner of boys everywhere, and offered to show them his bottom. Further words were shouted indecorously. This is not, dear readers, the kind of public record in which such improper public speeches should be recorded for posterity. It is recommended that you should undertake not to imagine the more unseemly details.

The growing number of assembled spectators warmed considerably to the subject of religious debate, which was turning out to be even more interesting than issues of theoretically dead workers. Some especially ambitious young apprentices had brought overripe fruit, to emphasize key points in their arguments. As a consequence, no one was able to hear Mister Edwards' speech on peace and brotherhood for the enthusiastic squeals of youthful combat.

Temperance soon learned that her grandmother was not especially impressed with this turn of events.

"You just don't think things through properly," Alice pointed out, tone acidic, as she dragged a tomato-splattered Temperance away from the mayhem. "Of course they were going to throw things at you. Silly girl! Why didn't you load your pockets with eggs before you set out?"

"Sorry, Granny." She had to admit, it was a shameful lack of foresight on her part.

"I'm far too old to have to go around thumping young men, and I resent having to do so on your behalf, miss."

Temperance giggled. "Sorry, Granny."

Alice snorted. "You're an absolute disgrace."

In an ideal world, Justina felt, all archaeology would be undertaken in precisely this manner. Digs should be invariably be situated in convenient proximity to large, well-appointed houses belonging to gentile hosts. The superior dig could then be depended upon to pause for afternoon tea, and allowed sufficient time for one to bathe and dress for dinner. The future of archaeology should include far more opportunities for evening dress, and far less scope for bodily suffering, she felt. If it was to all be about dirty holes and shabby clothing, one may as well employ poor people to do the job instead.

With the wonderful Roman baths nearby, and all the delights of a fashionable town, Bath was Justina's idea of heaven. She knew that one day, her mother would leave this life, an event which would free the tragically bereaved daughter to take her proper place in the world. In the meantime, she might yet make her fortune by other methods. One superb dig could set her up for life. She could not help but feel that it was all too sordid, having to think about money all the time, but how else was a person to afford the essentials of life?

"Why do you not marry, my dear girl?" suggested Lady Armitage, her kind hostess. "There must be some charming old fellow out there with plenty of money who would let you pursue your own interests."

Justina put down her cup and saucer. "I have yet to find a man I did not soon come to imagine I would want to smother in his sleep, should I be obliged to remain in sufficient proximity for long," she confessed. "And as I have no wish to be hanged, it seemed prudent to avoid the matrimonial condition altogether."

Lady Armitage chuckled at this. "I have always found that a room of one's own is a great precaution against the temptation to commit murder."

Justin nodded, seeing the wisdom in this. However, there were too many other shortcomings in the scheme for her to consider taking it further. A husband might expect her to obey his wishes, and, technically, would have a good deal of power over her. There were, granted, ways around that particular problem. Her mother had found physical restraints very much to her advantage. But that required so much dedicated effort. The ideal husband would live long enough the write a will in her favor, and then choke upon his bread and butter within a matter of days.

Had she felt confident of such an outcome, matrimony would have held no anxieties at all.

"Of course, with a little discretion..." Lady Armitage began, "A gentleman with no other heirs, no one to be offended by a sudden demise... Not that I am advocating murder as a solution to your difficulties," she added, eyes twinkling.

"Of course not," Justina said, recalling that before Lord Armitage, there had been a short marriage to Mister Henry Cantata Beak. His fatal fall from a third floor window had all been very sad, and unfortunate, but had done his newly wealthy widow's social career no harm at all.

That afternoon there were four of them digging in the garden; her old friend Amelia Scuttlecote, an elderly gentleman by the name of Parsimonious Bush, and a slightly younger fellow called Barnes, whose stutters discouraged him from participating in conversation. Lady Armitage came out from time to time, to observe their progress and be companionable, but had no desire to exert herself. They dug from ten in the morning until noon, and then from three in the afternoon until five, an arrangement they all agreed should henceforth be adopted at all excavations. Frequently servants undertook the actual digging, on close instruction, but the noble archaeologists all took pride in dirtying their own trowels a little along the way.

"It is hardly proper for us to be in the soil for hours at a time, as though we were merely common laborers," Mister Bush observed.

Lady Armitage had indicated her hopes that they might uncover a pagan shrine, around which she could then undertake to redesign her entire garden.

"We ought to be quite literally falling over them round here," she said, more than once. "My dear friend Mrs. Grantham has one in her garden, and it is a most pleasing feature. I shall be vexed indeed if nothing of the same is buried here as well."

"We shall not spare ourselves in any way," Bush promised. "We shall do all that mortal man can do to discover whatever ancient remains lie beneath your garden."

Lady Armitage nodded encouragingly. "You dear, dear man," she said. "I do appreciate you so very much."

They worked with all due diligence, not sparing themselves at all, save for essential pauses necessitated by civilized life. Meals, baths, balls and afternoon tea were rigorously upheld, but Lady Armitage would have expected no less from her hardworking crew and was keen to bestow cake, and immaculate pieces of bread and butter as soon as anyone looked even slightly fatigued. On the whole, it was a very jolly sort of unstinting labor.

Given the charming and generous dimensions of the garden, Justina dared to imagine they might spend all summer digging holes in it. There were plenty of gardeners to tackle the more vigorous jobs, and small holes soon grew into larger, and far more impressive ones. They could pass many delightful weeks in this adventure, arguing amicably over their discoveries, and enjoying the pleasures of Lady Armitage's benevolent hosting. It was the life she had been longing for.

However, just one week into the happy arrangement, the cruel hand of fate reached out to pour something rank over her joy. At first it seemed like a potential triumph, as Justina's trowel clinked against metal. For a few innocent minutes she pictured the pagan statue beneath and imagined the consequences of her success. Then followed the unavoidable effort of seeing what she'd hit. Justina kept quiet, in case it turned out to be something worthless. They had already dug up one mediaeval drainage system.

In the space of about an hour, Justina lifted a number of uncomfortably familiar pieces, her heart growing heavier as each segment emerged. She knew Lady Armitage would delight in the find, but even that failed to smother her acute feelings of discomfort.

"What could it be?" Parsimonious Bush pondered aloud. "Plaques for a wall, perhaps?"

"Regard the curve," Amelia said. "It is not meant to lie flat at least. I see the potential for this to be the remnant of a curved, pagan font. There are some images there, if you look closely. Yes, I have no doubt we've uncovered our first altar piece here. Well done, Justina! "

"It gives one such a thrill," Parsimonious Bush replied.

"Mmmm," added the invariably quiet Barnes, offered in a tone that suggested great enthusiasm.

They were all handling the pieces now, rubbing off earth and commenting on possible interpretations. How long would it take them to see the cauldron shape? How long before they assembled it? She knew it was pure superstitious nonsense to imagine that finding the item could invoke the man. Ridiculous to think that he would manifest now, or that the find in any way connected with her previous discovery. And yet, the thought would not quite go away.

"Please do excuse me for a little while, I feel a touch unwell," Justina said.

"Too much sun, my dear?" Amelia asked. "Take a little rest, we can manage, I'm sure."

She felt certain they could, all of them far more interested in the muddy bits of metal than her personal plight. She felt dreadfully nauseous now.

In the cool and quiet of her temporary bedroom, Justina found no relief. Slightly feverish, she lay and turned continually, her mind in turmoil. She did not suffer from the sun, normally. This indisposition seemed far more like the tornado of personal crisis than a mere biological setback. Much as she loved her current situation, it seemed impossible to think of staying. The cauldron had cast a dark spell of dread upon her. Finding a soiled handkerchief amongst the freshly laundered ones could not be more distressing. There would be no more dressing for dinner. No more charming exchanges with the lady of the house. She must go back to her social exile in Bromstone, and lick her wounds.

Justina felt as though the whole world intended to mock and punish her. Could she even dare to wield a trowel again, if these monstrous cauldrons kept coming into her life? She felt certain that if another dig resulted in one coming to the surface, she might become hysterical. Doctors would be called for. Blood would be let. She had heard tales of women whose families sent them away because their minds were disarranged. Who knew what her mother might do? Why could she not just dig up fascinating corpses, like everyone else?

I shall turn to books, she decided. *I know something of books. That will be a far safer arena in which to seek my fortune. It is a little too close to trade for my tastes, but what else is there? I must do something, and it would not be so very vulgar to buy and sell a small number of the rarest, most unusual and interesting volumes. It must be possible for a woman to make an income without entirely degrading herself.*

Mournfully, she packed her bag, and sought out Lady Armitage.

"So soon?" her hostess enquired. "And after your great success today?"

The risk of slighting her benefactress seemed great. "Please forgive me," she begged. "You have been so kind, and I fear I may seem ungrateful, but I may have brought on an old affliction and must waste no time in seeking out my doctor."

"You would be very welcome to avail yourself of mine, if it would help?" Lady Armitage offered.

Having waded so far into falsehood, Justina did not dare to about face. "It is…delicate… I am sure you understand, and just so much easier for me not to have to explain the details." God alone knew what Lady Armitage would make of that.

"I wish you well, my dear. Let me arrange transportation for you."

"I would be most grateful, and thank you. If I feel better, I shall write to you at once."

She fled the town that day, regret and relief vying for dominance within her breast.

Chapter fifteen

On the benefits of undertaking enlightening debates in public spaces

The ironmongers and the cobblers both had signs up that said, "We endorse and support local business. Mister Anderson's biscuits are very fine and nourish both the body and the soul."

Charlie glanced at both statements of allegiance, and headed towards the grocers. His window bore the legend, "Lacrimous cakes, a great comfort to anyone in times of woe and strife." The grocer had an array of the aforementioned items in both black boxes for those who had been bereaved, and a more cheerful red and blue box for those whose sorrows were not socially prescribed in their expression.

"You look glum today, Miss Rowcroft, can I recommend that you enliven yourself with some of these fine cakes?" the grocer suggested as she approached his counter. "Just the ticket, these, such an excellent idea." He pointed meaningfully at the red and blue boxes.

She'd only meant to buy tea and sugar, but had never been good at resisting the sweet allure of cake. And the grocer was right, she needed cheering up.

"Much better than those unspeakable Penance Biscuits," he added, handing over her purchases.

If felt like a little gesture of defiance against Mister Anderson, spending his payment on other people's confectionary.

Further down the street, she saw the baker had his own, handwritten sign in place. "All of our cakes and biscuits are baked on this very site! Wholesome food from a local business that does not employ dead people or in any way condone the disturbing of the deceased."

On impulse, Charlie bought some of their cakes too. There

were a number of things bothering her and cake seemed like a passable alternative to genuine solutions. She had no idea what to do with her dog-faced lodger, he made her uncomfortable but she didn't have the heart to throw him out. And there was supposed to be a public meeting about the biscuit factory. While she wanted to know what was said, she feared being drawn into it. Repeating the phrase "it's not my fault" didn't seem to be helping. If the cake didn't work, she seriously considered the possibility of resorting to gin. Laudanum was reputedly helpful for that kind of thing too.

* * *

Public Assembly to be held at Bromstone
In the upper room of the marketplace on the 27th of this month.

The meeting has been called for the purposes of discussing certain accusations about the factory belonging to Mister Anderson, formerly of Torquay, and to consider the legal and moral implications of any facts that can reasonably be established.

* * *

Squire Abbots, opened the proceedings with a speech about the noble history of Bromstone and our town's pristine reputation, reminding us all that we have a duty to uphold the good name of the town and not to bring a most excellent place into needless disrepute, through careless talk or dishonorable behavior. Mister Edwards, independent minister of this town, commenced the discussion by asking Mister Anderson to give the names of his employees, since not a living soul has ever been seen at his factory. Mister Anderson then gave the names of three working men who take care of his gates, saying, "I do not have to justify myself to you, Mister Edwards. My factories are sound, scientific and highly beneficial to one and all."

The assembled body of people booed him for this remark, and Squire Abbots, who had kindly agreed to chair the proceedings, was obliged to intervene and restore peace. There will now follow a transcript of the various comments made by gentlemen at the meeting, published for due public consideration.

Squire Abbots: Mister Anderson, this assembly is not a court of law, but it may be the first step in a process that will see you in one! May I remind you that you have been accused of using human corpses in your factory. If you can satisfy us that there is no truth in the claim, then the matter will end today. Mister Anderson, by the laws of this land it is a crime to interfere with the rest of those departed.

Mister Anderson: Can I first say then, that I am not a grave robber. Let us be quite clear on this point. I have never disturbed a grave in my life, nor have I paid anyone to do so on my behalf. There are, however, a great many people who die each day in our nearby cities. I refer here to individuals who have no friends or family able to pay for a proper burial. These deceased paupers are a plague, a hazard to public health and a financial burden to the state. I have undertaken to make provision for these unfortunates that relieves pressure upon the public purse. I make no apology for this!

Mister Edwards: Mister Anderson, you admit then, that you have human corpses in your food-making premises?

Mister Periwinkle: That is a most disgusting thing to do. Lacrimous cakes, by contrast are made by proper, living people!

Mister Anderson: Yes, although before you judge, please listen to what this means in practice. I have discovered a most rational and scientific method for bringing a semblance of life back into the bodies of those who appear to be dead.

Mister Edwards: This is an abomination sir! An outrage against God and man!

Mister Anderson: I am merely making use of a resource that is otherwise a burden to our communities. Where is the wrong in this? My work does a great deal of measurable good.

Mister Periwinkle: It is an outrage against good patisserie!

Mister Edwards: It is not the proper work of man to mock the miracles of Jesus.

Mister Anderson: It is not my desire to mock God, Mister Edwards, only to alleviate human suffering in this life. Tell me, young man, have you ever ventured inside a modern factory?

Mister Edwards: I have not, but this is irrelevant.

Mister Anderson: It is highly relevant. You will not have seen the cruel exploitation of living human beings that is commonplace in other factories. Pale omen, near to fainting from exhaustion after countless hours upon weary feet. Children cut and bruised by unkind machinery. Men made blind, crippled of themselves killed for the profits of another. My friends, I put it to you that the dead are already beyond suffering. They feel no pain. There is no horror of distress for them upon the factory floor, and in time they become no more than untroubled dust.

Mister Periwinkle: There is no human suffering at the Lacrimous cake factory, let me assure you! It is a place of happy employment.

Mister Arbuttle: By using the dead, you deprive honest men of employment.

Mister Anderson: I employ several of the living in various capacities. I have increased employment in Bromstone.

Mister Periwinkle: I think you will find that Lacrimous cakes employ far more people to far better effect!

Mister Hermitage: How much more profit do you make in this way, Mister Anderson? I take it that you do not need to feed or pay your dead workers.

Mister Anderson: This is a correct assumption, reflected in the very low cost of my biscuits, which you must agree gives further benefit to everyone who wishes to partake of their excellence.

Mister Edwards: Profit and gain are not excuses for attempting to put yourself in God's place.

Mister Periwinkle: These biscuits are in all ways inferior to Lacrimous cakes!

Mister Anderson: Mister Edwards, I have every respect for God, but I am also a great believer in the vital process of human progress, a noble endeavor which you seem to set yourself in opposition to.

The same themes were then repeated in various forms as the discussion progressed, but little new insight was added by the following hours of debate. After an hour, Mister Periwinkle was bodily removed from the building, as being the only way of avoiding violence being done to his person. It was suggested that he had been hired to speak on behalf of the Lacrimous cake factory, but may equally have been an amateur enthusiast instead.

At the end of the meeting, Squire Abbot made the following pronouncement: As no corpses had been disinterred I can see no reason for taking this matter to law. However, I am uncertain as to whether a moving person can be properly understood to be dead, which complicated things. However, before we conclude our business here, I feel obliged to say that I do not like Mister Anderson's notion of progress one jot, and that no such perniciously fashioned biscuits will ever find their way under my roof.

The assembly disbanded with a great many grumbles, none of the people who had attended being any the wiser as to who had come out worst in the end. It was a most unsatisfactory gathering that seems to have strengthened local divisions and disagreements rather than promoting neighborly good will.

The man on her doorstep had a cheerful, eager facial expression and a rather battered hat clutched in his large hands. "Miss Rowcroft is it? Yes?"

Charlie cautiously acknowledged that he had indeed found the right establishment.

"The famous inventor, yes?"

No one had ever accused her of being famous before. It made her feel quite peculiar. "Yes," she said, for want of a better answer.

The man proffered a hand. "Godfrey Excalibur's the name. I'm in boots."

Charlie looked down at his feet, saw only a pair of shoes, and felt she had missed something.

"Boots for riding, for cavalry, and the adventurous life! Tough, sturdy boots for gentlemen who like to spend their leisure time shooting things. You know the sort of thing I mean?"

"I have some idea, but no firsthand experience."

"Miss Rowcroft, I was at the town meeting last week, about the biscuit man, and it was mentioned to me that you are the one he should thank for his great success."

Charlie's heart sank. She had been dreading something like this, and hated the idea of being in any way associated with Mister Anderson's gruesome enterprise. "I really can't claim anything of the sort. Mister Anderson's business scheme is entirely his own."

"You are too modest! 'A most rational and scientific method!' Mister Anderson said those very words himself. And I thought what a great deal of wastage there is in this world, with all the dead animals. If only we could find the means to render, say, dog skin, more suitable for the boot industry. How much progress we might..." He was cut short by a pained howl from inside the house. "What was that?"

"My dog," Charlie said quickly. "I'm afraid, Mister Excalibur, that you need a chemist for that line of work. I am more of a mechanical inventor, and it's quite a different thing, I assure you."

"Can you not at least try? I was of the impression you are a scientist."

"No, I can't help you. I'm sorry. Good afternoon." She closed the door on him, wondering why so many people assumed science could conjure anything they wanted out of the air.

"It's all right, Nigel, no one's going to hurt you. He's gone now." She felt sorry for the dog-faced boy and his entirely justified anxieties.

Nigel emerged from beneath the table, still looking nervous. "Are you sure he's gone?"

"Yes. You really don't need to worry. I wouldn't have offered to work for him even if I knew how to do what he wanted." She sat down at the table and buried her face in her hands. "Why do people always want the impossible?" she asked.

"They've already got the possible," Nigel said. "What's the point inventing things people already have?"

She smiled at this. He had such a simple and direct way of looking at the world.

The furry face also stretched with a smile. "Charlie, I've got an idea about this mechanical horse. It all comes down to the winding..."

The dog-faced boy worried her. Regularly, and also, a lot. However, he did have a certain kind of charm, and working alone had been lonely. Clearly this was not going to be the day when she asked him what he planned to do next.

In the moments after the sack went over her head, Justina reflected that it had probably been inevitable. Something like this had been bound to happen. One of her insane suitors had no doubt carried obsession to its logical conclusion. With hindsight, she supposed it was remarkable none of them had tried to kidnap her before. Her hands were bound and the heat inside the sack rapidly intensified. The kidnapper was quiet, offering no clues to his identity. She pondered the question, for lack of anything more productive to undertake. There were so many people it could be, that she could not begin to guess who had done this to her. Too breathless to attempt screaming, she listened for clues instead, and soon realized there was more than one man involved in taking her away. In the past, the men who courted her had tended to fight with each other. It came as a surprise to think some of them could be cooperating now. Darkness ate into her mind, and her final conscious thought was to wonder whether they meant to ravish her in some new and memorable way.

Chapter Sixteen

On recognizing our duty to honor and respect those in their twilight years

The four elderly women eyed each other in a moment of silent solidarity. Not one of them was under the age of sixty, but they were people of action none the less and took each other very seriously in matters such as this. Alice knew the other three couldn't be relied on to hold a pistol straight, much less to actually shoot anybody. As a consequence they had armed themselves with the tools they knew best – rolling pins and frying pans. They had hat pins as well, bags full of dried pepper and some small kitchen knives.

"I feel as though we should be wearing something special," said Dorothy Fustus from number ten.

Edith smiled, and patted her on the arm. "We're good enough."

"Clean knickers should always be enough," said Myrtle.

"We may be walking into the very mouth of hell. We may face unthinkable horrors and dangers," Alice began, wanting them to be ready for anything.

"But we've got rolling pins," said Edith.

Alice smiled. Maybe they didn't need serious mental preparation. "We do indeed, and we've got a job to do."

The four women filed out into the night and made their way along the road in near silence. Alice paused at the corner of the street to make sure Temperance hadn't followed them. Barker Street looked reassuringly tranquil, but the girl was adept at sneaking and hiding, it didn't pay to be overconfident. Alice waited, straining her ears. A small rodent scuttled across in the lamplight, and then all was still.

It took them a while to make the walk, but they kept a steady, manageable pace. No point wearing yourself out before the action began, Alice felt. Not that she had any clear sense as to what might happen once they arrived. Still, panting and needing a sit down wouldn't be a likely route to success. When they reached their destination, the new road was as silent as she'd expected, lit only by the glow of a half moon. The street lamps had not yet made it this far. At this time of night, most of Bromstone retreated quietly to its hearth and the streets tended to be peaceful. There were two public houses and occasional evening events, but Bromstone's lack of historical action had nourished a general lack of enthusiasm for causing drama of any kind. Recent excitement had been more than most of the locals could take. It would keep them in conversation material for years. Not being a lifelong Bromstonite, Granny Alice had a rather different attitude.

There were lights in the windows of the factory. Faint, cheerless glows that suggested activity. She hadn't been sure how late they would work, or where the dead would be at this hour. Alice had never been in a factory herself, but had heard a few unsavory stories from girls who wanted more lucrative and less dangerous lines of work. Like dressing as boys and joining the army. Thus far, her impression of factories was very low indeed. She entirely expected her worst suspicions to be confirmed by tonight's little raid.

The young man at the gatehouse had a small lantern in his hand and a worried expression on his face. "Can I help you at all, ladies?" he enquired as he stepped out to greet them.

Alice leaned her rolling pin against her shoulder. "We just want a little look round. We're simply a few nosy, harmless old women. Don't mind us. We won't give you any trouble at all."

The gatekeeper frowned. "Why have you got frying pans?" he asked.

"We like to cook," Edith replied, smiling innocently.

He didn't look wholly convinced by this explanation. "You

aren't trying to threaten me, are you?"

"Of course not, young man. How could four doddering old ladies like ourselves possibly threaten a big, strong lad like you?" Alice said, trying to look feeble.

"I can't let you in," said the gatekeeper. "I'm not supposed to let anyone in. That's my job in a nutshell really. Sorry."

Alice nodded sympathetically. "I quite understand. We are going in though. We're going to walk right past you. What you have to decide is whether you think it is your Christian duty to attack four grandmothers who just want to take a stroll, or whether it might be best to pretend you haven't seen us."

The gatekeeper appeared to be thinking. Alice gave him some time, they were in no hurry. She considered how best to knock him unconscious, hoping all the while that it wouldn't be necessary to do the poor boy any damage.

"I feel a sudden urge to make use of a water closet," the young man said, and turned his back upon them.

They walked in.

After three tries at unresponsive entranceways, the quartet found an unlocked door and finally stepped inside Mister Anderson's Biscuit Factory. There were only a few gas lamps illuminating the large and eerie space. Despite the poor light, Alice could see a great many figures in the process of biscuit making. Wooden spoons tapped against the sides of bowls, accompanied by the soft swish of flowing flour, the faint squidges of many hands rolling, and a host of other low pitches noises she couldn't identify. There was no sign of anyone in charge, directing or monitoring the work. None the less, every figure seemed busy. No one turned to look as they four women walked through, no one approached them or told them to leave. It was decidedly peculiar.

"It is a bit creepy," said Dorothy in a stage whisper. "Do you think they're all dead?"

"I think they might well be," Alice said. "It's too quiet for living people." She waved a hand in front of the nearest face, and met with no reaction at all. "They don't seem to know we are here. Or, they do not care in the slightest." She shivered. People were not supposed to be like this; placid automatons working in silence. She bit back the urge to shout at them.

Edith walked into something, the subsequent clatter making the whole space ring with noise. No one stopped or looked at them.

"Dead people," Myrtle said. "No doubt about it."

"Hello good people, I want you all to listen to me!" Alice called out.

The workers all stopped in their labors. Many of them turned slowly to face her. Apparently they were susceptible to instructions. She assumed they must be, or else harnessing them to work would have been impossible.

"We've come to set you free," Edith called out. Her words fell into the silence like a dying bird into a snowdrift.

"You work for no reward, you are slaves here. Come with us, we will liberate you," Alice said. The lack of response was making her nervous. Real people, surely, would have been affected by such words. *Or would they?* For all she knew, living factory workers might be no better. Crush a human spirit, and you may as well employ a corpse for all the life that will be in them. "Come on," she said, trying to coax them. "Come with me."

A few of the workers shuffled towards her. Once they started to move, everything seemed a good deal better. Clearly used to obeying orders, they just needed some plain instructions to follow. That would do for now, but already she had worries about the longer term.

It didn't take long to have them organized and out into the yard.

The four women left them the dead to do as they pleased, and carried on the quest for victims of industrial oppression.

Working their way around the buildings, they found other rooms and a few more confused and silent people. After a few hours, it become clear they had found everyone and taken them outside.

The scene outside the factory did not match Alice's intentions very well. Her liberated people just milled about in the yard until the four women directed them passed the stunned gatekeeper and on into the street. From there, they wandered away in twos and threes, still not uttering a single word. The soft pad of their feet was the only sound to be heard for some time.

"What will become of them now, do you think?" Myrtle asked.

Alice hadn't really planned that far ahead. She'd rather assumed that, once out, they would know what to do with themselves. "I hope they go on to wherever they should be," she said.

"I didn't see a cauldron anywhere in there," Dorothy pointed out.

None of them had seen anything like one, if you counted out the mixing bowls.

"We'll have to come back for it," said Alice. "I think that's all the adventure my bones can take in one night."

"He'll make more of them," Edith said, grim.

Alice nodded. "I know, but I think we've done all we can for now. It'll give him a warning at the very least."

She didn't like leaving a job half done, but between them they had a lot of bunions, rheumatism, and other debilitating features of advancing age to consider. Looking for the cauldron would have to wait for a bit.

The smell of incense was all too familiar. Frankincense, sandalwood, she knew them well. On regaining consciousness, Justina at first thought she must be back at her mother's house. Any moment now, there would either be some chanting, in whatever language was currently in vogue, or she would be offered a nice cup of tea. She had never quite grasped why religion and incense went together so often. Or, for that matter, why cups of tea so regularly entered the equation too. Ordinary, normal churches only went for the tea drinking, but after that debacle with the vicar, the donkey and the insufficient restraints, Justina's mother had stopped taking her to that sort of church. After a while she remembered the sack, and being hoisted, and wondered where she was.

"Would you like a cup of tea?" asked an unfamiliar male voice.

Justina blinked a few times, realized there were no restrictions upon her movement, and sat up. Feeling none the worse for her recent kidnapping, it occurred to her that she hadn't been in the least bit abused while she slept. This pleased her enormously. She would have hated to miss it.

"Yes please to the tea. Out of curiosity, who are you gentlemen, and why have you kidnapped me? My mother won't pay a ransom, I can assure you." To her relief, her voice was both clear and calm-sounding, despite a fair degree of inner disquiet over her circumstances.

The robed and bearded man who had proffered tea seemed surprised by her words. "We are not kidnapping you! What a frightful thought! We merely needed to borrow you for a little while. I do hope you understand?"

Justina accepted a steaming cup and looked around properly. She had four robed and bearded captors. None of them were visibly armed, nor did they look especially insane or dangerous. That might be a good sign. "So, what do you want with me?" she asked, hopefully.

"Signs and portents led us to you," one of the men said.

"We know that you are tremendously important. We have seen you in our dreams."

This was far more familiar territory, gentlemen were always dreaming about her it seemed. She was unsure whether to feel relieved, or disappointed by their turning out to be suitors after all. But four of them? Did they all want to marry her? That smacked of something foreign and exotic, but even so it did not appeal to her.

"However, we are unsure as to whether there is a great thing that you must do, to fulfill your destiny, or whether the critical moment lies in your past, as yet unrecognized. Our work may depend on whether you need our direct aid, or our skills in interpretation."

"Also," another chimed in, "We do not yet know what your destiny is, or was, only that it is of great importance to us."

Perhaps they weren't trying to collectively marry her after all. "Not a world-saving variety of destiny, then?" Justina asked, somewhat encouraged by this. She had never seen herself as one to perform heroic and dangerous acts for the good of mankind.

The four men appeared to be in various degrees of puzzlement over her question. Eventually, one of them asked, "Do you know who we are?"

Justina cheerfully expressed that she had no idea whatsoever.

"Ah," said another of them, far too sympathetically for her liking. It suggested condescension. Justina only approved of patronizing when she was able to do it to other people.

"We have brought you here so that we can understand your significance," the oldest of them said.

Based on previous inspections, 'here' was a very small room that suggested habitation by all four of them. She supposed they must be very poor, and that surprised her. Madness such as theirs must be very hard to maintain without a dependable income. She wondered if they might like living with her mother instead, but the hermitage was smaller than this, designed to house one man at a time.

"We must seek for guidance. Please remain seated, as guidance can be dangerous and we cannot be held responsible for anything that might happen as a consequence of sudden or imprudent moves on your part."

"I shall not interrupt you," she said, thinking that if she tolerated whatever silliness they had planned, they might then release her.

Years of witnessing her mother's trek through the religious and metaphysical systems of the world had equipped Justina uniquely for this moment. She sank into the calm and patient state that had brought her relatively unscathed through many a peculiar experience. She'd encountered it all before, she thought, the chanting and incense, glazed eyes, ungentlemanly postures and funny hand gestures. They waved feathers about, lit more incense, talked incomprehensible nonsense. Yes, this was the kind of spirituality she knew all about. It's theatrical foolishness had long since lost the power to surprise or alarm her.

"Yes," said a soft voice from somewhere behind her. Apparently they were a more mechanically astute species of mystic, like some of the mediums she had encountered. Justina was not afraid of voices produced by wax cylinders, and waited cheerfully for the knocking sounds to commence.

"There are many cauldrons," the voice said, conversationally. "She's dug up a few, but one was true."

Justina felt her entire body become cold. The situation had now ceased to amuse her. "Did Alain Chevalier put you up to doing this? Is it his joke, perhaps?" She stood up.

One of her captors made an unpleasant, gargling sound.

"Really, I've had quite enough of this foolish charade!" She looked around to see where their speaking deice was hidden. At her back there turned out to be a wall, covered with an ornate hanging. It was looking at her. There weren't any eyes, or even rumples that might suggest a face. Nonetheless, her impression of being regarded by the tapestry was irrationally strong.

"We require the true cauldron," said the tapestry. "The first cauldron, the battlefield and the raven. The changemaker. Let me see your mind."

Justina felt nothing at all. No icy fingers of dread poked deep within her skull. There was no sense of uncanny penetration, but apparently that wasn't necessary.

The tapestry began to speak again. "In the sacred land, rain soaked at moon dark, with lust and pride in your heart and a soul thinner than a long buried shroud." It stopped and she hoped that was it. The stop turned out to be just a pause. "A mind too narrow to turn pieces into a fair shape, a careless mind more troubled by longing for fame than visions of wonder. And then, the woman who makes and sells, and the man who takes what many would call holy, and makes biscuits from it. This is a story woefully lacking in brilliance."

Justina wondered if there had been opium in her tea, or some kind of herbal concoction to make her hallucinate. Either that, or perhaps madness was hereditary after all. The words stung her, but she felt determined to reject them. How could these people possibly know the things she most feared to be true about herself? A flicker of self-knowledge passed through her being, but she did her best to pay it no heed.

The tapestry apparently hadn't finished with her. "You have played your part. You will guide these men to the cauldron and then you will be free to continue with your life of irrelevance."

"Now, hold on a minute," Justina said, the words proving difficult to negotiate passed her lips.

"It is not your business to know. You are unworthy, and you would not understand," the tapestry concluded.

Justina sat down hard. Her chest hurt and she wondered if she might be about to have some kind of terrible fit. Perhaps she had gone mad already and none of this was real. She wanted to scream, but realized that wouldn't help at all. If she'd imagined men inside her own room, there could very easily be doctors outside of it, listening. Better not to rave or howl until she was quite certain as to what was happening. And of course if this horrible experience was real, the odds were good that raving and howling wouldn't improve her situation in the slightest. She closed her eyes, took a deep breath and crushed back down the rising scream inside her throat. *I will not degrade myself by showing distress. I will be icy and disdainful. I will not treat their words as important. They have no idea who, or what I may be, and their opinions re of no consequence.*

Having forcibly calmed herself, she determined to try and take more control of the situation. Looking around again, she saw that one of her captors appeared to have fainted. Blood leaked from his nose, the crimson shocking against the pallid hue of his skin. Another man wept openly, while the third remained frozen with one knee raised and his hands outstretched. Only one of the four seemed alert and fully present.

"I'd better make another cup of tea," he said. "More sugar this time, I think."

Justina stared at him in disbelief. "Did you hear the voice?" she demanded.

"Yes." The man rose unsteadily. "That's why I suggested tea. And some bread and butter, or a bit of cake. Afterwards, it's always best to do something normal and reassuring. How else does one remain sane?" He smiled benevolently. "You may have been shocked by this experience. If you become suddenly cold, or feel nauseous, do say. I have remedies."

She watched him fill a kettle with water from a glass bottle. Only when it had been set upon their tiny range did he start arranging his comrades into more seemly postures. "It's a funny sort of life," he observed.

"Do you have to do this a lot?" Justina asked. Polite conversation made the tapestry seem further away.

"Oh, fairly frequently. I don't really get visions myself, I'm more of a reading the signs man. I don't know why, but it doesn't seem to affect me as much as it does the other chaps. I feel a bit left out sometimes, but it's probably as well, they need me to straighten things out at times like this."

"I see," said Justina. She didn't, but it felt normal to say so. "Tell me, who made that charming robe for you?" Anything to not think about what had just happened.

Chapter seventeen

Moderation in all things: An excess of enthusiasm may be dangerous for the health of both your body and your mind

Had it not been for the necessity of purchasing food at regular intervals, Charlie could easily have gone days at a time without leaving her house. She did as much as possible with the various carts that brought goods door to door, but her odd hours, unpredictable eating habits and eccentric house guest conspired so that she had to seek further provisions. She had always been told that fresh air and society were good for a person, but had never entirely believed it. You only had to look at people to find plenty of evidence to the contrary.

Turning the corner at the end of Barker Street, she saw a perfect illustration of this very idea. A man had just walked into the side of the final house. After banging himself directly in the face, he lurched to one side and then tried to continue forwards in the same direction. This path took him straight back into the wall and a repetition of the previous encounter with it. Charlie assumed there must be drink at the root of his troubles, and decided to leave him alone in case he was dangerous.

Only a few minutes later, she noticed two women standing perfectly still in the middle of the high street. At a glance she could see they were not conversing, merely loitering. Several carts swerved to avoid them. Everyone else who had ventured abroad on foot, went carefully around the pair, trying not to notice this imposition. Both of the stationary individuals were somewhat grey of skin, and their clothing was dreadfully shabby. They stood out from even the poorest Bromstonite, for any respectable person would at least brush and mend their clothing to maintain a decent standard. It looked as though the stationary pair were either lost, or confused. Unlike the drunk man, they did not suggest any kind of threat.

Charlie, being no great respecter of social niceties, when she might be able to offer assistance, walked up to them. "Excuse me, ladies, are you lost?" she enquired.

Neither woman spoke or moved in response to her question. Both had their eyes shut. If they didn't even have the manners or sense to react to her, what did that say about their prospects? You couldn't help people if they ignored you, she supposed, and went on her way. Her intended destination was the bakers, and to get there necessitated climbing over a person of indeterminate gender who had decided to lie down directly outside the door. It had turned out to be a rather unpleasant and troubling sort of day.

No, fresh air and meeting people could not be said to contribute greatly to a person's wellbeing.

The gang had congregated in their favorite wet-weather spot – an old summer house at the end of an overgrown garden belonging to a house that had almost completely disappeared under a blanket of ivy. Rumor had it that a crazy old lady still lived in the house, but no one had seen her in years. Friday Bob claimed to have broken into the property once, and found her bones where they had fallen after her solitary death. He also liked to tell people that he'd seen her ghost in the garden. It was the sort of garden that suggested haunting, but Temperance hadn't seen anything yet. She had thought about going into the foliage-draped building herself, but it was so overgrown she hadn't been able to locate a door, or even a window to break in through.

"You all know where all these creepy new people have come from," Friday Bob was saying.

"My Dad says they must be poor workers from Birmingham, looking for jobs," Rapunzel offered. "That's why they're so queer-looking and pale and don't know what to do. It's the coming from Birmingham."

Friday Bob nodded sagely at this unassailable truth. "I reckon they might have come from the cities, once," he said, "But I'll tell you, they were dead when they left them places."

Temperance grinned. She'd been sworn to secrecy and was trying very hard not to say anything that would constitute breaking her promise to her grandmother. But it would be entirely different if Bob worked things out for himself.

"On our streets, right now, are the dead people Mister Anderson was going to make into biscuits," Friday Bob concluded.

"Do you think they've killed Mister Anderson and escaped?" Albert Nose asked.

They debated the possibilities for a while, until Friday Bob said, "You're being very quiet Temperance," and stared at her, accusingly.

"Granny says I'm not allowed to say anything to anyone about what really happened," she said, virtuously.

"Your Granny never went and let them out!" Friday Bob replied, but it was more question than assertion.

Temperance said nothing. She just smiled and let Friday Bob wonder. The more he pestered her with questions, the more important her silence felt, and the more she enjoyed it. "I can't say anything, Bob, I made them a promise."

"Them? So it's not just your Granny?"

"Can't say," Temperance replied.

When it stopped raining, they went out to search for dead people. It wasn't hard to find lost looking, grey-faced men and women. There were a lot of them, milling about in every street. If you poked them, they didn't seem to notice. You could snatch their hats and not even get shouted at. You could roll these people into puddles and they'd just lie there, eyes firmly shut, not even trying to get up again.

"It's a bit creepy and I'm not sure I want to play this game anymore," Rapunzel said after they'd walked their latest victim into someone else's garden.

For once, Friday Bob agreed with her.

There were letters to the papers of course. Not merely the modest Bromstone Herald, which normally saw the equally modest airing of local concerns, either. Several prominent gentlemen of the district put their names to a piece that was dutifully sent to The Times for consideration. Alice didn't read that sort of publication herself, but she heard about it in the baker's.

"Dead ought to mean dead," the baker commented. "With the exception of Lazarus, and Jesus, and the end times of course. But for general everyday life, it ought to be one thing or another, I always say. You can't go round halfway between life and death."

"No indeed," said another customer. "Some people have no manners at all."

No one could quite agree on the nature and status of Mister Anderson's former workers, which made it harder to decide what should be done about them.

"Something should be done, though," the baker said, repeatedly. "Someone really must do something. What good are the gentry if they won't lead the way in matters such as this?"

"That sounds a little like dissent to me," Alice said.

"I don't know about that," the baker hurried to reply. "I just think they ought to do something. It's not our place, is it?"

The whole town was buzzing with confusion.

"Oh, people would never have dreamed of doing such a thing when I was a lad," the grocer told her.

"Quite so," said Alice. "In my youth, I only ever heard of one dead person who got back up again and they always said that was the doctor's fault for being too drunk to get it right in the first place."

"The dead are not what they used to be," said the grocer,

shaking his head. "It's falling standards all round, that's what it is."

All of the wandering workforce had been declared dead at some point in their recent history. At least, that was the confident opinion of those who discussed such business at the fishmongers. No one quite knew where this intelligence originated, but everyone had heard it from someone else who ought to know the truth of such things. Of course, with each repetition, the story became a little larger and more certain. Mister Anderson himself had confessed to sourcing his workforce from the departed, had he not? Raking over foggy memories of the recent meeting, no one could quite recall who had declare what to be dead at which moment in the proceedings, much less agree over whether it mattered. As all of the previously deceased appeared capable of independent movement, their status remained uncertain as well. Could one die and be considered alive again? Did movement equate to life? Bromstone remained undecided, and uneasy.

Alice watched the unfolding drama with concern. At the outset, she'd felt certain she and her friends were making the right choices in their liberation move. The more opinions she heard, the more confused she felt. The dead people seemed wrong, and there was consensus there, but no one knew what to do about them.

"It is unholy," proclaimed Mister Edwards from his pulpit. "When the body dies, the soul departs to God's hands. The shell may be animated in some grotesque way, but it is not life, and there should be a proper, Christian burial for the unquiet remains."

Edith reported and discussed his sermons at length, which did nothing to cheer Alice up.

They soon discovered, locally, that no matter how legally dead a person may be, burying someone who is still moving, it too uncomfortable a business to conclude. Alice had been along for that episode too, watching the blank face of the man lowered into the ground. When the first shovel full of dirt fell upon him, he raised an arm, then a foot. For some minutes, these random movements continued and when at last he was still, everyone else had gone, leaving her as a lone and troubled witness to the scene. It felt shameful, but what could a person do?

Charlie noticed, in her foraging trips, that some of the locals saw mortlessness as more of a political issue than a spiritual one. Soap boxes started appearing in the market place and rare was the day when you couldn't be thoroughly confused on a number of political points whilst trying to find a little something for supper. Charlie's relationship with things political bore a strong resemblance to her spiritual views – these were things that mostly happened somewhere else, to other people. Only now she seemed to be falling over politics on a daily basis, along with individuals who had lain down in the street unexpectedly.

Quite a crowd had gathered at the market place that day, sufficient in number that getting around them was almost impossible. There were things she needed, but even so, Charlie seriously considered giving up and going home. Large gatherings always oppressed her, and she did not want to meet Godfrey Excalibur, or anyone else with similar ideas. A cluster of large, less than sober fellows backed up into her, cutting off her means of escape with their large frames. There seemed to be nowhere she could go. Charlie felt panic rising within her. Losing self-control in so public a space was an awful prospect. She turned her head frantically, looking for an escape and finding none. The men were oblivious to her, and pushing her back towards the wall.

"Miss Rowcroft?" A firm hand alighted on her arm, and guided her into the safety of a small alleyway. "Forgive me, but you seemed distressed," said Edward Edwards.

"I don't like crowds of people," she confessed.

"We've had no fewer than seventeen speeches in the last five days from this chap," Edwards said. "Ezekiel Pots, Trade Unionist, so far as I can establish. He's not from round here, he's come to stir up trouble, no doubt."

"I wouldn't know," Charlie said. She wanted to leave at once, but could not. A lecture from the minister was not much of an alternative to the one going on in the street, even if it did come with less risk of being trampled.

Apparently her face gave her thoughts away, "I'm not going to harangue you," he said gently. "We've enough of that already. I think he's near the end, if you are happy to wait here with me, the crowd should depart soon."

"Very well," she said, and lapsed into the relative comfort of not speaking.

"If you feel faint, you would be welcome to take my arm, for support," Edwards offered.

"Thank you, but I think I am safe from swooning now."

From his soap box, Ezekiel Potts finished the speech. "This is yet another way of abusing the poor. These people move. They have labored in your factories, they should have rights like any other human being. How long will it be before the very definition of 'alive' depends upon the land a man holds or the quantity of money at his disposal?"

"Much as I dislike the fellow, I fear he may be right," Edwards said.

Charlie didn't want to be involved in any of it. She just wanted to buy bread, and some cheese and go home.

The following day, Mister Potts was forced to stop his public speeches, as the local dignitaries became concerned that his words might provoke the dead into rioting. Someone had indeed undertaken to do something, but it was far short of fulfilling local demands. If the dead had ever paid heed to the philosophies of the trade union movement, no one ever saw much evidence of it. They just kept shuffling about, and occasionally falling apart. Even in his absence, crowds continued to form around the market place on the off-chance of further drama. After a long history of gentle apathy, at least some elements in Bromstone had finally developed an appetite for action, and appeared keen to make up for lost time. Who knew what reckless and problematic acts might ensue? The civilized, retiring portion of the town watched nervously for signs of revolution, with no idea what the early stages of insurgency could possibly look like. A new kind of hat? Little medallions on ribbons? Who could say?

Fractious and anxious parties alike were not called upon to wait long for the next great event to shake their once-peaceful town. New banners came, new posters appeared in windows, new shouting matches happened spontaneously in the street as rival perspectives clashed.

"If it's good for business, it's good for everyone," was the slogan adopted by Godfrey Excalibur and his associates. This resulted in a brawl between the aspiring tradesman, and a curate from the Quivering Chapel. Myrtle had seen the entire encounter, and had been shocked to discover that any churchman could throw a punch.

"The world has gone mad," she confided to Alice. "But he knocked the gentleman out cold. What would Jesus say to that?"

On the following day, adverts went up in which Mister Anderson tried to hire men to collect up his workers. Alice and Myrtle considered them together.

"I'm thinking the dead aren't very good for business," Myrtle said.

According to the fishmonger, everyone was too caught up in the ethical dilemmas to want to do anything practical about the issue. The baker said they had all fallen from grace and that this signified the coming of the end times. At the grocer's they were told that in his day, people would have known their civic duty. He didn't mention what, precisely, that civic duty might involve. Alice counted no fewer than six new posters asserting beliefs and suggesting solutions that morning, the lowest number for a day so far. Meanwhile the steady stream of pamphlets stacked up in her privy against future opportunities for use. At least some good had come of it as she hated using decent reading material in this way.

The personages of uncertain mortality status were a considerable nuisance in Bromstone. Aimless and devoid of reason, they ambled into all manner of unhelpful and unlikely places. Not a day passed but she heard a tale from one of her neighbors. There was a universal feeling that the responsibility to sort it all out lay squarely on someone else's shoulders.

In Barker Street, three women did not participate in this general view. Each knew her own role in the mayhem of the arguably not dead. Knowing you have done a thing and seeing how to deal with it, are unfortunately unrelated issues. As though conscious of their shared guilt, Miss Fairfax, Miss Rowcroft and Mrs. Perry avoided each other, and said nothing. What else could they do?

Walking in to town to shop became a trial. Alice dreaded it, but was too proud to send her grandchild instead. She dreaded what new development would be waiting to affront her. More than this, she dreaded seeing the mortless. In daylight, they were soul destroying. Their blank faces and lifeless eyes made her sick. She took to crossing the road whenever they were in view, and noticed a great many others adopting the same methods.

On Tuesday of that week, she noticed that Mister Anderson's new advertisement posters read, *Anderson's biscuits, eaten for certainty about the state of your soul in the hereafter.*

The presence of his former employees appeared not to have reduced people's concerns about the state of their souls. Chapel attendance went up, according to Myrtle and Edith. There had been a brief disruption to production, but Anderson had fresh offerings for the cauldron, and it was back to business as usual.

The factory chimneys smoked, and lights showed in windows after dark.

While speeches were made and lengthy pamphlets exchanged, no one asked the mortless how they felt about any of it. This was probably as well, because the mortless could not have answered them.

By slow degrees though, the problem resolved itself. The dead could not continue forever, and once they fell apart, movement ceased and discreet burial became easier. Some of them, however, lasted for a remarkably long period.

Chapter eighteen

The necessary features of a spiritual life

The unmistakable, rumbling sound of a traction engine rattled its way into the kitchen long before the vehicle itself appeared. Alice was pressing shirts and in no mood to be distracted. Oblivious to this, Temperance ran out of the house, and then ran back inside again, so excited that she made no sense at all.

"Slow down," Alice commanded. "You sound like a mouse that's been in the snuff box."

"It's them! It's them! It's the Druids I told you about. The Ancient Oder of Bears, or whatever they are. They're here, coming down Barker Street!"

Although Temperance clearly felt no alarm at the return of the men who had kidnapped her, Alice had a few things she wanted to say to them. Iron in hand, she followed her granddaughter out into the street. The traction engine crawled towards them, its caravan bumping audibly over every lump and indent in the road. There were two robed and bearded men riding on the contraption, while the other two perched in the caravan door. Alice positioned herself directly in their path and waited for them to stop. Seeing the huge machine crawling towards her did not alarm the old woman in the slightest. She had seen such mechanical beasts stop before and was reasonably confident it would not crush her. Even a woman of her years could hope to outrun the lumbering monstrosity, should the need arise.

There were all manner of strange, graunching noises as the smell of hot oil assailed her nostrils. The traction engine slowed, pistons still pumping. It came to rest a few feet from her, the great wheel halting and steam erupting sporadically from the pipe work.

One of the men waved. "Hello, Temperance."

Granny Alice grimaced, trying to radiate disapproval through every part of her body. Unfortunately, Temperance had long since developed a tolerance for this technique and hardly even noticed it any more. The girl would respond to direct orders, but was willfully blind to anything subtle, and quite a few things that weren't. On this occasion she quite predictably failed to notice her grandmother's displeasure.

"I've taken up being a Druid too," Temperance shouted up to them. "We're now calling ourselves The Ancient Order of Beards."

They took this in good humor, Alice thought. You never knew with religious types. Some were accommodating, others flew off the handle at remarkably little provocation. Normally, Alice enjoyed trying to provoke God botherers, but she had more serious issues on her mind.

"Young man, I want a word with you," she said, brandishing her iron at the first one to descend from the engine.

"Madam?" He pressed his hands together and did a funny little bow.

"If you make a habit of taking other people's children away, you are going to wake up one morning and find you've got a bullet lodged in your skull. I can assure you that life becomes a lot less enjoyable after something like that happens."

"Are you threatening me?" the Druid asked. He sounded more curious than accusatory.

"Yes," said Alice. "Well spotted."

"Note taken," said the Druid.

"They didn't take me on purpose," Temperance put in, looking very worried. "It was an accident. You don't need t shoot them Granny! Really, it was mostly my fault and they didn't mean to do it."

"No, indeed," the man replied. "Once we grasped who she was and where she needed to be, we lost no time in returning her."

He seemed genuine enough, but trust did not come readily to Alice. Their presence in her street disconcerted her. "What are you doing here, if not looking for my granddaughter?"

The Druid smiled at her. "We had someone to deliver, and a keen sense that we should ourselves be in this place, at this time."

"Well then," Granny began, but didn't get any further.

The caravan door emptied of Druids and to her considerable surprise, Alice saw Miss Fairfax behind them. One of the Druids unhooked a set of steps from the underside of the caravan, and set them in place for the archaeologist to descend. There was a woman whose honor probably didn't need defending with death threats, she thought. Alice reasoned that Miss Fairfax was probably at least as much to blame for anything that befell her, as the Druids were. This was none of her business. Even so, she watched as her neighbor staggered inelegantly towards number seven, clearly the worst for drink. A woman who couldn't hold her liquor had no business being out in public, Alice felt.

"What are you lot doing then?" Temperance asked, jumping up and down with sheer enthusiasm.

"We have discovered something of great importance for our quest, and we have come to resolve the matter of a cauldron," one of the Druids explained.

"Do you mean the one Mister Anderson has got?" Alice asked. "The one he makes dead people come alive with?"

The Druid nodded. "Indeed, the very same."

"So this is because of me?" Temperance asked, beaming.

The Druid looked puzzled by this.

"I was the one who told you about Mister Anderson and the bucket, wasn't I?" she pressed.

"Ah." A look of recognition dawned, followed by a benevolent smile. "Of course, yes. You were a great help to us. And also, thanks to Miss Fairfax, we now have a better understanding of where the precious item might be found, and have come to see that we are called upon to act in this matter."

"Are you going to take the cauldron away and stop Mister Anderson making dead people come alive? Only they've been wandering all over the town and they're so sad, and wrong. Something needs doing about them," Temperance said.

"We will undertake to solve this problem," the Druid replied, evidently serious.

Alice eyed them up, and considered the possibilities of the traction engine. "Just the four of you, is it?" she asked.

While the other Druids set about doing all manner of incomprehensible things with their machinery, the one standing before her nodded.

"I'd hold on a moment if I were you" she said. "Mister Anderson has guards now, and we've had a lot of troubles round here in the past week or so. I very much doubt you'll be able to walk in here and just take it."

"It is what we must do," he replied.

"You need more people," Alice said.

The Druid frowned at her. "My dear lady, a woman of your years, surely…"

Alice didn't let him continue trying to put her off. "I've been in the factory before, and I've probably killed more men than you have during my lifetime, so you can wait up and let me find a few other people to help."

"This time, you are clearly not going to surprise them at all," Temperance pointed out. "What with the traction engine and the daylight and everything. I'm coming too."

Alice weighed up her options. "Fair enough."

"And I can get others, too," she said, then directed her next question to the nearest Druid. "Do you think we're going to need our robes and beards for this?"

He chuckled, "Probably not."

"I just thought it would be a good opportunity to wear them in public," she said. "With people noticing and everything."

He patted her shoulder. "It's not about what people notice, it's about what you do, and how you live your life."

"Oh!" said Temperance. Alice could tell that thought had not previously crossed the girl's mind.

"We've got work to do," said Alice. "Come on." She hurried back into the house.

"I thought you didn't approve of Druids," Temperance said, trotting along behind.

"I don't, particularly, but I approve of Mister Anderson a good deal less and your Druids don't seem to be going round moralizing. Sometimes, my girl, we have to pick our friends according to our enemies."

Temperance nodded sagely, and asked what she could do to be useful.

The desire to avoid whatever madness had overtaken Bromstone, had kept Charlie in the house. Work seemed even more appealing than usual when the alternative was Ezekiel Potts or Godfrey Excalibur, or whoever had put themselves in charge today. She had no desire to be trodden on, shouted at, or presented with awkward questions. Speculation in the various shops had long since moved beyond the realms of sanity, and she could not bear the prospect of having to nod and smile politely in face of utter nonsense.

Fuelled by this desire to be very busy, the work had flowed as never before. Neither she nor the dog-faced boy had slept for several nights. It hadn't been intentional, they'd just never come to a natural stopping point, and oddly, she hadn't been tired. Light from beyond the windows came, and went, and came again, the changes marked only by the lighting and extinguishing of lamps. Charlie had lost track not just of the day, but the time. She didn't register the passing hours at all. Never before in her life had she worked with such fever. There was a fire in her head, and it seemed they could do nothing wrong.

She and Nigel had long since stopped talking about what they were trying to do. At first it had just been an experimental foray into the idea of the mechanical horse: A means to pass the time as much as anything else. But then it had magically taken off. Problems that had previously vexed her now seemed to resolve themselves. Had she ever before thought so well, so clearly or at such speed? Charlie thought not. Perhaps at last the genius of true invention had fallen upon her like a cloak dropped from a nearby building. It wasn't quite the metaphor she'd been looking for, but most of the time she was too busy making to indulge in a great deal of reflection.

The unlikely workmates had fallen into a strange rhythm, passing each other tools and pieces, not needing to talk about it at all. Nigel had a knack for things mechanical, but none of the language with which to describe it. In the early hours of mechanical horse making, he'd talked about 'this thing' and 'some of those things with things on them' and on the whole it had slowed them down. Whilst not talking, their communications seemed flawless. Had Charlie given herself time to think, it would undoubtedly have occurred to her that this was a touch unusual.

Between the sleep deprivation, lack of food and creative passion, she was in something like a state of ecstasy. Half mad, half inspired she felt as though they were somehow working from the same design. It was as though the pattern existed as a magical, ethereal thing just beyond conscious grasp, presenting itself one piece at a time. She imagined that the idea of this machine had always existed, separate from human thought and just waiting for the right minds to pour itself into. Had she been in her usual frame of mind, Charlie would have found such notions laughable and embarrassing. Fortunately for the mechanical horse project, normal thinking had long since been encouraged to sit quietly in a corner and not make a nuisance of itself. Rationality was for days without inspiration! Reason had long since melted away in face of the overwhelming nature of what they were doing. It felt right, and therefore, surely, it must be right? At last she had entered the fairytale world of invention where creations sprang from the hands like... frogs... where genius exploded into the world, its shape and nature defined. The sensation of being caught up in this enthralled her.

They oiled, tested, polished, tightened what was already built, and waited for the knowledge of the next part to come to them. Knocks to the door were ignored, if they were noticed at all. The machine grew, impossibly. From time to time, Charlie paused to look at it, wondering what they were doing and what had happened to her mind. A little voice at the back of her head still tried to tell her that invention did not happen like this. It was not, and never had been a flurry of mad genius leading to sudden, inexplicable creation. You thought about problems and solved them logically. Designs were drawn in advance, and then were modified through experimentation along the way. Most importantly, you tended to have some idea of what you were doing, and why. The mechanical horse idea was running away with her, and she didn't have the faintest idea what half of its insides were for, or how it was supposed to work. The mechanisms they had painstakingly constructed made no sense at all.

As she tried to think about it, Charlie realized that for much of the time, Nigel had been leading the work. Did he know what he was doing? He hadn't said a word. She'd felt drunk almost, not quite in control of her own mind or body. The more she wanted to think about it, the harder it became to concentrate. Charlie had a keen sense of something being very wrong. The closer they came to finishing, the less euphoric she felt, as though recovering from the effects of alcohol, or an excess of tea. Blaming the sleep deprivation did not make this feeling go away. Tired and unfed as she was, she lacked the strength to wrestle with these ideas, or resist what had overtaken her.

Hands moved, wielding tools, working and turning. The

voice at her head pleaded with her to stop, to think, but she couldn't. Fingers had to move. Oil. More cogs. Part of the bicycle frame. She had the lid from an old biscuit tin in her hands now, and no idea what it was for, but that didn't make any difference. Out into the yard, in the gloom. What days was it now? Dawn, or twilight? She couldn't tell. Looking for something, hand wet amongst items long abandoned. Something found. An old chain, heavy in her arms as she staggered back like a somnambulist. Tighten. Oil.

She was so tired now that the room flickered in and out of focus continually. Her eyes closed for seconds that could have been hours, and the pillow upstairs seemed to be calling her name in a whispery, seductive sort of voice. It ought to be possible to stop and lie down, but she couldn't.

Now, in a final insult to sanity, the room was filling up with mice. Hundreds of mice, whirring and squeaking, with feet and wheels. The walls between wakefulness and nightmare had become so thin that she could see right through them. Only she didn't know which side was which any more. Where had the mice come from? Surely they hadn't got through this number of rodents? Had they been breeding behind the cupboards? What had they been eating back there? Surfaces undulated with mice, a living, squeaking wave of abnormality.

Slowly at first, the mice climbed into the machine. They clicked and shrieked amongst the moving parts, working their way into the mechanism. She'd never seen mice this organized before. Were all mice like this, once you got to know them? Were they all thinking independently, or was someone telling them what to do? At last, her hands fell still, with no more work to be done. Like a puppet that is no longer held up from above, Charlie flopped. Strings finally cut, she drooped in a chair and stared at the nightmare reality of mice before her. They came from the cupboards in numbers beyond counting, heading for the machine with a most eerie certainty.

"I see mice," Nigel said, voice quavering.

"Could be worse," Charlie replied, repressing the urge to giggle because she knew it would be a short step from there to screaming. "Could be dead people." She desperately needed to eat and sleep and drink tea, and wash. A bath of tea might answer all needs at once, with a loaf of bread instead of a sponge.

She slept in the chair for long enough to feel more like a person again, but could not tell if she had really woken up, or just fallen deeper into an even more extravagant dream.

If anyone had asked Charlie to design a giant mousehorse that would inspire feelings of both horror and utter hilarity at the same time, she would not have known how to achieve the effect. Looking at the giant mousehorse that had taken over her workspace, she couldn't decide whether to laugh maniacally or vomit. Nigel appeared to be doing both. The mechanical mousehorse turned its head towards her, showing of fearsome teeth. She couldn't remember what they had made those out of.

"The wheels, and the feet," Nigel said. "For the girl who wanted a horse?"

Charlie shook her head, having no desire to let Temperance get anywhere near this abomination. It seemed to have a mind of its own, if the uncanny movements of the head where any indication.

"What do you suppose it's for?" She didn't get an answer, because Nigel had already curled up under the table and gone back to sleep. The mousehorse appeared to be in no hurry to do anything. Even so she kept watching it, worried that at any moment it would start doing something absolutely dreadful. She was too tired to run away. Her eyes were painfully heavy, and the mousehorse hadn't done anything yet. She'd just rest them for a moment, and then check again. Sleep had been lying in wait for just such an opportunity, and wasted no time in pouncing upon her weary form.

When she next surfaced, Charlie kept her eyes tight shut for a while, determined that when she looked, it would all be fine and normal out there. No mechanical monsters. No dog faces. No unspeakable horrors perpetrated in her sleep. When she opened her eyes there would just be an untidy room and nothing more disturbing in it than a Penance Biscuit.

If there is a God, now would be a really good time to take an interest in me, Charlie prayed, half-heartedly.

"Mousehorse wants to go out now," Nigel said, shattering her fragile hopes.

Chapter nineteen

Mrs. Eggton's guide to arranging public celebrations and civic events

Wearing fresh attire, and revived by the cheerfully banal features of her own home, Justina knew herself much improved in mind and appearance. For weeks now she had carried a burden of fear and uncertainty, but she felt lighter, although she did not know why. Memories from her time in the caravan were inspiring, and alarming, and neither response troubled her. This too struck her as representing a change in her own character. *How fascinating and original I am becoming!* she reflected happily.

Looking into the street from her front window, she observed that the eccentric Druidical gentlemen were still parked before her home. The traction engine rumbled like a sleeping dragon. She had previously been of the impression that the Druidical gentlemen would leave her so as to continue in their quest. Something had changed the plan, evidently. Around their caravan and engine, a considerable crowd had gathered. There were old ladies bearing kitchen implements and vagabond children brandishing sticks. Many of the faces were familiar and therefore probably neighbors, but she knew few of them by name.

"Will you be needing me again today, miss?" her maid enquired, having come quietly into the room.

"I don't know," Justina said. She had no plans at all. "For tea, certainly."

"Could you spare me for a few hours now to go on the protest? It's going to be a very big one."

"Is that what they are doing?" She wondered how that fitted with the Druidical gentlemen's other plans. "Perhaps I should come as well." She was weary, but curiosity drew her out. How could she rest and let others take central stage in her absence? This was all about her cauldron, after all.

"I can go then, miss?"

"You can," she said, feeling tremendously benevolent. "Fetch me my shawl, I shall come as well."

She descended to find the street was full of noise and activity, but no one appeared to be in charge. As she wondered whom to approach for information, a rather gaunt young man strode up to her.

"Miss Fairfax?" he enquired. "Do you intend to join us?"

She didn't recall having seen him before, but then, one young man looked very much like another, in her estimation. Common young men apparently did not feel the need for formal introductions anyway. Unsure as to his class and significance, she smiled, and hoped her behavior would not be considered vulgar by anyone significant who might, even now, be watching her.

"I'm not quite sure what I am doing, but was curious. What is happening, can you tell me?"

He smiled. "It is a crusade, dear lady, a striking out against wickedness. We go to prevent Mister Anderson from creating any more horrors."

"Oh," she said. She could see how that would connect with the Druids. She had thought they meant to do it alone, but apparently a small army was gathering to support the cause.

"Forgive me. I am Edward Edwards and entirely at your service." He took her hand and kissed it. "We have met before, but I do not imagine that a fellow such as myself could hope to have made much impact." He bowed.

Justina wondered if she should have the words 'kindly do not propose to me' embroidered onto the front of every dress she owned. It might save a good deal of time and trouble. However, she feared it would look ghastly. It would flaunt her consciousness of attracting such attentions. So easy, in defending oneself, to become an object of ridicule, she reflected. Better to try not to notice these things, and to ward off the proposers with icy disdain.

"Hello, Mister Edwards," said Mary, her servant girl. The creature had the audacity to approach them, and from her tone, clearly viewed this Mister Edwards as an equal. "I'm going to come along," Mary added.

"That's excellent, Hephzibah," the young man replied. "I'm so glad."

Justina disliked the idea of her maid being known in this way, to this gentleman. She bristled, meaning to say something to the girl about the impropriety of it, but at that moment the side door on a house across the road flew open with a crash.

She turned at once, the whole crowd drawn to this ominous sound. To her amazement, an absolute monstrosity merged from the building. A great, heaving mass of metal and fur, it stood taller than a man and pulsed with unnatural energy. Justina shuddered at the horror of it, and wished herself to be the sort of women who was reliably able to faint in adverse circumstances. Her stays had never been sufficiently tight to encourage such collapses: The price of being an adventurous sort who favored free movement and already possessed a naturally slender middle. However, at times like this she could see distinct practical advantages to a swoon.

A human figure emerged from the house. A human figure with a most inhuman face.

"It's the dog-faced boy!" shouted one of the children.

Even with this cry in the air, nobody moved apart from the dog-faced one. He climbed onto the back of the first monstrosity saying, "I think it's safe." His voice sounded very small and nervous.

Pale and bedraggled-looking, Miss Rowcroft also emerged from her house to complete the scene. Justina could not imagine what it signified, and hoped someone else would decide what to do about it.

The monstrous pair leaped forward, very slowly. It was the most unnatural movement Justina had ever observed. Nothing, surely, should pass through the air at such a ludicrously languid pace? She had the alarming impression that time itself had slowed. Metal and fur produced a second, improbable bound, then a third, with the dog-faced boy clinging to what might have been the mechanized creature's neck. The monsters claimed Barker Street, and, as though they had been waiting for this cue, the Druids fell in behind them. The traction engine crawled along, its pace well-matched to that of the leading beast. Those on foot began to follow. No speeches had been made, no leadership offered. Justina feared they were approaching a condition akin to socialism. She had no idea what genuine socialism looked like, but poor people without authority to guide them seemed highly at risk of such heresies. Still, if she wanted to know what was happening, she would be obliged to continue with them.

Once they were moving, proceedings gained their own momentum. Justina could see that the people around her were confused as well, but marching meant protest, whatever the thing at the front signified. Protest, they already had some experience with, and that had a soothing influence. The lumbering traction engine represented a very solid, reassuring counterpoint to the madness at the head of their column. With steam and engineering on your side, of course all would be well! She tried to convince herself that the Druids knew what they were doing. They had other kind of insights, and her experience of them left her inclined to trust what they did. Somewhere along the way, her resentment of all things irrational and religious had evolved into a curious respect for mystery. That, and a desperate hope that someone knew what was going on and what should be done. The idea that all was now chaos, did not bear contemplating.

"For God, Humanity and all that is good!" shouted Mister Edwards.

There was a rousing cheer from the marchers in response to

this. The alarm generated by the appearance of the dog-faced boy and his steed melted away.

The protesting throng had to walk slowly to keep pace with those at the fore of their column. It was, without a doubt, the slowest heroic charge in the entirety of human history.

As the procession wove through the town, it swept up even more people. In the weeks of building anticipation and patisserie warfare, Bromstone had transformed from a place of sleepy disinterest to one ripe for action. Something was happening, and it barely mattered what form the development took, only that it served to give a sense of making change. People from all walks of life attached themselves to the procession, from ragged children to stout pillars of the community.

It was like fete day, the Easter parade and a circus all mixed up together, Temperance thought. The town had been buzzing for weeks, very much like something about to boil over, or explode. She had plenty of firsthand experience about that kind of thing, mostly due to Charlie, and knew a bit about the importance of letting off steam. Until this year, her hometown had been a really boring sort of place. It had taken a lot of imagination to come up with any adventures at all. People in Bromstone didn't like adventures, and quietly resisted them, never making too much fuss for fear of over exciting themselves. Or at least, that had been the size of things. Now, everything had changed, and she liked it immensely.

There were a lot of thoughts swirling around inside her head as she walked – pride at taking her own Druids out in public was at the fore. She felt important, and essential to the unfolding drama. These fellows on the traction engine were also her Druids, because she had found them first. Other things were worrying her, though. At the front of their procession lurched something that could have been based on a horse. If you'd never seen a horse and were trying to construct one based on hearing stories about them. She was sure there were bits of bicycle in there. The horse bothered her, because she hadn't seen it, or the dog-faced boy before. They'd come out of Charlie's house though. Charlie must have made the horse without telling her. And how long had the dog-faced boy been in Barker Street? Charlie had been keeping secrets, and that didn't feel good. Better not to dwell on it now. She'd have to ask Charlie about it all later.

As they walked, the remaining mortless people came to them. Seeing them made Temperance shiver, but none of them came to close to her. Slow moving, blank-eyed and silent, they seemed to belong in this unhurried crusade. The adults were coping with the dead, and she didn't want to stand out by making a fuss. She wondered what made the mortless folk move. Their faces were so empty and their eyes never seemed to look at anything. But if they weren't thinking, or feeling, why did they do anything at all? The more she thought about this, the more uncomfortable she felt. Being a sensible sort of girl, Temperance decided to think about something else instead.

Even with the walking dead amongst them and the alarming duo at the front, the day had a festive feel. Albert Nose had his beard on, Friday Bob was wearing the most ridiculous hat she had ever seen. Someone had got a drum, then a couple of people turned up with brass instruments. As the musicians came from rival chapels, they insisted on playing entirely different tunes and neither of them paid the slightest attention to the drummer. The result was a jolly, messy sort of noise. It was a pity, Temperance thought, that no one had a dancing bear to bring along.

Of course Mister Anderson was ready for them. He'd had a good half hour of warning as they'd made their slow and noisy progress. There were seven of his living employees stood alongside him in the new road as the crowd approached. The holiday mood started to evaporate as the procession came to an awkward halt. Some of the grannies had frying pans, but Temperance didn't think most of them meant to start a fight. Seven against this many wasn't good odds, but whatever the people of Bromstone were spoiling for, it wasn't bloodshed. All of Anderson's living workers were local men, everyone knew somebody on the other side.

"Stay there," Alice hissed, and left her to push forwards.

Alice probably would start a fight, Temperance reflected, and tried to get herself a better view, wondering what her Granny had in mind, and expecting it would be good.

The exceedingly wrong horse was sidling about in the middle of the road, and two of the Druids came to flank it, limiting its erratic movements. The drummer stopped, and the trumpeter followed him into silence. A few moments later, the French horn trailed off with the fading, wilting sound of public embarrassment.

"Who is in charge of this rabble?" Mister Anderson demanded. "You will disband at once or I shall have you all prosecuted for rioting and trespass."

During the moments when everyone else was wondering what to make of this, Granny Alice stepped forwards. "I'll do," she said. "I'm not in charge, no one is. But I'll do the talking."

Anderson stared at her for a few seconds, sizing her up. "What do you people want? This isn't a bank holiday! Shouldn't you be doing something productive?" Mister Anderson shouted his words so that everyone could hear. He was red in the face, his skin stretched so tightly that Temperance thought he might pop like a boil.

Granny didn't seem in the least bit put out by any of this, and her reply was much quieter. Even so, her voice carried well. "We've come for the cauldron. We don't much like how you use it."

"That cauldron is mine, bought and paid for. I break no laws, and you have no right to enter my private property. I am warning you people to leave, because I will see every last one of you behind bars if you do not."

"You break God's law!" Mister Edwards shouted from somewhere in the crowd.

Temperance thought they were going to get into yet another of those pointless grownup arguing contests. She'd hung around the market place enough times recently to know that adults could spend hours at a time shouting the same things back and forth at each other, never getting anything done at all, and apparently never getting bored with repeating the same, tired explanations. If that happened today, she might as well go home.

The very wrong horse folded in upon itself. It brought instant silence. Then, as all eyes were upon the actions of the strange contraption and its equally peculiar rider, the whole device opened out like a giant spring, rising lowly and dramatically into the air. When it landed, the crash was deafening. It looked to Temperance as though the horse monster was melting. The dog-faced boy hopped neatly from the machine's horse-like back, and then all the fur started dripping out of the huge metal frame. Temperance gasped, overwhelmed by what she was seeing. She pressed forward, which was easy enough because most people were going the other way, clearing the space for her. A river of sinuous fur washed down the road, swarming around the windowless houses until a door opened and they rushed inside like a dark tide.

The spell broke. All around her people were shouting. Some of them tried to run towards Mister Anderson, others attempted to run away. There were screams. Temperance clambered under the Druids' caravan, dragging Rapunzel with her. From somewhere in the distance she could hear a sound like a French horn being strangled.

"We'll be fine here," she promised her friend.

"Adventures aren't supposed to be like this," Rapunzel said. "Adventures are supposed to be fun. I want to go home."

"We will, when it's safe," Temperance answered.

By the end of the New Road riot, all of the dead people appeared to have returned permanently to that condition. Some of the rioters who had recently been alive in the normal sort of way, were now flirting with other states of being. The majority of people had gone, leaving the wounded, the traumatized, and a few souls intent on helping them. Charlie staggered towards Edward Edwards, where he was helping a man to stand up. She'd been knocked down and trodden on a few times. Her skirt was filthy, her shawl gone, and her hair had come loose, and was getting in her face. She felt awful, but had clearly got off lightly compared to some of the prone figures she could see in the road.

"Are you hurt?" Edwards asked.

She shook her head, then wished she hadn't because it didn't help. "I haven't slept in a while. I can't think what to do, I'm so slow. This is all my fault. I didn't know what was happening." She was close to tears.

"You look as though you need to rest," Edwards said gently. "Let the Druids make you a cup of tea." He took her arm and guided her gently to the steps of their caravan.

"This is all my fault," Charlie said. She was close to tears. "The horse, the mice, the dog-faced boy, even the cauldron. It's all my fault."

Edwards put a hand on her arm. "Did you mean any harm, in what you did?"

"No, but that doesn't make any difference. It's still happened."

"Did you strike a blow today?" The young man persisted.

"No, but..."

He shook his head at her. "No buts, Miss Rowcroft, you are not to blame for what others do. You are shocked and distressed, that is all. Please, do not cause yourself any more pain." He paused, his eyes full of compassion. "Perhaps afterwards, if you have need of spiritual guidance and reassurance..."

She had no idea what to say. One of the Druids pressed a steaming cup into her hands. "I believe the only dead people are...redead," he said. "If that's any consolation, miss?"

At this moment, Temperance and another girl crawled out from under the caravan. "Have you seen Granny?" she asked.

No one had, they soon realized. The last sighting of Alice had been just before everyone went mad. There was no sign of Mister Anderson either. It wasn't easy to tell who had fled voluntarily.

"Would Mister Anderson harm Alice?" Charlie asked, anxiously.

The girl grinned up at her. "Not much chance of that. I expect she's kidnapped him and is making him tell her all his secrets. Granny's good like that."

There was a long silence during which none of the adults were able to come up with any kind of response to the girl's assertion.

All they knew was that Granny Alice and Frederick Benevolence Anderson had been the two people worst placed to make an escape. Whatever had happened to them, neither was lying bleeding and concussed in the road, and neither had been taken up by the dog-faced boy when he departed.

"Why did the dog boy take the cauldron?" Temperance asked. "I saw him do it."

The nearest Druid patted her on the head. In other circumstances, she would have bitten his hand, Charlie knew from experience.

"I don't know, little friend, but two of my companions are in pursuit. That beast may be alarming, but it can be out run," said the Druid.

"I feel very confused," said Charlie.

"That's all right," the Druid replied. "We never know what's going on. It's all to do with energies of the inner planes, the magical realms and the deeper mysteries. You bend a spoon and somewhere in another realm, a butterfly flaps its wings."

"That's silly," Temperance said.

"Yes," the Druid agreed, "But most of the time it works perfectly well. Certainty is an illusion brought on by not thinking enough."

"Do you chaps know what the cauldron actually is?" Charlie asked. She was conscious that both Edward Edwards and Justina Fairfax had been drawn closer by the question. Miss Fairfax looked slightly rumpled, but somehow far more intact than Charlie knew herself to be. How did the woman do it?

"There are many ancient tales of cauldrons," the Druid said, cautiously. "Myths of magical happenings, tales of the old gods." He sighed. "We've all been reading for years of course, but there are only a few, specialist scholars in our field and none of us are properly qualified, and it's all very difficult to say. New texts from ancient times are being discovered every day. It's amazing how many people turn out to have something pre-historic tucked away in the family attic." He sighed. "And one has to wonder how much of this scholarship is really dependable."

"I heard your tapestry talking not so long ago. I think we're a very long way from books and matters of scholarship now," Justina said.

The Druid shook his head. "It's fine when we're doing it, or talking with each other, but trying to explain to you... I fear anything I say will sound foolish, and it is a most serious business that we are about."

Edward Edwards said, "I do not pretend to understand what you do, but I do understand what you mean. That which is most sacred cannot be explained to those who do not already under-stand it."

"You have the essence of it there," the Druid agreed.

Charlie rubbed her aching temples with her equally sore fingers. "Let's try this another way then. What do you want the cauldron for? We all know it gives a kind of life to the dead, so what do you intend to do with it, if you get it back?"

"Destroy it," the Druid said.

They were so shocked by his words that none of them spoke for a while.

"It is an ancient artifact! A treasure!" Justina exclaimed, dumbfounded. "It is magical, I suppose it must have some Druidic significance. You never even mentioned this before. Why on earth would you want to destroy it?"

"We believe it was made for battle, so that soldiers could be restored to fight again. It was, I think, made in dark and desperate times, and it was not meant to continue. There is too much power in it to subvert what nature intends."

"Well, on that part, I heartily agree with you," Edwards said. "I'm all for destroying it."

"What about all the other cauldrons that have been turning up. Are they the same?" Justina asked.

"There are many copies, but only one of any true power, as far as I know. Of course, I could be entirely wrong on that score. Still, it would not hurt to have the other ones, just to be on the safe side."

Justina brightened visibly at this. "I could do that! I could collect them."

"That would be most helpful," said the Druid.

Charlie wondered what could have happened to cause so radical a change in the other woman's character. "I doubt there's much I can do to help you," she said, relieved by the prospect.

"You could tell me about how the... whatever that was with the mice, came into existence," the Druid suggested.

And so Charlie began relating the tale of the mousehorse. As she spoke, she understood what the Druid had meant. Some things seem very foolish indeed when you try to explain them. In hindsight, she could not provide any good reason for what had happened. She felt shaken to the core by the whole experience. The more she thought about it, the less sense it all made.

"It sounds to me, as though you were in a state of rapture," the Druid offered.

"Like a religious delirium?" Edwards enquired, "When one loses track of the material world and draws closer to the divine?"

The Druid nodded. "Exactly."

"I felt inspired, I remember that much," Charlie said.

"Uncanny possession," the Druid and the minister said, in perfect unison.

"Overtaken by some other presence," The Druid added, for clarity.

"Would you like an exorcism?" Edwards asked. "I have some prior experience. Although mostly in the past I've been called upon the exorcise thunder storms, and to pray worms out of sheep. I was in a rural parish before I came here."

"Thank you for the thought," Charlie said, momentarily thrown by this glimpse into a wholly unfamiliar world. "I think whatever it was, has passed on. All I want to do is sleep."

"I'll look after you," Temperance promised.

Tears stung in Charlie's eyes, and she stopped trying to fight them.

Chapter twenty

Honing your investigative skills for personal gain and the public good

Inside the factory, mortless people worked in silence. None of them paid the slightest attention to Alice as she hurried after Mister Anderson. Evidently he'd not wasted any time in finding fresh corpses and putting them to work. Alice couldn't have argued a logical case against what she saw as she hurried through the building, but she felt the wrongness of it. That was enough to keep her fighting the architect of it all.

She passed through an unmarked door and found herself in a small office. Mister Anderson was clearly expecting her. He looked calm and unflustered, while Alice was conscious of being too hot and somewhat out of breath. He did not offer her a chair, and remained seated behind his own desk. Oh yes, Mister Anderson was entirely the powerful businessman now, and Alice knew she was supposed to feel inferior for being made to stand while he sat. She'd never been obsessed with social niceties though, and took the snub as a sign of his ill breeding rather than any possibly shortcoming on her part.

"Why have you followed me?" he asked. "These are private premises, woman. Leave, or I shall have you removed." He sounded very tired, as though the fight had gone out of him and he was just repeating words from a script.

Alice stared at him. "What are you trying to do, Mister Anderson?"

"I am saving myself from an angry mob," he replied, still unflustered for all his obvious exhaustion. He met her gaze. "Really, if I had any interesting plans at all, do you think I would take this opportunity and reveal them to you?" he enquired.

"A fair point," Alice said. She hadn't followed him with any real plan in mind, but having seen Anderson's hasty escape, had hurried after him. When the dog-faced boy went one way and the factory owner the other, she suspected something was up. She supposed he'd just been more concerned about saving his skin, than his property.

"My only plans involve considering where I shall dine this evening," he added. "There is nothing under this roof but legitimate business. I rather imagine you have indulged in too many works by hysterical, female authors and imagine gothic schemes at every turn," he said, evidently enjoying the observation and his own sense of self-important.

Alice wanted to slap him. Only the desk prevented her from such a gesture. "I suppose you'll have to start employing the living now," she said, making clear her own amusement at this prospect. "No more unpaid slave labor for you, Mister Anderson."

"If you want a job, you will have to apply by the usual means. Now, kindly make yourself absent."

She didn't like his tone in this remark, and was tempted to say a few choice words. But, he was clearly so comfortable in his high opinions of himself, that anything she said could only reinforce his prejudices. However, there were bigger things afoot than Mister Anderson's manners, and she needed to do some thinking. She closed the door to his office and made her way back through the factory.

In the room of the working dead, Alice paused to have a proper look at this gathering of human misery. They were all very thin and sad-looking. Life had not treated these people kindly. Death did not shock Alice. She had seen a great deal of it over the course of her long life. Sudden death was very much a part of existence for her. Without the dead, there might have been equally thin and silent living people at work here. That was a grim thought. Anderson wouldn't treat the living any better. They too would face long hours for little pay. Morally speaking, was that any kind of improvement?

Better to live wildly and die young, in Alice's estimation. The only trouble was, she'd accidently got old and started caring about things. It was causing her no end of trouble. She wanted to encourage these mortless people to go outside as well, but remembering what had happened with the first lot, there didn't seem to be much point.

As a younger woman, she would have run off after the dog-faced boy, or challenged Anderson to a duel. Stiff of knee and not as impulsive as she'd once been, Alice hesitated and thought about things. She could go back outside and throw herself into whatever mayhem remained. She could go back to the office and make sure Mister Anderson never put another slave, living or dead, on his factory floor. It wouldn't save the world from all the other Anderson's predating it though. The frying pan was a handy weapon and she had few qualms about the idea of beating him to death with it. *And what would happen to Temperance?* Murder might not be the best solution for the days troubles. Instead, she decided to go after the dog-faced boy. The fiendish young woman she had once been was still very much alive inside her heart, and seeing the mortless workers gave her a sudden appetite to go out with a bang.

Sat in Charlie's kitchen, Temperance felt utterly miserable. Her Granny had vanished. Despite her bold words earlier about what Alice might do, she felt worried. Granny should have been back by now, should have kicked Mister Anderson in all his most delicate places and returned triumphant. That she hadn't seemed like a really bad sign. All the other things she'd been carefully not thinking about came back to haunt her now that there were no decent distractions. Charlie hadn't told her about the dog-faced boy, or the mousehorse, or anything important. Having been deliberately excluded from so much, she felt betrayed, unloved, and unwanted. Sitting here now, with all the mess of the mousehorse project around her, with the leisure to notice dog hairs and other such details emphasized to her the sheer awfulness of her own predicament. To make matters worse, Charlie had fallen asleep in a chair so Temperance couldn't even complain about the unfairness to anyone.

"This is so unfair," she said out loud. It didn't help, and Charlie didn't wake up.

The house was messier than she had ever seen it before. There were bits of metal all over the place, and tools left where they'd been put down. Some were on the floor, under the table. Charlie might be careless about plates, but she looked after her tools, normally. Apparently the whole world had gone mad today.

Although Charlie had invited her back, Temperance had been offered nothing to eat. She hadn't eaten since breakfast. Well, apples didn't count, did they? Or the cake the Druid had given her. But that was ages ago. How long did it take a person to starve to death? She pictured Charlie waking to find her skeletal and lifeless form, wasted away from lack of nourishment. She'd be sorry then!

There was no fire laid even. It was stupid of Charlie to be asleep in the chair. Temperance wanted to scream at her until she woke up. It would serve Charlie right, and show her how unkind and thoughtless she'd been. Just as she drew in a breath ready to howl, the inventor shifted slightly in her seat. Her head turned slightly, and Temperance could see how pale the woman looked. Charlie was really thin; the kind of thin that tended to go with being ill. Maybe Charlie was dying. If anyone in the room was at risk of really starving to death, it might in fact be Charlie. In Temperance's melodramatic frame of mind, that prospect seemed all too real. Granny had gone forever, Charlie would die. Then what would happen to her? Temperance felt like crying.

Before the tears came, she remembered that highwaymen and pirates wouldn't cry. She tried to think like one of them. It was no good sitting around feeling sorry for herself. There might be something to eat in the cupboards. Food would make her feel better, and looking for it would give her something to do. If that didn't work, she'd go back to Granny's house. There would be cheese, apples and bread at the very least. Charlie had told her to stay, but Charlie was now snoring intermittently. Temperance didn't see any reason to follow orders.

The first cupboard contained saucepans and plates, badly stacked, and a box of Penance Biscuits. Temperance was not quite desperate enough to eat them yet, but supposed they would do in direst emergency. The second cupboard she explored was full of empty packets, boxes and paper bags. She found one, lonely aniseed ball and decided it would only get damp if left there, then ate it with no remorse at all.

The third cupboard was entirely empty, but she could see a sizeable hole in the back panel. Temperance had the kinds of fingers that couldn't help but poke into things. She tested the hole. It turned out there was a space behind the cupboard, and as she probed, the back panel shifted slightly. That made her curious, and with very little effort she discovered the whole panel could be persuaded to pull away. It wasn't a very well built bit of furniture. There wasn't much light in the back of the cupboard, so she fetched a candle. The scene revealed to her by flickering light, came as a surprise.

In the space behind the cupboard were three mice. They had some of Charlie's smallest tools. With these implements, they were carefully putting together a mechanical device that looked like it could be a fourth mouse. The four furry workers showed no sign of concern over being discovered and paid no attention to Temperance as she watched them. When their construction had wheels attached to it, they pulled a little fur coat over its neat, mechanical body. She had been right – it was another mouse. The four then emerged from the cupboard, passed under her left knee, pottered across the floor together and departed via the crack under the door. Temperance shivered. They were the most disturbing mice she had ever seen.

The New Road houses had been built on an old and barely used lane. In no sense was it really speaking either new, or a road. Until the houses came, no one had paid it much attention for years. It was just the lane no one used that went on a rather eccentric meander leading eventually to Hethrington, and had been replaced a long time ago by something more direct. Alice hadn't walked that way in a fair few years, but she remembered it well enough. It was a pretty sort of lane and usually had primroses on its bank, in the spring.

Once the mud took over, it became easy to see where the shambling mousehorse had gone. There were signs of other human feet as well. Perhaps someone else had followed the monster. While Alice could spot a footprint readily enough – especially tracks this obvious, she couldn't tell much about them beyond that. Age of print, for example, was a mystery to her, unless there was fresh snow or something equally straight-forward. She followed along at a gentle pace, pleased that the most obvious direction had turned out to be the right one. When the mousehorse showed signs of having doubled back, taking a little detour into a wood, Alice could also see that no human footprints had followed it. Apparently, is anyone else had been pursing, they weren't very good at following tracks, or had been shaken off somewhere further ahead. They could be halfway to Cheltenham by now. Or possibly, they'd come through that morning and had nothing to do with any of it.

It occurred to Alice that if she caught the dog-faced boy and the mousehorse on her own, she'd be about as much use as she had been in Mister Anderson's office, if it came to a fair fight. But this was a wood, there would be no witnesses and she could claim self defense. Alice had no intention of getting into anything even slightly fair. An approach from behind with a frying pan would settle matters quickly, she felt. At least where the dog-faced boy was concerned. She assumed that with him out of the picture, his mechanical monster wouldn't give her too much trouble. It was a machine, therefore it could be switched off.

Even with the troublesome nature of her knees to contend with, Alice was still very good at creeping up on people. She found the dog-faced boy and the mice in a clearing and watched from behind a tree. The mice were about half way through the complicated process of getting out of the horse mechanism and into the cauldron itself. Killing the dog-faced boy would be easy. He was a freak. Thirty years ago, she wouldn't have given it a second thought. Of course, she realized that if she beat him to death with the frying pan, she might never find out what was going on. She also started to wonder whether the mice would retire quietly in such a scenario, and there were a great many of them. If they weren't under his command, there was no guessing what might happen if she launched an attack.

Why were all of those mice swarming into the cauldron, she wondered. They weren't dead, so what could they possibly hope to gain? Once all of the mice had disappeared from view, the dog-faced boy followed, folding himself right down into the large, metal pot. Holding her breath, Alice watched. She'd never seen the cauldron in action, but expected drama at any moment.

In a nearby tree, a blackbird broke into song. A few spots of rain came down through the leaves. The dog-faced boy stood up again and clambered out of the cauldron, covered in mice. He turned, and kicked the great object over, using some very colorful language as he did so. Alice understood that he felt thwarted in some way. The mice poured back into the horse, which took as long as the unloading process. It was not the most enlightening of scenes.

Alice crouched down, pressing against the tree trunk in the hopes of not being seen. The clanking, squeaking monstrosity passed her by, but she could not tell which way it went. After the sound had faded away, she emerged and went to investigate the abandoned cauldron. It had been made from a single sheet of metal, and was both large, and lightweight. No wonder Mister Anderson had made no effort to save it – the dog-faced boy had stolen a rather shoddy replica. How he could have failed to notice the difference, she didn't know. Perhaps in the heat of the moment, he hadn't looked properly. Perhaps he wasn't smart enough to work out that this wasn't the real thing.

The more interesting question, was why Mister Anderson had installed a fake. There had been a lot of unrest, which made sense of hiding the cauldron, but did not explain knocking up this funny creation. It was all a bit esoteric for Alice. She dragged the ersatz cauldron to the road, then went in search of Druids. She could direct them to the fake, and leave them to it. Even this lightweight replica was too heavy for her to carry back to the town. It would take too long, and she didn't want to abandon her frying pan. Then, once the Druids ere organized, she'd have to sort out her granddaughter, wherever the girl had got to. Temperance would be fine, she felt certain. The girl had a keen sense of self-preservation.

After the mice had gone, Temperance decided that sometimes, it might be better not to know what was happening. Whatever had occurred here with the dog-faced boy and the mousehorses was starting to look very complicated and troubling. Not that she was forgiving Charlie yet. She let herself out and examined the street for signs of change or danger. The Druids had brought their caravan back, and it sat in the road outside number seven. The traction engine stood silent, and unattended. No one else was in sight. Temperance stopped feeling hungry and sorry for herself, and instead made her way over and climbed up to the driver's seat of the great engine. There was a wheel to turn, which she knew connected to the chains that tugged the front wheels round. You had to spin it a lot to make anything happen. There were also some levers, one of which was probably a brake, and a thing to pull that made it whistle. She could feel warmth from the fire box, which meant it might be persuaded to get going again, but didn't know how to get any of it started. Still, with a bit of time, she could probably figure it out.

"Do you want to learn how to drive it?"

She hadn't heard the Druid approaching, and jumped, then looked round guiltily. "I was only looking," she said.

"I know. But I could tell you how it all works."

"Yes please," said Temperance, the enormity of her woes instantly forgotten.

They were still discussing the mysteries of levers and steam when the two other Druids returned, with Alice between them.

Temperance folded her arms. "And where do you think you've been?" she asked in much the same tone Alice always used with her.

Alice smiled up at her. "I didn't mean to," she said.

Temperance nodded. She understood entirely.

There were more local people who wanted to talk than could reasonably be squeezed into Alice's kitchen. As several of them were from the Chapel of Quiet Independence, Mister Edwards decided they may as well use the church. Given that plenty of those wishing to converse belonged to other chapels, or none at all, it spoke of the extraordinary nature of their circumstances that no one complained about the choice of venue. The combined effect of mortless people, stolen cauldrons, biscuit conflict and public disorder created an unusual atmosphere. Then there was the business of mousehorses, or micehorses, no one felt wholly certain what it should be called. The absence of clear grammar only added to general discomfort.

Previous experiences of Edward Edwards and his enthusiasm for her company made Justina wary of the whole assembly. She kept to the back of the room, and for once, tried not to draw any attention to herself as she watched the initial proceedings. After a little while she realized that the young minister hadn't even tried to reason with such obvious targets for conversion as the Druids. Apparently, on this day of misrule, nothing usual could happen.

"You didn't catch fire," the little girl from next door pointed out to the Druids as the four of them entered the house of God.

"We never do," one of the men replied.

"I keep thinking God's going to smite Friday Bob, but that never happens either."

Justina watched them with interest. It seemed as though everyone else here knew someone. There was a cheerful, communal atmosphere, no doubt stemming from the shared sense of being menaced by unnatural forces. She had no idea how to be part of the friendliness though, even if she had been beset by the same woes. It had never previously occurred to her that there might be some kind of society amongst the poor. For most of her life, she had given no thought at all to the lives of those less affluent than herself. So long as they knew their place, and behaved accordingly, they held no interest. Now, she had the curious sense that these dowdy, coarsely spoken, socially irrelevant creatures, were people too. They had opinions. There were a great many of them at large in the world, and Justina supposed that if they all decided to suddenly heave in the same direction, the rest of England might well be obliged to follow. She couldn't begin to imagine what that would look like, but the idea created a pleasant frisson of mild alarm in her breast.

Part of Justina wanted to take over the gathering, and give it some appropriate direction. No one seemed to be doing anything of note! Furthermore, as far as she could ascertain, there were no men here suited to the task of leadership. As far as she could tell, no one was organizing anything, although a lot of people were talking enthusiastically. Before she had quite decided that something ought to be done, one of the Druids climbed onto a chair, which resulted in a hush. He spoke to them for a while, his warm and friendly voice describing much of what they had all shared that day. She felt reassured just listening to him.

Once they had caught up to the present moment again, the Druid said, "My brothers and I have a sacred task; to destroy the cauldron. We are more grateful than we can say for the help you have given us this day. Many dangers and uncertainties lie before us. We shall try to bring no more misfortune to your town as we rid you of the cauldron's pernicious influence."

Miss Rowcroft stood up then, her ungloved fingers awkwardly entwined as she spoke. "Why did the dog-faced boy want the cauldron? Do you have any idea what was happening out there?" She sounded distressed.

"We do not know who he is, or for that matter, where he is" one of the Druids replied. "However, he was a member of the freak show called Mister Clamhorn's Human Horrors. There was another of that party known to be seeking the cauldron and for whom we have been searching. We believe there to be a connection, although we are not yet certain what it is."

"Alain Chevalier," Justina said, more loudly than she had intended. Even voicing his name sounded to her like the casting of a dark spell.

An uneasy silence settled on the room. She imagined the name could not be meaningful to these people, but then again, perhaps he had appeared to them all. Her mind spun out fantastical, labyrinthine plots.

"He has many names, in which he hides magics that we barely comprehend. But something in your face, Miss Fairfax, makes me think you have some knowledge of the man we seek."

"How did we miss that before?" one of the other Druids asked.

"We must have been distracted, we thought we knew what we were looking for."

Justina was amused to note that they were all blushing.

Certain aspects of their recent history would not be discussed publically. They had been very distracted indeed. She forced her mind back towards the subject in hand.

"He directed me to the location where I discovered the cauldron," she admitted. If only her audience had consisted of scholars and princes, this experience of holding every gaze in the room would have been rapturous. As it was, she still felt cheered by it.

"We do not think he would dare to lift it from the soil himself, nor would he risk being the one to put it back together," one of the Druids said.

"Was that a dangerous thing to have done?" Miss Rowcroft asked.

"Very," the eldest Druid said. "The cauldron draws upon what it comes into contact with, both the living, and the dead. It is complex, unpredictable and dangerous. It is remarkable that you ladies survived the lifting and reconstructing unscathed."

"If we knew what this Chevalier chap wanted it for, we would stand a better chance of working out what to do," Miss Rowcroft asked. "Is he going to make another factory, like Mister Anderson's?"

The Druids exchanged glances. "We are not certain. Given what we know of him, he may intend to raise an army of the dead, and conquer Britain. I gather that's traditionally what people want it for, and he seems the type."

"So why on earth wasn't it destroyed long ago?" Justina asked. "Whenever the person who first made it worked out what it did, why didn't they just take it apart again?"

"These things can get away from you," Miss Rowcroft said, softly. "Like the mousehorse."

One of the Druids nodded. "There is always someone who imagines it will come in handy, or that they will be able to control the uncontrollable."

"We should write to The Times at once. No one will tolerate

the creation of a corpse army," Justina said. There were sounds of encouragement and agreement from those around her.

"I'm sure if we inform the proper authorities, it will all be taken care of," an old fellow pronounced.

"Who do you suggest we appeal to?" asked Edward Edwards. "The government? The army? Who would believe us, until it was too late?"

"It is a significant point, and we agree with you whole-heartedly, Mister Edwards," the eldest Druid replied. "It is our belief that Chevalier, or his minion will return under cover of darkness and strike once again for the real cauldron." The others nodded agreement. "Once we are all topped up with cake, we shall return to the biscuit factory and make another stand."

"Well," Mister Edwards replied, looking eager, "We should waste no more time and head back."

"There may be violence," the Druid warned.

One of the local men stood up, fist clenched over his heart. "We are patriots here, Mister…Mister Druid! We shall not stand idly by while England is threatened by its own dearly departed!"

Justina found herself cheering too. There was nothing like a bit of noisy flag waving to stimulate the blood.

"Cry God for Harry, England and Saint George!" someone shouted.

In the quiet, after the cheering, Temperance enquired, rather too loudly, "Who's this Harry chap then?"

Chapter twenty-one

What a sweet and proper thing it is to cause other people to die for one's country

Charlie provisioned herself with an old blanket, an umbrella, several rather pointy hand tools and the means to start a fire. Never having been on a mission to save an ancient artifact from evil misuse before, she had no idea what else to bring. Her parent's brief attempt at sending her to finishing school certainly hadn't provided a useful grounding for such occasions. She could picture Miss Joshing and Miss Beaucroft explaining the correct attire one should wear for moments of civil unrest, and the right etiquette to employ when in verbal confrontation with one's superiors. If the tone of lessons on matrimony had been anything to go by, girls would be sent forth to riot with a very precise shape of bonnet and no warnings about the possibility of stones being thrown. Charlie had spent much of her youth stealing books in order to compensate for the many inadequacies of her upbringing. The book stealing had contributed to the briefness of her stay with Miss Joshing and Miss Beaucroft, as well.

New Road looked empty when the first Bromstone patriots approached it. They spread out, doing their best to surround Anderson's biscuit factory. Not that anyone knew where the real cauldron had gone, but it was the only plan they'd got, so they stuck with it. The dog-faced boy and Alain Chevalier didn't know where to look either, it only made sense that they would come back here.

Once the organizing had been done, Charlie found herself positioned on a low brick wall, with one of the Druid quartet for company.

"Charlie Rowcroft," she said, offering her hand. "Professional inventor, frequent troublemaker." Her voice sounded bolder than she felt, which was probably a good thing.

"It was you who assembled the cauldron?" the Druid enquired.

"Yes."

"How did it feel?"

Charlie pondered this question for a while before working out how to answer it. "I was too busy thinking to notice feeling anything at all."

"Perhaps that is as well. You shaped it with your curiosity, not malice. It may be less dangerous for that."

They were both silent for a while. Charlie pulled the blanket tighter across her shoulders and hoped she wasn't going to have to spend too long making polite conversation.

"Do you and your friends have names? Only, no one has introduced anybody, and it might help if we did," she said.

"We had names, of course," the Druid began. "Names are things of power. Chevalier, if we are all referring to the same man, makes much use of the power in names. If there is a silent letter in a name, you can bind power into it."

She stared at him in disbelief.

"No, really," said the Druid. "I'm quite serious. It's more your sorcerous tradition than Druidical of course. Do you have any idea how many great wizards have names like Nicholas, and Thomas? Those silent haiches come in very handy, I gather."

"I had no idea." She wondered if he was joking at her expense.

"Names like Malcolm, Graham, and Phoebe are very good, too. Change your name, and you change your destiny."

"That all seems a bit farfetched to me," Charlie confessed.

The Druid raised one eyebrow at her. "I think you know more than you suspect. For example, I imagine Charlie Rowcroft must have a very different sort of future from the Miss Charlotte who must have preceded her."

Charlie could see there was some logic in this, and so agreed with him. "Do I take it then that your names are all secret?"

"You are close to the truth. We have all renounced personal names. It is part of our dedication to an uncertain fate, and our determination to be mobile agents within the fixed threads of destiny."

"Doesn't that make things confusing?"

"No more than anything else does."

Charlie was so tired from the mousehorse experience that she fell asleep not long afterwards, curled against the wall and wrapped in her blanket. It was not, she reflected on waking, the kind of action calculated to improve one's reputation. However, her Druid companion remained awake, and didn't appear to mind. Apparently destiny had not been creeping up on her while she napped. At least, not this time.

Early morning brought the Lacrimous Cake Factory's marching band. They all wore black, with dashes of cheerful color about their persons, but were otherwise a selection of unremarkable people. The band was evidently as new to the world as the cakes they celebrated. As a consequence, they made more of an impression by dint of volume than force of talent.

Half an hour later, seven assorted priests and vicars turned up to protest to Mister Anderson about blasphemy. They were followed by a man selling baked apples from a cart, a tinker, four bored apprentices and a group of trade unionists who were supposed to be rallying elsewhere and had been confused into making a detour by the scale of the existing assembly. As the day wore on, food, hot tea and gulps of restorative substances found their way into the patriot's hands. There was no sign of attempted cauldron theft, or the massing of a mortless army to overthrow natural order. As a consequence of having nothing better to do, the gathering took on the air of a street party, during which neither the dog-faced boy nor Mister Anderson put in an appearance.

In the mid-afternoon, of the first day of standing about, an unfamiliar personage appeared on horseback and made a rousing speech. He looked every inch a gentleman, from the prim, starched whiteness of his collar to the excellent soles of his shoes. The only trouble was that between the Lacrimous Cake Band and the three people purporting to be "Tromboning for the Good Lord," no one could hear a word he said.

Justina spent most of her time trying to see how she might be important. She had long, erudite conversations with the Druids, in which many serious words were spoken, and no conclusions reached. Mister Edwards discussed with her at length about the ethical dimensions of the problem. The trade unionists were all eager to explain their cause, the details of which confused her enormously. At almost every other point they made, she found herself saying things like "but surely, such things would never occur!" They were like emissaries from a foreign kingdom and she did not speak their language.

Finally, one of the Druids took her aside in a manner that suggested significance. "The signs tell us that you know where the cauldron now resides," he said.

She was sorely disappointed by this. "I can assure you that I do not. I haven't the least clue as to its whereabouts."

The Druid scratched his head. "It was very clear. The voice of the honey pot spoke to us, and said that our lady of autumn had been sent word, that she would know the way."

"I have two questions," Justina began. "Firstly, why do you assume that I am your lady of autumn?"

At this, the Druid smiled. "We believe it to be a reference to your glorious hair, Miss Fairfax."

Justina was especially proud of her auburn tresses. "That makes a degree of sense. My second question is, why does one of your oracles not direct you to the correct location? Surely that would save a lot of time and confusion."

"I have asked myself the same question, many times. My

belief is that the mysteries do not think as humans would. They may come to us with little sense of our own place, and our time. They try to speak to us in ways that we would understand, but it is like…oh, how would you explain a tree to someone who had never beheld one, or explain death to something eternal?"

She frowned at these unfamiliar ideas. "I suppose that would be very hard."

"I think that is approximately what happens when the spirits try and speak with us. They are not all-knowing. Sometimes, they make mistakes, and sometimes only in hindsight do we realize what was meant. It may come clear in time. It may not. I've spent the last few years wrestling with the words 'you are the missing sock of the gods and you can only be found when you have forgotten how to be lost'. I offer this as illustration. I am not sure how important the sock part is."

Justina wondered, and not for the first time, if the fellow was mad. He seemed calm and serious; at odds with her assumptions about lunacy. "That must be rather trying for you."

She looked around, hearing the rhythmic thump of feet. A column of shovel-bearing young men were making their way down New Road, and the resident throng had opened a little to let them through. It took her a moment to place them.

"Diggers," she explained to the Druid. "I met a few of these chaps weeks ago. Younger sons and gentlemen of leisure for the greater part, playing at political radicalism with retro-action, as they like to call it. They evoke a movement whose day has long passed. Ultimately harmless, frequently annoying." She shrugged.

"The earthmen cometh!" pronounced the Druid, clearly pleased. "I'd been trying to decipher that one all morning. Prophecy, it's only coherent once things have happened."

"Perhaps not the most useful subject to study, then," Justina observed. He wasn't listening though, ad she felt horribly super-fluous again. Perhaps the Diggers would need her to explain to them what was going on and who was in position already. She hurried towards them.

Unable to face a second night smelling like an old cat and sleeping in her clothes, Charlie went home. All of the momentum of the previous day had gone. There had been no dramatic confrontation, and no clear solution. No one could tell what had happened to the cauldron, much less what would happen next. Increasingly it seemed that in fact, nothing at all would come as the sequel to previous dramas. The whole situation seemed pointless and she wanted little more than to crawl away and hide.

When Charlie passed through the side door that led straight into her kitchen, she found the room was swarming with mice. They had taken over every surface. A frantic look around showed her no signs of the dog-faced boy, or even the horse contraption.

"Hello," said the mice. The sound of their voices shocked her. It took her a moment to realize that they were using one of her own machines, somewhat modified. It had been intended to amplify the human voice and pick up speech sounds from a great distance. Now it had a mouse wired into it, and another one running in a little treadmill alongside to provide the necessary power.

"Where is the dog-faced boy?" she asked them, taking a few cautious steps backwards as she spoke.

"We ate him," said the mice.

They were all looking at her with tiny, dark eyes. It wasn't good. Behind her, the door clicked shut with a hollow and ominous sound. She wanted to believe they were lying, but her stomach clenched with fear and dismay none the less. For all the problems he had caused, the dog-faced boy did not deserve to be eaten by mice. If that had really happened, she was going to be very upset. For now, she concentrated on being entirely calm and sensible. The current situation did not suggest that she could afford to mourn, or otherwise become distracted.

"But you are going to be much more helpful," said the mice. "We won't need to eat you, will we?"

The gang of children moved quietly through scenes that would have made adults shudder. The dead were still going about their work inside the factory. Or at least, they were trying to. Hands, fingers and sometimes whole arms had dropped of various cadavers, and fallen into the giant bowls of biscuit mix. Crumbling bodies lay on the floor where they had fallen. Others of the laboring dead stepped over and upon the prone ones, oblivious to everything but the job in hand. Where someone had become unable to continue their part in the manufacturing process, finger-laden biscuit mix piled up, burned, fell in boxed piles on the floor and otherwise made a nuisance of itself.

"Stop it!" Temperance screamed at them all, unable to stand what she was seeing.

At her command, the mortless stopped moving. Their stillness turned out to be just as horrible as the previous activity had been. Stationary, they looked even more dead. The children kept moving, huddled close together for the comfort of being near other living beings. After a while, they found Anderson's office. The door was shut, but not locked, so they piled in.

The great entrepreneur was under his desk, singing to himself.

Keen to prove himself after his recent display of fear on the factory floor, Friday Bob strode forwards. "Where's the cauldron, Mister?"

"Bring me my chariot of gold!" sang Mister Anderson, painfully off key. "Bring me my something, something of desire."

"The cauldron. Where is it?" Friday Bob asked again.

Mister Anderson responded by undertaking to mangle another hymn. It wasn't until he got round to the bit about hobgoblins and foul fiends that they had any idea what he was on about.

"Is he crying?" Rapunzel asked.

Friday Bob leaned down and poked Frederick Benevolence Anderson. "He's crying, like a girl."

"I don't think he's going to be any help," said Temperance. "The cauldron's not here. That's why all the dead people are falling apart and he can't make any new ones."

"Who took your cauldron, Mister Anderson?" Friday Bob asked.

"Daddy wouldn't buy me a bow wow," Mister Anderson proclaimed. He was still signing as they left.

"I suppose," said Temperance, "Whoever it was took the cauldron must have done the stealing before we even turned up, or the dog-faced boy got here, or anything."

"So who is it, then?" Friday Bob demanded as they crept back through the realms of the dead.

"Dunno," Temperance admitted.

Behind them, the singing grew louder. "I dillied and dallied, dallied and dillied, lost my way and don't know where to go…"

The blaze created a fitting finale to the New Road protest. After all of the arguing, waiting and feeling put out, people were glad of a bit of drama to round thing off nicely. The children watched from a safe distance. Fire always looked so cheerful. It also served to take the chill off an otherwise damp evening. From the speed and ferocity of the conflagration, it seemed that someone had gone to considerable effort to make sure the place was reduced to ashes.

"They'll blame us," said Friday Bob, looking around nervously. "Lots of people know we went in. They can say how they tried to stop us, but we were always no good. We'll probably be hanged."

"Only we didn't do it," said Temperance. "It must have been Mister Anderson. He was bat shit crazy, from what we saw of him."

"Do you think he's dead?" Rapunzel asked.

Inside the factory, something exploded.

"I think he must be," Temperance said.

The fire engine turned up in time for its crew to watch the final stages of the blaze. No one had run buckets as they would have done in the event of a house fire. No one had come out of the factory, either. It seemed a suitable end for the last of the mortless.

After the fire, Justina was invited to dine with some of her neighbors. Having never broken bread with the working classes before, she marveled at the way they prepared and served their own meals. The food itself seemed wholesome enough and tasted good, if a little bland. They were all terribly impressed by her learning, and by tales of her adventures in archaeology. It made a pleasant change from the company she usually kept. The fashion of reserve and witty cynicism hadn't reached these tables yet.

It was quite late in the evening when she finally returned home. As a consequence, it was not until the following morning that she finally opened her mother's letter.

My dear Justina, the cause of enlightenment has been set back in a most deplorable way. My guiding light has left me, by means that I am unable to fathom. They all talk a good deal of magic, but none so far has shown the slightest capacity for performing any wonders. I know I have often lamented to you before about such setbacks, but I swear to you that this is by far the worst I have endured. I am distraught. You cannot begin to imagine my torment. Truly believe that I had finally discovered a man of genuine power and insight, but his one conclusive proof of this has been to flee from me. You must advise me! I insist that you come home at once to help me. I am determined to seek out Mister Jones. I cannot live without him. I shall die, or go mad, or take up croquet at the very least if I cannot secure this man once again. In unspeakable anguish, your mother.

The second letter said:

You are a cruel and cold-hearted child. I shall leave all of my worldly wealth to your cousins! You leave me no choice but to set out alone into untold danger, to do what I must. If you do not hear from me again it will most likely be because I have died as a direct result of your carelessness. There. I hope you are satisfied! Ungrateful, unnatural wretch of a girl.

There had been plenty of other letters like these two in the past, and Justina allowed the words to slide away from her awareness, making very little impression at all. Gradually, a few new thoughts began to nuzzle against each other in her mind. She thought about Druids and Henry Caractacus Morestrop Jones. Not so very long ago, she had told him the entire history of the cauldron. He'd been highly enthusiastic about helping her when they spoke, but he's also been locked in a cave and keen to secure an ally who could facilitate his release. At the time she had supposed he would have enthused upon any topic she cared to mention and thus had not read anything into at.

As a Druid, she supposed he might have some professional interest in the matter of ancient cauldrons. Especially one from Wales. Her knowledge of Druidry had advanced considerably in recent weeks. She understood their precise relationship to the Abrahamic faiths now, along with the reasons for their innate superiority. It had been explained to her that both Pythagoras and Joseph of Arimathea were Druids, and who could be more venerable than those esteemed gentlemen?

The timing, of ArchDruid Jones's escape and the cauldron theft were so close as to be suspicious. Could it be mere coincidence? So few people knew about the cauldron and its uncanny

magic, after all. Just everyone on Barker Street, all of the aforementioned people's friends and families, the chaps who had
gathered corpses, and whoever Mister Anderson confided in. On
reflection she felt that, as secrets went, it lacked a critical ingre-
dient.

Then there was the issue of the nameless Druid with the
traction engine and his belief that she held the answer to the
cauldron's whereabouts. The first letter from her mother would
have been on its way by then, making the assertion that bit less
silly, if Henry Jones was indeed the culprit. *I am becoming as mad
as they are,* she realized. Did any of it make sense? Having seen
her mother through so many magical and spiritual obsessions,
Justina's capacity for belief had been sadly eroded. Yet now she
was considering the same kind of enthusiastic belief she had
always derided in her mother. With so many frauds and
charlatans in the world, what could one possibly trust? In their
defense, her Druids had sought neither donations nor payments,
where so many others were transparently motivated by a desire
for wealth. Mother's spiritual gurus always needed little money
to facilitate the holiness, she had observed.

No, the traction engine Druids were people of a wholly
different order. She felt certain they were only a little insane, and
not really dangerous or deceitful. Her best course would be to
seek them out once more and share her insights.

Chapter twenty-two

Fin de siècle science and its role in bringing about the Armageddon, a treatise

"Make us a new cauldron," demanded the mice.

"Gladly," said Charlie. "If you can give me the precise designs, materials required and dimensions necessary, that should be no trouble at all." She was trying anything to buy thinking time. Or at least, not being eaten time.

"Do you not remember it all?" the mice asked.

"No, I have a very poor memory for that sort of thing, I'm afraid. Also, I expect it's the sort of contraption where, if I even got it a little bit wrong, it wouldn't work properly."

There was pause, during which she assumed something must be happening, but could not quite fathom what it might be. The mice did not appear to be communicating with each other by any normal means. They were all staring straight at her still, but she had the uncanny feeling that nevertheless, they were considering her words collectively.

"In which case, we want a man shape. Like the horse shape only easier to hide. We want to look like a man again."

Nothing in the world would make those mice look human. No matter, time could be purchased this way. "I'll get straight onto it," Charlie said.

She had no idea how the mousehorse had been built, and little desire to create a new monster, but the mice kept opening their mouths and showing her their teeth. Admittedly, these were small teeth, but multiplied by so many mice, they represented a significant capacity for biting. Charlie considered making a run for it, but how far would she get before the mice swarmed her, and put the teeth to work? Not far enough, she suspected. Palms sweating, and slightly nauseas, she tried to formulate a cunning plan.

For several hours Charlie put on a complex show of gathering materials together, taking old devices apart, oiling, polishing and sharpening tools in ways that they had never been intended to experience, screwing things together in random combinations and making a lot of noise. All being well the mice would be fooled by all this activity and not be able to figure out that she wasn't really making anything at all. She just hoped the mouse-horse experience wouldn't repeat itself. The idea of discovering she'd accidentally fulfilled their commands during what was supposed to be illusionary labor, worried her, but she was certain nothing she had pieced together so far could do anything but jam up. For the first time in her life she felt grateful for all the malfunctioning, exploding machinery she'd been required to contemplate in recent years.

The stares of the multitudinous mice made her very nervous indeed. She hoped they were convinced by it all. She couldn't keep pretending to build things forever. At some point she would have to make a bid for freedom, and risk the conse-quences.

"Well mice, we're progressing very well here, and this isn't going to take long now, but I don't have enough cogs or sprockets and some wire would really help," she said.

"We will find them for you." Some of the mice moved towards the door.

Her heart sank. Charlie paddled frantically for a means to get out of her house. "It needs to be the right grade of wire of course, not just any old wire. We need left- and right-handed sprockets for the joints and, oh! How could I forget? We need some ansels, at least a bag of smorit and a couple of bahoojas. Do you think you can manage all of that?"

The mice who had been heading for the crack beneath the door, stopped moving.

"What are they?" asked the mice who controlled the speaking

machine.

Charlie sighed. "It'll take me a while to explain. I can draw you some diagrams, if that would help? If you confuse hashleys for smorits we'll have no end of trouble."

"We do not have time." The mice went ominously quiet and still for a while. Charlie prayed silently to any benevolent deities that might be listening. *Just let me get out, I'll try not to work on Sundays and I'll try and remember what day it is so that I remember not to work on Sundays and…*

"You must go," said the mice.

"If you're sure?" said Charlie. Better not to appear too keen.

The power-mouse ran in the treadmill, producing the only sound for the few seconds it took the speaking-mouse to decide on a response. "Four of us will come with you, in your pocket, to make sure there is no funny stuff."

"Hop in," Charlie said, holding her jacket pocket open to make it easy for them. "We'll go for the smorits first."

It took a lot of self-control not to cheer on leaving the kitchen, but Charlie knew she had a way to go before real safety might be achieved. She walked casually across the road, even though her heart raced with anxiety. The door to Alice's kitchen opened for her.

"Evening," said Alice.

"Granny, I need to borrow a big saucepan with a nice, firm lid and I need you to put a couple of bags of smorit in it for me." Charlie kept her voice even, but pleaded with her eyes.

"What's smorit?" Temperance asked.

"Very important for inventing," Charlie said quickly. "And I know Granny has some. And a big saucepan."

Alice gave Charlie a look that could have meant almost anything, and put her largest saucepan on the table. "Lid off?" she enquired.

Years of running away from exploding mistakes had given Charlie a fair turn of speed. She whipped her jacket off and threw it into the saucepan before the mice had chance to notice anything was afoot. Alice slammed the lid down on it.

"Are you going to tell me what this is all about?" Granny asked, staring at the pan with a worried sort of look upon her face.

Inside the saucepan angry banging commenced. Charlie rested a hand on the lid, just to be on the safe side.

"Remember the mice?" Charlie began, then, seeing movement through the window, changed direction. "We may be going to need to bar the doors."

She could see the mice swarming out of her house. Up until that moment she hadn't thought about what they would do, in response to her escape, or the implications of how they talked to each other.

"Battle stations," said Alice, her tone perfectly calm.

Temperance jumped to her feet and set to work. Charlie watched as the door was barred and the table set against it. Wooden boards went into the window frames, clearly designed for that specific purpose. It looked entirely slick and well-practiced. Charlie wondered about her neighbors, and why on earth they had such arrangement in place, but had no time to ask.

"Upstairs," said Alice. "We can see them from up there, but they can't scale the outside of the building. I keep the upstairs windowsills greased."

Stunned, Charlie followed. Had she missed something? Did everyone have a few defenses at their disposal? Charlie knew her education had been inadequate...even so, she wasn't sure this kind of behavior could be classified as 'normal'.

Temperance put a flat iron on the saucepan lid, and they left the four captive mice as prisoners.

From the bedroom window they could see the mouse swarm as it battered Alice's house.

"There's rather a lot of them," Alice observed, her mind racing. Taken as individuals, the mice could easily be dealt with, but in such numbers she felt a good deal less confident about their chances.

"They've been making more," Temperance said. "And before either of you tell me I'm being silly, I saw their workshop in one of Charlie's cupboards. I saw them, they make each other."

"She's right," Charlie said, morosely. "They're mechanical mice. I do wonder who made the first one, and how, and, for that matter, why?"

Alice bolted the door at the top of the stairs and reached up to release the trapdoor in the ceiling. It rolled open.

"We may have to do some wondering about all of that later, but for now, I think we should move." She hooked down the attic ladder and creaked her way up it. This kind of swashbuckling activity had been a lot easier back in the days when her joints didn't protest so much. When she'd set up this emergency escape route, she hadn't really envisaged needing to use it. *Old habits die hard,* she reflected. Her fondness for having such resources to fall back on had contributed significantly to her not dying young. Being wild and impulsive is easier when you have a few tricks lined up and ready to use.

She led the younger pair through the empty attics of her neighbor's houses. Temperance had been up here before of course, and knew what she was doing, with a bit of prompting. The inventor's eyes were wide and glassy, as though she had descended into a state of shock. No time for that now. At least Charlie showed enough sense to keep moving rather than flapping her arms and asking awkward questions.

The journey required walking carefully along the joists, punctuated by frequent ducking. Living in an end-of-terrace property next to the detached number seven, Alice had four otherwise unused attics at her disposal. No one else ever came up here. The final house in the row belonged to Alfred Pears, who had been deaf and distracted for years. He knew nothing about the little trap door Alice had set into his roof. Nor did he know about the carefully positioned ladder hidden by the shape of that same roof, which took a person safely down the tiles, and over his outhouse to a rope ladder that, admittedly, had seen better days. It held together while they lowered it and made the final descent into Alborough Road.

"Where are we going now?" Temperance asked as they set off at a brisk trot.

"No idea. Any suggestions?" Alice enquired. She hadn't planned the escape route further, reasoning that if she needed to use it, a lot of what happened next would depend on who, or what, she found it necessary to run away from.

"Mister Edwards lives down this way. He'd take us in. He'd have to, it's his Christian duty," Temperance said.

"It's cynical, exploiting the faith of good people like that," Alice replied. She paused, and added, "It's nice to know you've been paying attention."

"I can't help it," said Temperance. "I take after you."

Alice smiled to herself. "He's a nice young man. Just the right sort of insane for something like this."

The four Druids listened in absolute silence as Justina explained about Henry Caractacus Morestrop Jones. They asked no questions until she had finished, which of itself was moderately unsettling.

"Henry Jones. Didn't he used to be Henry Pendragon Jones, working out of Leeds with Great High ArchDruid Emanuel Merlin and The Most August Order of Venerable Druids?"

Justina listened, bemused, as the four discussed a Veritable Druid Order, The Only Genuine Druid Order, The Order of Most Ancient Druids and other variations upon the themes of authority and antiquity. Apparently Druids were as fond of these things as archaeologists, and just as happy to extol their own virtues. Or perhaps it was merely a masculine thing. There were all so terribly fond of making themselves seem important.

The four eventually concluded that Jones could have been one of several highly disreputable people.

"Miss Fairfax, our noble tradition is frequently besmirched by charlatans. Any fool may call himself a Druid, and rather too many do. It takes more than a beard and a borrowed name."

They all had very fine beards, but it seemed diplomatic not to comment upon this, so she merely nodded.

"Do you have this gentleman's address, by any chance?" one of her bearded companions asked.

She did not.

"No sense of where he might go, or what he might do?"

Justina pondered this. "I suppose he'll either be doing everything he can to remain free from my mother, or he will go back to the house and attempt to murder her. I don't know him well enough to say which is most likely."

"Could you direct us to your mother's abode then?"

"It will take you a few days at the speed of your traction engine. Would you need me to come with you?"

The Druids exchanged glances. "Ours is but a small caravan," one said.

"It has been our habit to share everything."

"I can be shared," Justina said. "I mean, I can manage, in the circumstances, as the cause is a noble one."

Her sleep patterns had been erratic for so long that Charlie found herself awake late in the night. There was very little she could do, and lying still made her feel like screaming. Edward Edwards' home entirely corresponded with her expectations of an unmarried, independent minister. It was a small, neat and Spartan space. He had accepted the three refugees with absolute grace, surrendered his bed to Granny Alice, made up what he could for herself and Temperance, and was now sleeping downstairs in his chair. As a consequence of being asleep, he looked far younger and more vulnerable than his waking self suggested. She'd watched him for a while until the anxiety that he would wake and notice this, caused her to move away.

Afraid that her restlessness would disturb the others if she stayed inside, Charlie crept out and sat on the front doorstep. It was a chilly night for the time of year, but mercifully quiet. Still, her nerves were raw and she expected the mouse swarm to appear at any moment. Listening for unfamiliar noises, she picked through recent memories, trying to find links and lines of logic that would bring it all together. Why did mechanical mice want a cauldron of rebirth? What was their connection with the dog-faced boy? Why was any of this happening? And, for that matter, how was any of it happening? There were a great many things she could not explain.

Her own presence in the mystery puzzled her even more. Her own actions had shaped several key developments, but she had no motives that she knew of, no personal involvement in any of it. Was it just fate? Charlie did not like the idea of being a pawn in destiny's game. She wondered if there were any choices she could now make of her own free will. None of these thoughts were conducive to seeking her bed, and she began contemplating the relative merits of gin, and laudanum. Not that she had either, and Edwards didn't seem the type to keep any such things, even for emergencies. But one never knew. Could she wake him up and ask him, or would that be going too far?

There came a soft, shuffling sound, like the tap of miniscule boots moving together. Her first thought was to envisage a diminutive fairy horde trooping down the road. Then she pictured the mouse swarm, creeping forwards on an unholy combination of wheels and feet. Her pulse raced. They had found her before, and could do so again. She stood up, preparing to run, but not sure which direction danger lay in. Would they come at her from all sides, cutting off escape? She had visions of her own torn flesh, as the horde moved on into the house to shred her companions in an act of cold vengeance.

Scanning the road, she saw a large hedgehog, pottering towards her. Spines rattled against cobblestones, creating the sound of many tiny feet. She laughed, nervously. The hedgehog paused to look at her, then continued untroubled upon its way.

Charlie decided that she couldn't worry about the bigger picture. She had no idea what any of this recent chaos was really about. However, it made a good deal of sense to worry about dying, and becoming insane, and seeing people she loved being eaten by mechanical mice. So many other people who were caught up in this mess seemed to have grandiose schemes and epic ambitions. Charlie didn't. She wasn't going to go around trying to save the day. She was going to figure out how not to be eaten by mice. The rest would have to take care of itself.

Once they were all settled in the dry space under the bridge, Friday Bob announced he'd seen the mouse swarm on Soulier Road, heading north. "They've killed seventeen people already. They take you right apart, even your bones, so no one ever finds anything to bury, or to say who's been eaten. All they leave is dust and maybe just one tooth or your door key or something small like that."

There had been a lot of stories recently, but no one, as far as Temperance knew, could name a single person who had actually been eaten by mice. Or, for that matter, anyone who had vanished in mysterious way that suggested a mousey consumption. Not that such details really counted when it came to a good story. At least she didn't have to try and make something up this time.

"I heard that," said Albert Nose. "If you see something lying in the road, you never know if it was dropped by accident of it the person it belonged to was eaten up by the mice."

"Mister Edwards says they are like a plague from the Bible," said one of the twins.

Temperance cleared her throat importantly and waited until they were all looking at her. "Charlie says we have to make a giant trap and catch them. She says we have to do it today because the mice will be looking for her."

"Do they eat cheese?" Rapunzel asked. "You said they were mechanical mice, so what do we catch them with?"

"Magnetism," Temperance announced, grandly.

"What, that funny look into my eyes you are feeling very sleepy stuff? When I clap my hands you will think you are a chicken? Like at the circus last year? How're we supposed to learn that in a day?" Albert Nose asked, tone petulant.

There was a silence while the others thought about this.

"I think that's mesmerism, you numbskull," said Friday Bob. "Magnetics is one of those funny, jerky exercises like your mum does."

"I thought that was caltrops," said Rapunzel. "Or calligraphy, maybe."

They collected big words and hoarded them, as other children might collect marbles, but it had never been with an eye to precise and immediate use.

"Castanets?" tried one of the twins.

"What, like a fishing net? That might work," said Rapunzel.

Chapter twenty-three

Holy fools; reflections upon the wisdom of insanity

It proved embarrassingly easy to find Henry Caractacus Morestrop Jones, formerly Henry Pendragon Jones, formerly Halleluiah Jones. No one quite knew what he'd been before that, and Mister Jones himself had very carefully forgotten and never mentioned it. As Justina led her quartet of Druids through her mother's gate, she noticed that the front garden had finally been cleared of abandoned furniture. Instead it now held the physical presence of a very much sought after gentleman. He was sat in the cauldron, with exposed chest and shoulders suggesting the full horror of nudity. Fortunately, the worst of it was covered by water and shadow. He looked for all the world like he was taking a bath.

As they approached, Henry Jones broke into song. The tune consisted more of enthusiasm than melody, while the words were a strange amalgam of prayer, classical Latin and nonsensical improvisation. The five of them paused to listen, but once it became evident nothing important was being expressed, they continued forward.

"Hello Henry, old chap," said one of the Druids, stepping closer to the cauldron.

The ArchDruid looked up, blinking. "Is that you, Bob?"

"I have renounced my worldly name," the Druid who might once have been Bob replied.

"Splitters," muttered Henry Jones. "I'm going to ignore you until you go away."

"What are you doing in that cauldron" one of the other Druids asked.

"I am ignoring you, did I not mention this already? And I am experiencing rebirth. Kindly leave me to my rapture."

At this point, the butler emerged from within the house, and sidled up to Justina. "I do apologize, Miss Fairfax, he's been here for two days already. We would have removed him, only we understand that Mrs. Fairfax wished him returned. He's been quite cooperative and so, lacking any clear instructions, I thought it best to leave him in his current condition."

"He has not offended our neighbors, with his...his enthusiasms?" she asked, nervously.

"We have had a few visitors, but no complaints, Miss Fairfax."

"I am glad to hear that. Where is my mother?" Justina enquired.

"I'm afraid I have no idea. She left no forwarding address," the butler said.

Justina turned to her companions. "Gentlemen, how do you wish to proceed? I believe this is the right cauldron, although it is unfortunately occupied."

They began the slow and now familiar process of discussing the problem. Justina and the butler waited. Henry Jones continued to soak and pretended he couldn't hear them. The Druids were, she felt, a little foolish in some regards, but they possessed considerable charm between them. Their interest in pagan fertility cults turned out not to be wholly academic and theoretical in nature, but did not center excessively on an interest in reproduction. Two days in their company had served to rouse her curiosity rather than dampen her ardor. It was an experience Justina had never known before, although she still expected to tire of them eventually.

"It is my cauldron. I cannot get out. I refuse to get out! Can you not see I am in the process of being magically reborn?" Henry Jones shouted at the other Druids.

"No," one of them replied. "Did you not realize that death is a necessary pre-requisite for literal rebirth in this cauldron?"

"It is a spiritual rebirth I seek, you cretinous, narrow-minded fools."

"Ah yes, but as far as we know, the cauldron requires an entirely literal, bodily demise takes place first, before it works any magic upon the flesh," another of the Druids said cheerfully. Justina could tell they were enjoying themselves.

"We would be more than happy to assist you in this regard," another of the four suggested.

Henry Jones gripped the cauldron's rim with his white and wrinkled fingers. "This is private property!" he boomed.

"Henry dear," said Justina, making every effort to sound like her mother. "You are making an ass of yourself on my lawn. I will not stand for it. You will be provided with a towel, to spare our eyes from the horrors of your exposed and waterlogged flesh. Then you will retire and dress yourself in a manner more becoming of a gentleman. After that, you will undertake either to remove your personage back to the hermitage, or from these premises. I leave that for you to decide."

"It's not working, is it?" Henry Jones asked. He stood up in the cauldron.

The butler, experienced in covering moments of social embarrassment, whipped his jacket off and protected them all from the unwanted view.

"It is not working in the least," Justin assured him.

"It's not fair," Henry Jones said. He sounded childish and petulant, almost as though he might cry. "I want to be transformed! I want to be special."

Justina reflected that his time in the hermitage may have unhinged his mind. Assuming it needed any additional unhinging. He had never struck her as being a model of sense or reason.

"I would like my trousers," said Henry Jones, climbing out of the cauldron.

"Just come with me, sir," the butler encouraged.

"Can I have my old room?" asked Jones. "The one in the garden. I think I would feel safe there."

"Absolutely, sir." The butler raised an eyebrow at Justina, and then led the house guest away.

"It's tragic, really," one of the Druids observed. "His mind has quite gone."

"Did I not prophesy as much four years ago, when I said, he who claims the head will find that the mind has fled?" the eldest of the quartet said.

"I thought that pertained to old Fastidious Monkspotter and that business with the statue."

She could see another discussion brewing. "Gentleman, shall we empty the cauldron and depart, or do you wish to dismantle it here?"

"I should be happier if we put a little distance between ourselves and Mister Jones before we consider the cauldron," the youngest said. "His state disturbs my equilibrium."

Yes, Justina thought. *We are all a little closer to joining him than might be advisable.*

They emptied the cauldron onto the lawn. It took all four of them to carry it back to the caravan, although they were being extremely careful with the item. Justina wondered how on earth Jones had managed his act of theft.

"I dislike lying, but we needed him to remove himself," one of the Druids said to her.

She had no idea what he meant. "Oh?"

He continued. "I do not think it is merely a cauldron for rebirthing the dead. It is a cauldron of transformation."

"Whatever it is, I do not think it has significantly improved Mister Jones," Justina observed. "Rather the opposite."

"It is said that certain places or experiences might transform a man into either a poet, or a lunatic. I had always assumed that the direction of change must come from within, while the energy to drive it comes from outside. But even so, I would not test myself by placing my living flesh inside this cauldron. I am too aware of my own imperfections."

As they began the next stage of their journey, Justina wondered whether she would be worsened, or improved by a sojourn in the cauldron. She rapidly came to the conclusion that her anxiety outweighed her curiosity about the subject and that she found her current condition to be wholly acceptable.

"Are we to destroy the cauldron now?" she enquired.

"It does need to be destroyed," one of the two still with her replied. He seemed nervous.

"We hadn't planned that far ahead," the other admitted. "And obviously we should not attempt so delicate a task whilst on the move. There might be unforeseen consequences."

She touched the object's rim, feeling the unyielding strength of the metal. "What tools do you have?"

"I think we have a shovel, for the coal," one of the pair said.

"Clippers for the maintenance of beards. Some cooking implements, a cooking knife, and a golden sickle."

"It's not real gold of course. Far too costly, and far too soft. It's brass, and largely ornamental."

She nodded. "So we conclude that you do not have the means to unmake this item, and that it might be dangerous to do so."

"That would be the size of it, yes. But it should be taken apart and buried, I think."

Justina could see an obvious flaw here. "That only works until someone finds it, and puts it back together again. What is to prevent Chevalier from locating it, unearthing it and reassembling it? Why don't we melt it down, or throw it in the sea?"

"There is a lot of power in the cauldron, dear lady. We have no idea what would happen if we tried either. Burial has worked before, and diminishes the threat for now. But yes, we should consider some strategy for dealing with Chevalier."

As solutions went, it seemed rather thin to her. "Miss Rowcroft assembled it, therefore perhaps we might assume that she could safely dismantle it, and perhaps mangle it a bit for good measure."

"That seems the best solution," the Druid agreed.

Where Alice had found four cage crinolines in so short a time, Charlie didn't like to think. None of the old women of Barker Street seemed like the sort of people to have worn such extravagant dresses in their youth. For that matter, the inventor struggled to imagine any of her elderly neighbors as ever having been young. She would never have considered utilizing such things either, but when Alice had presented the contraptions, it was obvious that they might serve. Bell-shaped and enormous, their steel hoops, designed to hold out vast skirts, would not need much encouragement to stand up by themselves. Just a few supporting rods should do the trick. Charlie tried to imagine wearing one, and felt very glad to have missed that particular fashion.

"Are you sure four's enough?" Granny Alice asked.

"I think that should do it. The bigger problem is going to be getting enough magnets. Temperance collected everything I had from the house. No sign of the mice there, she said." Charlie shivered at the thought of them. She hadn't wanted the girl to go, but as Temperance pointed out, the mice had little reason to take interest in her, and Charlie needed tools. "Her friends have found a few," Charlie added, "but nothing like enough."

"Well, I gave that a bit of thought too." Alice hefted an enormous wooden box onto the table. "You remember old Augustus Neville? We buried him a bit back, but he'd been ill for years. Mind you, I think he imagined a lot of it, but I would never say so to Myrtle."

Charlie waited patiently through the pre-amble, knowing that when Granny Alice talked, it always went somewhere, even if it did go there slowly.

"Well, Augustus was always trying new cures for all the ailments he thought he had. Pills, potions and I don't know what. And of course Myrtle was never one for throwing things away, so all his medicinal items are lying around in her house. It turns out that Myrtle still had this, and she says you're welcome to it." Alice whipped the box lid off with a flourish.

Leaning closer, Charlie read: *Doctor Von Schnidt's guaranteed restorative machine. Eases aches and pains, and soothes the body. Instructions included within. Do not use whilst bathing, during thunderstorms or for non-therapeutic purposes.* Inside the box lay a strange, metallic device that looked in no way suitable for any kind of contact with the human body. There were far too many spiky things sticking out of it, for a start.

"Myrtle said it was a bugger for getting spoons stuck to it, so I thought it might do for you," Alice said.

Charlie reached for a fork, and tested the machine. Instant adhesion. There were magnets in there somewhere, and powerful ones at that. She whooped, and started trying to work out how to take the thing apart. Whoever had constructed it evidently had a sick mind, and a penchant for sharp edges. Still, it was the first time in several days that she'd felt optimistic.

"What are these?" Temperance asked, joining them in Mister Edwards' kitchen. She climbed inside one of the cage crinolines and pulled it up over her head.

"Child traps," said Alice.

Temperance eyed it critically. "You'd have to be pretty useless to get trapped in one of them."

"They tie you in," Alice said. "It's so big and heavy that you can't run away and so wide that you can't get through doorways."

"That's evil," said Temperance.

Alice nodded, but did not reply. No, Charlie really couldn't imagine her adopted granny ever wore that kind of dress.

"You could always hide a lot under those big skirts," Alice said, a gleam in her eye.

"What, like weapons?" Temperance asked.

"People even," Alice replied, then added. "Or so I imagine. I wouldn't know."

Temperance chuckled. It was easy to see where the girl got her penchant for silly stories from.

Chapter twenty-four

Pest control in the modern household: Advice for anxious wives and mothers

It looked like no mousetrap Alice had ever seen. But then, these were not your typical, cheese-eating mice. They called for something special, and they were going to get it. One of the loaded crinoline cages hung downwards, resembling its former petticoat role. The other three clustered around it like giant flowers. All of them were attached to an old but solid piece of furniture. It might have been a chest of drawers, but the drawers were entirely absent now, and something had been living in it. They didn't know how Temperance and her friends had sourced the item, or the wheels now attached to the bottom corners. On the whole, Alice felt it was better not to ask.

"You're the cheese then," Temperance said, plainly enjoying herself. She had her cluster of friends in tow, and was showing off for their benefit.

Charlie didn't look as enthusiastic. "It only works if they still want me, but if they don't, I suppose that solves the problem for me at least."

"I can't say I feel comfortable with this," Edward Edwards confessed. "I would prefer it if I could go in your stead."

"As far as we know, the mice were interested in me. They aren't looking for you," Charlie pointed out. "It's kind of you to offer, but I don't think it would work."

Edwards sighed. "Let me come with you, at least."

"Well, you can help me wheel it out, but if the mice come, they could be all over you. I have no idea what it might occur to them to do if you're with me, and I don't want you getting eaten. They told me they ate the dog-faced boy."

"I believe that," said one of the children. "I've heard they ate loads of people."

Alice shook her head. "I don't think so. Not loads of people. Maybe one or two children though."

They squealed at this, but she could tell the idea appealed to their macabre sensibilities.

A most uncharacteristic grin appeared on the young minister's face. "I have a plan," he said, and went back indoors.

"I want to come too, with the mousetrap," said Temperance.

"And me," demanded one of her friends.

Alice and Charlie said 'no' in perfect unison. Before Temperance and her gang had time to start protesting, Edward Edwards returned to them, carrying what looked like two long poles. In moments, he swung up onto these. They were stilts, and with them he towered over the wheeled cabinet.

"I greased the lower part of the poles. I do not think it likely that any mice, mechanical or otherwise, will be able to climb up them." He took a few steps. "Beyond that, I shall trust to God and my own dexterity."

The gang of children stared, eyes large. They were clearly impressed by this development.

"Well obviously we could go too if we all had stilts," said Friday Bob.

"No," said Charlie. "Amaze me, Mister Edwards, how did a minister come to stilt walking?" She was eager to think about anything except the imminence of mice.

Edward Edwards blushed. "In my younger days, well…it is fair to say…my upbringing…" he hesitated. "I grew up in a circus."

"An odd place to find a religious calling," Charlie said.

"It was the tightrope walking. I came into the habit of praying a great deal. Then later, when I started learning the trapeze, it occurred to me that I liked payer a good deal more than I liked aerial gymnastics. From that moment, my way was clear to me."

"We'd better go," she said, conscious of her desire to abandon the plan. "You lot are not coming," she added, for the benefit of the children.

"We could go to my house," said the other girl. "If you're going back to Barker Street, my house is right on the corner. That would be safe, wouldn't it?" She squinted up at the adults, in a manner that was probably meant to be endearing, but mostly had the effect of making her look half blind.

"That seems safe enough to me," said Alice.

"We haven't seen any actual mice in ages," Friday Bob pointed out. "They've probably all gone anyway. This is a stupid plan."

With Friday Bob's vote of no confidence ringing in her ears, Charlie set off. Perhaps she was being silly about the mice. It might be sheer arrogance on her part, thinking they would still be looking for her. But she hadn't wanted to risk going home, and Alice had opted to stay put as well. Mister Edwards had been so kind to them all, but now she felt like a bit of a fraud. She glanced across at him, looking for signs that he thought her silly.

"Can you manage all right, with the pushing?" he asked, from the other side of their contraption.

"I'm fine, thank you."

"You're being very brave," he said. Which rather answered her question.

Charlie had opted for the junction between Barker Street and Alborough Road as the place to make her stand. There was a little triangle of grass where the roads met. The children had dashed off ahead to Rapunzel's house, and Alice had started doing the rounds to warn people to stay inside. Charlie could have wished them all further away, but she needed to be readily findable to lure in the mice, and no one seemed convinced that it would be dangerous to be in the general vicinity. After all, no one on Barker Street had been eaten, yet. The trouble with mice, she reflected, was the difficulty of making them sound sufficiently dangerous.

"I suppose all we can do now, is wait," Mister Edwards

observed.

"I hope they find me. It's funny, I've spent the last few days hoping they wouldn't. Now I just want it to be over, one way or another." They were both silent for a few minute, then Charlie added, "Don't you have any good Bible quotes to comfort us with while we wait?"

Edward Edwards shifted his weight continuously from one stilt-foot to the other. It gave him an air of uncertainty, which Charlie suspected he did not deserve. "I do not think that Jesus had a great deal to say on the subject of mechanical mice. In fact, when it comes to conflict, his words can be condensed into something very much like 'please be nice to each other.' But these mice are, I feel certain, ungodly abominations, so I do not feel we owe them a great deal of sympathy."

"Try and convert me," Charlie suggested.

"What?" he replied, teetering round to face her.

"I'm not much of a Christian. Convert me. Well, talk to me a lot about God, because frankly I'm terrified and I'd rather listen to anything you might say than think about the mice or my immediate future."

Edward Edwards cleared his throat, and commenced reciting the Bible, from the beginning. King James version. He skipped over the bits he didn't like, including a lot of the begats, never having been able to keep them all in his mind, but Charlie had no idea that he had missed some of the less exciting bits out. She let the sound of his voice wash over her, the cadences of language soothing. She imagined it must be very reassuring to believe in something.

When the machine was in motion, two people could comfortably travel on the traction engine itself, and a further two could sit comfortably in the open door of the caravan. In their days as a quartet, this had worked well for the Druids, but Justina complicated matters. Those on the traction engine needed to be familiar with the workings of the levers. Justina intended to learn, but the opportunity to do so had not yet arisen. She discovered that, with a little assistance, the caravan roof offered a most charming seat on sunny days. Riding at this great height, she could imagine herself as a gypsy queen, a bohemian adventurer, a pagan goddess. Basking in sunlight, conscious of curious stares from passersby, and ducking occasional low branches, she had never been happier.

They were just entering Bromstone when she noticed a peculiar darkness on the road ahead. It appeared to be undulating. Justina had never before paid much attention to the surface of roads, and the veil of smoke from the chimney before her did not help her ascertain whether this might be perfectly normal. As a consequence, it took her some minutes to realize this was not the proper behavior of a public thoroughfare. The road surface appeared to be moving towards them.

She shouted this observation to her companions in the caravan door, who in turn shouted at the two on the engine. However, thanks to the noise from their steam powered beast, communications were slow, and not very accurate. They were only just considering that there might be a problem when the dark tide washed in. Some of the mice attempted to climb up the traction engine, but the majority hurled themselves at the caravan. From the roof, Justina could do little but watch, and shout advice. Several mice made it inside the door, but most were thwarted by either the motion, or the determined efforts of the Druids.

"They want the cauldron!" she screamed. She supposed the Druids should have figured that bit out already, but in the absence of anything else to do, it felt a bit like making a contribution.

Despite the ongoing assault, the traction engine still rolled forwards. Justina turned to the back of the caravan, to see how many mice they had crushed. Against all the odds, there was no sign of that kind of carnage in the road. All they could do was keep going, and hope to beat the mice off. Outrunning anything was improbable.

As they rolled into Barker Street, a surreal scene greeted them. There was man pacing about on stilts, and at the cross-roads, perched on a most bizarre-looking wheeled contraption, sat Miss Rowcroft. The Druids ground their contraption slowly, inevitably towards the pair. It seemed almost as though the tableau in the street had been constructed with this very moment in mind.

"They've snarled up the engine somehow," one of the Druids shouted up to her. "We're going to stop. Stay up there. Hopefully you'll be safe."

After the first couple of hours, the wait had become very dull indeed. Temperance and her friends had spent some of the time amusing themselves by making bets and guesses about what would happen and who would die. Temperance had enjoyed that bit. Friday Bob was really good at coming up with hideous, unlikely death scenarios. He'd created a complex series of imagined accidents for them, involving an escaped pig, a pothole, sudden distraction due to an airship and Mister Edwards being impaled upon one of his own stilts. The description of the ensuing slow and bloody slide to ground level, followed with consumption by angry mice, had been inspired. After a story like that, reality was only going to disappoint them, so they had wandered off in search of food. Friday Bob was always hungry, especially when in other people's houses.

Then there had been the big argument because the twins were supposed to go home for tea, but Rapunzel's parents wouldn't let them out.

"Mam will kill us," they whispered in discordant unison.

"The mice will kill you more," Temperance said. "They're going to be really angry, when they get here."

"I don't think they're coming at all," said Albert Nose. "It's a stupid plan, Pie Face. You're stupid and your friends are stupid and the stupid mice are..."

Temperance halted the tirade by punching him in the stomach. While Albert rolled noisily on the floor, she went back to the window and resumed her observations. Charlie looked very pale and worried, which Temperance considered to be rather a shame. The waiting might be boring, but Temperance knew she'd have loved being the cheese in a giant mousetrap. It was a waste, being miserable like that. *Next time,* she promised herself. When she grew up, she was going to do a much better job of having adventures. She was going to be like Granny.

Temperance heard the distinctive sounds of the traction engine before it came into view, and waited for it, hardly daring to draw a breath. She knew it had to be the druids. Or at least, she didn't think anyone else bringing a traction engine to this corner of England. It had to be them, and they had to be coming here, surely? What kind of an adventure would it be if all the important things went off and happened somewhere else? That wouldn't be fair at all.

It felt a bit like holding on for the first roll of thunder in a storm. If it didn't come, she would be horribly let down. They'd waited long enough. Something ought to happen. It was well past time for a few flashes and bangs. Only, she was trapped in a house and Rapunzel's parents wouldn't let her out either, and it might not be the druids after all. Finally, the traction engine rolled into view, surrounded by the long awaited mice. Rather than call out to alert the others, she watched the unfolding scene in silence. Let them miss it. They deserved as much. They were all being horrible and it would serve them right.

The Druids stopped right underneath the window. It was like a sign, Temperance thought. She considered the size and distance of the caravan roof, the height above ground, and the ease of getting onto the window ledge. It would be no harder than the jump from the twins' room above the shop to the roof of Mister

Holibart's shed, and she had managed that plenty of times before. Even the time when she'd missed, she hadn't broken anything, or died. Temperance opened the window, climbed out onto the sill and threw herself into the air.

The slow approach of the Druids, flanked by the mouse swarm, had been hellish to watch, but Charlie didn't dare move. She made eye contact with Edward Edwards, who had spontaneously run out of Bible quotes and turned a pallid hue. No backing out now. No thinking better of it. The mice seemed intent on overwhelming the caravan, but a few separated out and raced towards her instead. She bit her lip, glad that at least this time, they weren't talking. The first mouse vanished under the crinolines. There was a sharp 'ting' sound, then a second and third such noises ensued, followed by a tirade of furious squeaking. The mouse trap was working, at least when the mice came close enough. The only trouble was, they were far more interested in the caravan and consequently most remained out of range.

Charlie watched with dismay as Temperance made her demented leap from the window. The thud of her landing almost made Charlie's heart stop. The girl stood straight away, hooted, and then started throwing things at the mice. From a distance, it was impossible to see what the projectiles were, but Temperance had a lot of pockets. Swarmed by mice, the two Druids from the caravan clambered across to the relative safety of the traction engine. There wasn't really enough room, but they huddled together as the great rodent tide swept into their home.

Charlie felt powerless, her plan had come to nothing. The only way the mousetrap could work, required getting a lot closer. Heart pounding, Charlie leapt to the ground and wheeled her contraption towards the mice. The little 'tink' sounds soon came thick and fast as the metal in their bodies responded to the magnetic former petticoats. There were far more mice inside the caravan though, and most were managing to escape from her. She felt a few of them climbing her legs, tiny teeth razor sharp in her shin. She tore them off, yelping, throwing their small, aggressive bodies into the trap. From the caravan roof, Temperance shouted encouragement and Justina called out warnings when stray mice headed for her ankles.

By the time she stopped the campaign of mouse harassment, Charlie's clothes were soaked with the sweat of terror and her hands were shaking. The mice were all either in the caravan, or in the undergarments. Those held by magnets fell quiet, and Charlie could hear little beyond the sound of her own breathing.

"What is happening?" Justina called down.

"They've all gone into the caravan," said one of the Druids. He climbed down to have a look "I can't see anything."

Charlie held her breath as the man ventured inside. Her legs were bleeding and sore from just a few mouse attacks. She had no doubt the ones in the caravan could take all of this fellow's skin from his bones if they wanted to. Time seemed to be moving far too slowly. She supposed he'd have screamed, if there had been a few seconds between attack and annihilation. What would it sound like, if all the mice pounced at once?

The Druid poked his head out of the door, and she breathed out again. "They're all in the cauldron, and they aren't doing anything at all now."

The mice in the traps squealed, and seemed to be trying to escape again.

"Now what?" Charlie asked. Her voice sounded distant in her ears.

The four Druids fetched the cauldron out into the open. This took several minutes and a lot of effort, but not a single mouse deigned to poke its furry head over the rim to see what was going on. Then, one of the men helped Justina and Temperance down from the roof.

"I don't know what this means," the oldest look one said.

"Well, obviously something has to happen," said Temperance. She stared at each adult in turn, the challenge in her gaze unmistakable. It was their job to come up with a solution.

Charlie took a deep breath. "I think we need to put all the mice into the cauldron."

"Isn't that what they want?" Justina replied. "Wouldn't we be helping them? Doesn't that defeat the object rather?"

"Possibly," said Charlie, "But I think it's the only way we're going to find out what's going on." After everything she'd been though, she really wanted some kind of explanation.

Temperance reached into the nearest cage crinoline, and pulled off a mouse. It stayed limp and passive in her hands. She dropped it into the cauldron. There wasn't so much as a squeak. Within a few minutes, everyone else was elbows deep in old undergarments too, pulling mechanical mice from the magnets and sending them to their fate.

"Being in the cauldron had no discernible effect on Mister Jones," Justina pointed out as they worked. "And these mice are not, and have never been living creatures. I can feel the machinery in them. I can see a distinct practical advantage to having them safely contained in one place, though." It was a good argument, and it gave a logical validity to what they were doing, even though Charlie suspected they were all driven by curiosity alone.

Somehow, all of the mice fitted into the cauldron.

"Well, now we can dispose of them," Justina suggested.

There was no actual explosion, no pyrotechnics, not even a theatrical puff of smoke. For a few seconds, Charlie felt as though her body had been turned inside out and back again. There was a man standing up in the cauldron. He had ebony hair, a ruthless smile, and eyes that seemed to be looking right into her soul. Nearby, Justina gave a little scream, and staggered backwards. The Druids whipped assorted symbols out of their robes, brandishing them like weapons.

"Aren't you the frozen demon from the freak show?" Temperance asked, calmly.

Before the man could answer her question, or undertake any other action for that matter, the sound of a single shot cut through the air. The clear, crisp explosion of it rang out and at once, the mouse man slumped.

A few minutes passed during which no one moved.

"Is it safe?" Justina asked.

"Wait," suggested one of the druids.

Charlie glanced around nervously, but couldn't work out where the shot had come from.

The man rose up again, showing no signs of having been recently penetrated by a bullet. His presence somehow seemed diminished. There was a second shot. What rose up after the third impact was grey and blank eyed, like their previous mortless people had been. After the fourth bullet hit home, the contents of the cauldron remained quiet.

One of the Druids stepped forward nervously, to take a look. "Just dust," he said.

Charlie felt her limbs unfreeze a little. Looking around, she could still see no sign of the marksman. She felt dreadfully cold, shaking suddenly, she struggled to think or breathe. Someone put gentle arms around her and murmured words of assurance. Closing her eyes, she waited for the world to stop spinning.

Chapter twenty-five

Superstitions of the urban working class and their contribution to falling standards

The mice had overturned almost everything in Alice's house, and there were breakages, but she assessed the damage as being superficial. It did not take her long, with a broom, and a monologue of mouse-abuse, to put her home back to some semblance of order. She was still sweeping when Temperance pushed the door open. Edward Edwards came in behind the girl, bearing Charlie in his arms. The inventor appeared to be in a dead faint. Alice righted a chair, into which the young minster descended with his precious burden.

Alice hunted about for a feather to burn.

"I have absolutely no idea what just happened," Edwards said. "My mind cannot quite grasp what my eyes are sure they have seen."

"It was amazing, there were mice and druids and a gun and a dead man who was in the cauldron and..."

"Temperance," Alice interrupted. "Take a moment to compose yourself, and then tell me, please."

"Yes, Granny."

"And how was Miss Fairfax?" Alice enquired, watching the young man's face carefully.

Apparently Edwards had to think about this. "I believe she was quite unharmed. She's telling people what they should be doing, which is probably as well."

It looked as though his old fixation had broken. But then, Alice reflected, her neighbor had changed somehow of late. The burned feather did its work, and Charlie spluttered back into consciousness.

"Are you alright, my girl?" Alice demanded.

Charlie managed a small nod, and carried on leaning her head against Mister Edwards' chest.

"You be careful with my Charlie, she's a different sort of creature altogether," Alice said.

The pair looked confused, glanced at each other and launched into a most telling array of protestations and denials. There followed an embarrassed dance of trying to get Edwards out from under Charlie, during which both of them blushed fiercely and apologized to each other far more than was necessary. Alice didn't say anything else, she just put the kettle on and waited for them to figure things out.

The Druids came later, to check on Charlie. They stood in a row just inside the kitchen door.

"Are you quite well now?" one of them asked.

"I'll do," said Charlie.

"We wish to be on our way shortly."

Charlie nodded. "That's nice." She wanted them to go away. She wanted everyone to go away.

"The cauldron," one of them said.

"It needs to be destroyed," another added.

"Righty ho," said Charlie, thinking this wasn't really her problem.

"We thought you..." one of them began.

Hearing the hint of an unwelcome suggestion in those words, Charlie sat up a little straighter and stared at them. "You thought I could do it? Didn't you tell me, or one of you did, that the cauldron is dangerous?"

The Druids shuffled their feet. One of them spoke. "Uh, yes."

"Why, exactly, do you think that the job of taking it apart is my problem?"

"We thought that, as you had assembled it safely, you stand a good chance of dismantling it without any trouble either."

Charlie huffed. "Well, that would be a very tidy solution for you, wouldn't it?" She thought about this. If she said no, they would take the cauldron and do something with it. Destroy it. That didn't strike her as being the best idea. They might get themselves killed. She remembered the cauldron. It was such an interesting contraption. "You haven't really given me a lot of choice though, have you?"

"Charlie, you don't have to do this," Alice said.

"Oh, I think it's a job with my name on it," she said, wearily. "Leave it in my kitchen, the door's probably still open. I'll sort it out."

"Do you want any help?" Edward Edwards asked.

She shook her head. "I'll be fine."

It took Justina a few minutes to scrawl a letter to her landlady, and to tell Mary that her service was no longer required. She contemplated her books, possessions and wardrobe. It looked like the property of a stranger. That old life, and the person she had been felt so distant as to be unreal. Quite when everything had changed, she did not know. It didn't seem to matter. After a few moments of thought, she pulled out her smallest travelling case and packed into it her most sensible, hard-wearing clothing. There were a couple of books worth taking, the rest was just pretentious nonsense. There might be some food worth removing from the kitchen, but she needed no more than this.

"Mary?" she called. The servant girl duly appeared. "I shall be leaving shortly, as I said. Take anything of mine that you want. Have a look now while I write another letter."

While the startled girl explored jewelry and clothing, Justina took a second piece of paper and settled down to write again.

Dear Mother, I have no idea when I shall see you again, although I am sure that I must. I am writing to assure you that I am well, and safe. I have finally found my calling, and a place in the world that suits my nature and gives me a sense of purpose. I have given up the house on

Barker Street and can offer no suggestions as to my likely whereabouts in the future. Today, I am also giving up my worldly name and becoming one who is mobile within the threads of destiny. I shall go out into the world with my friends and let the path take me where it will. I realize there is an irony in this; that after years of berating you for your spiritual questing, I have now chosen to go so much further than you ever dared. I shall see you when fate decrees. I know we have not always been friends, but I part from you in peace and good humor. Always, your daughter.

She folded the letter, placed it in an envelope and handed it to Mary, for posting. "Help yourself to anything you want," she reiterated. "I will not be needing any of it again."

"Thank you, miss."

Bag in hand, Justina walked purposefully down the stairs and made her way back to the other four Druids.

"Are we ready to go?" she enquired.

They were.

The gang were back in the summer house, listening to the dull thud of rain on the roof, and burning old boxes of Penance Biscuits for warmth.

"You never shot him," said Rapunzel. "You were right there with me in the kitchen, Friday Bob, that's a bare-assed lie and you know it."

Friday Bob's version of events had not been as successful as usual.

"And you can't shoot straight, and you don't even have a pea shooter since we broke it, much less a pistol, or a musket or anything," Albert Nose added.

"You don't know the half of it," Temperance said, softly.

They all turned to look at her. It wasn't just the old gang members in the summer house today, there were a few new recruits too. The legend of the mousetrap had spread, and

Temperance's fame with it.

"It all began at the freak show," she said. "The demon, frozen in ice. An ancient history from hundreds of years ago, from before there even was history. He was evil. He was French. That's how evil he was. But while he was frozen, that was no problem. Only Miss Fairfax looked at him. There was a spell on her, from birth, and any man who looked at her went a bit mad. I lived next door to her, I saw how crazy she made people. But this wasn't a normal man. This was a demon. He'd dreamed about her even before he saw her, and when she turned up and looked at him, it made his ice melt." Temperance paused for dramatic effect. Her audience was riveted. "Before he froze himself in the ice, the demon made mechanical mice. He had to freeze himself because he was so old, and his body was going to die, so he was buying time, but he wanted the cauldron all along. His plans went a bit wrong and when Mss Fairfax melted him, his whole body fell apart so he had to possess the mice and the dog-faced boy just to survive. If we'd been at the freak show when he melted, it could have been one of us he took over. We were lucky. So he used the mice to make more mice so they were like his army, and then he had to steal the cauldron only the first time he tried, Mister Anderson or someone fooled him and he stole the wrong one. But he got it in the end. It's a cauldron of change, not rebirth, that's why he wanted to get all of the mice in it. He used some of his own demon magic to have the cauldron turn him back into himself."

Temperance closed her eyes and leaned back against the summerhouse wall. It had taken her ages to get the story this straight, and she knew it was full of holes. Not that it mattered. It was a good story. Some of it might have been true.

"So, did you shoot the demon?" one of the new boys asked her, reverentially.

Temperance had considered a really complex explanation about a machine that let her fire a gun from somewhere else, but that stretched even her powers of imagination. She fell back on her favorite theme instead. "Didn't I always say that my granny had been a pirate and a highwayman? She's a crack shot. What I've never told anyone before is that she's part of a secret group of demon hunters. They've been around for hundreds of years too. I'm training to be one myself, as it happens. But that's why she knew he was a demon, and she shot him. Only we can't tell anyone because it's a really secret society."

"Can we be demon hunters too?" asked the new boy.

Temperance smiled indulgently. "I've started teaching Rapunzel. But I could probably find some time to teach you lot as well."

The circus was due in a few weeks time, and Temperance knew there would be plenty of scope for playing demon hunters then. The version she had concocted of recent events was, in her own humble opinion, her best story yet. She'd tried it on Alice first. She always did.

"I'm just a harmless old granny," Alice said at the end. She always said something like that, only this time she added, "Not that I know anything about demons of course. But you could see anything those mice turned into wasn't going to be very friendly."

For the first time since she'd moved into Barker Street, the entire kitchen was perfectly clean and tidy. Even the mouse workshop behind the cupboard had been dealt with. Charlie wasn't normally one for housework, but in the aftermath, there had been something very healing and soothing about getting rid of accumulated grime and rubbish.

There had been a steady stream of visitors. Temperance brought outlandish stories. Granny Alice brought cake, and useful tips on getting rid of stains. Edward Edwards had been round twice, apparently for the sole purpose of standing about awkwardly and asking how she was every two minutes. Now that they weren't fighting for their lives, he had returned to being his previous youthful, ungainly self. She had become rather fond of him, and had the feeling he was trying to work out how to court her, but was that enough? She'd seen so much, and felt so much. The experience of turmoil made her crave the comfort of clinging to someone. The logical part of her mind did not consider this to be the best idea.

All the other houses in Barker Street lay in darkness now. She'd been out to check, looking for something human, something that made sense. Now it was just her, a solitary gas lamp, the tidy kitchen, and the cauldron. Before swanning off, the Druids had said their piece about taken it apart. So far, she hadn't even started. The manic cleaning session had been partly an excuse for stalling, but it had also given her a lot of thinking time.

Charlie didn't want to raise an army, or live forever, or do any of the things the cauldron might be used for. Or misused for. Of course, none of the Druids really knew what it was, all she'd heard was guesses. No one knew what this item meant, who had made it or where it really came from. It was all stories, when you got down to it. Stories, fear, and apparent messages from the spirit world. No proper science at all, when you got down to it. She had put it together in the first place, and that connected her to it. She didn't want to take it to pieces and put its carefully worked remnants back into the ground. That prospect felt very wrong indeed. It would be like killing someone.

What were the alternatives? Keep it as a flower pot? A large ornament? Start exploring what it could do to other things? She had enough money to dedicate her life to researching it. Was that the life she wanted?

Charlie could see one possible future very clearly. The path that carried on in the way she had been going, and led only to small inventions and small triumphs. There would be an awkward courtship from Edward Edwards, to which she would eventually succumb out of sheer loneliness. Then babies, raising children, burying children, worn down like all the other aging women of Barker Street. Assuming she lived that long. The obvious path would give her the kind of life she was supposed to have: One just like everyone else's.

The other path she might take began with a choice. It might kill her, or drive her insane. She might reach the morning and watch the sun come up with nothing changed on the outside. But even if that were the case, she suspected a lot would have changed on the inside, because she had chosen. When she considered it like that, it didn't seem to be a very difficult decision at all.

Charlie extinguished the flame in the gas lamp and waited for the gloom to resolve as her eyes adjusted. She took off her shoes, drew a slow, deep breath and climbed into the cauldron.

It was very, very dark inside, but not as cold as she had expected. The silence was absolute, but had a peaceful quality to it. She closed her eyes and settled into the most comfortable position she could find. One way or another, everything would be different by sunrise.

Author's Note

There are nods to actual history in this story, but mostly I made it up. Because I am a Druid, I feel particularly obliged to mention just how much I made these Druids up. There is an embarrassing history of Druidic societies from the 1700s onwards giving themselves silly titles, fantasy histories and prancing about in public, so some of that content in the story has a little bit of almost truth in it. The spiritual side is purely my invention, having very little to do with either the historical versions of Druidry, or modern Druidry as I practice it. Although I really would like a traction engine.

**TOP HAT
BOOKS**

Historical fiction that lives.

We publish fiction that captures the contrasts, the achievements, the optimism and the radicalism of ordinary and extraordinary times across the world.

We're open to all time periods and we strive to go beyond the narrow, foggy slums of Victorian London. Where are the tales of the people of fifteenth century Australasia? The stories of eighth century India? The voices from Africa, Arabia, cities and forests, deserts and towns? Our books thrill, excite, delight and inspire.

The genres will be broad but clear. Whether we're publishing romance, thrillers, crime, or something else entirely, the unifying themes are timescale and enthusiasm. These books will be a celebration of the chaotic power of the human spirit in difficult times. The reader, when they finish, will snap the book closed with a satisfied smile.